Meet...

Mrs. Joline B. Newhouse, who writes a "fortnightly" newspaper column called "Between the Lines."

Georgia Rose, the girl whose life is more like a soap opera than the TV serial she's addicted to.

Martha Rasnick, the young housewife in "Dear Phil Donahue" who writes all her troubles to the TV personality "because you talked to me, Phil, all those mornings."

Florrie, the cake lady in "Cakewalk" who causes her prissy sister no end of embarrassment by "wearing running shoes, at her age, and wooly white athletic socks that fall in crinkles down around her ankles."

"Lee Smith has held the mirror up to a certain slice of life and if the image seems a little manic or crazy, well, it's because the life's that way, not the glass...For those of us tired of the witless caricatures of Southern folks in *The Dukes of Hazzard* or *Dallas,* here is the real thing, potato salad and all."

Michael McFee
The Spectator

W9-CFJ-525

CAKEWALK

Lee Smith

BALLANTINE BOOKS • NEW YORK

Nine of the stories in this volume, some in slightly different form, first appeared in the following magazines, to whose editors grateful acknowledgment is made. "Artists" and "All the Days of Our Lives" in *Redbook*, "Georgia Rose" in *McCall's*, "The French Revolution: A Love Story" in *Ingenue*, "Heat Lightning," "Between the Lines," and "Mrs. Darcy Meets the Blue-Eyed Stranger at the Beach" in *Carolina Quarterly.* "Horses" originally appeared in *Love Stories by New Women*, a collection published by Red Clay Books. Cool Club Rules made up by Josh Seay and David McLeod, members of the original Cool Club.

Library of Congress Catalog Card Number: 81-8501

ISBN 0-345-33950-9

This edition published by arrangement with G. P. Putnam's Sons

Manufactured in the United States of America

First Ballantine Books Edition: October 1983
Sixth Printing: March 1991

For my mother
Virginia Marshall Smith

Contents

Between the Lines

"Peace be with you from Mrs. Joline B. Newhouse" is how *I* sign my columns. Now I gave some thought to that. In the first place, I like a line that has a ring to it. In the second place, what I have always tried to do with my column is to uplift my readers if at all possible, which sometimes it is not. After careful thought, I threw out "Yours in Christ." I am a religious person and all my readers know it. If I put "Yours in Christ," it seems to me that they will think I am theirs because I am in Christ, or even that they and I are in Christ *together*, which is not always the case. I am in Christ but I know for a fact that a lot of them are not. There's no use acting like they are, but there's no use rubbing their faces in it, either. "Peace be with you," as I see it, is sufficiently religious without laying all the cards right out on the table in plain view. I like to keep an ace or two up my sleeve. I like to write between the lines.

This is what I call my column, in fact: "Between the Lines, by Mrs. Joline B. Newhouse." Nobody knows why. Many people have come right out and asked me, including my best friend, Sally Peck, and my husband, Glenn. "Come on, now, Joline," they say. "What's this 'Between the Lines' all about? What's this 'Between the Lines' supposed to mean?" But I just smile a sweet mysterious smile and change the subject. I know what I know.

And my column means everything to folks around here. Salt Lick community is where we live, unincorporated. I guess there is not much that you would notice, passing through—the Post Office (real little), the American oil station, my husband Glenn's Cash 'N Carry Beverage Store. He sells more than beverages in there, though, believe me. He sells everything you can think of, from thermometers and rubbing alcohol to nails to frozen pizza. Anything else you want, you have to go out of the holler and get on the interstate and go to Greenville to get it. That's where my column appears, in the *Greenville Herald*, fortnightly. Now there's a word with a ring to it: fortnightly.

There are seventeen families here in Salt Lick—twenty, if you count those three down by the Five Mile Bridge. I put what they do in the paper. Anybody gets married, I write it. That goes for born, divorced, dies, celebrates a golden wedding anniversary, has a baby shower, visits relatives in Ohio, you name it. But these mere facts are not what's most important, to my mind.

I write, for instance: "Mrs. Alma Goodnight is enjoying a pleasant recuperation period in the lovely, modern Walker Mountain Community Hospital while she is sorely missed by her loved ones at home. Get well soon, Alma!" I do not write that Alma Goodnight is in the hospital because her husband hit her up the side with a rake and left a straight line of bloody little holes going from her waist to her armpit after she yelled at him, which Lord knows she did all the time, once too often. I don't write about how Eben Goodnight is all torn up now about what he did, missing work and worrying, or how Alma liked it so much in the hospital that nobody knows if they'll ever get her to go home or not. Because that is a *mystery*, and I am no detective by a long shot. I am what I am, I know what I know, and I know you've got to give folks something to hang on to, something to keep them going. That is what I have in mind when I say *uplift*, and that is what God had in mind when he gave us Jesus Christ.

My column would not be but a paragraph if the news was all I told. But it isn't. What I tell is what's important, like the bulbs coming up, the way the redbud comes out first on the

hills in the spring and how pretty it looks, the way the cattails
shoot up by the creek, how the mist winds down low on the
ridge in the mornings, how my wash all hung out on the line
of a Tuesday looks like a regular square dance with those pants
legs just flapping and flapping in the wind! I tell how all the
things you ever dreamed of, all changed and ghostly, will come
crowding into your head on a winter night when you sit up late
in front of your fire. I even made up these little characters to
talk for me, Mr. and Mrs. Cardinal and Princess Pussycat, and
often I have them voice my thoughts. Each week I give a little
chapter in their lives. Or I might tell what was the message
brought in church, or relate an inspirational word from a magazine, book, or TV. I look on the bright side of life.

I've had God's gift of writing from the time I was a child.
That's what the B. stands for in Mrs. Joline B. Newhouse—
Barker, my maiden name. My father was a patient strong God-
fearing man despite his problems and it is in his honor that I
maintain the B. There was a lot of us children around all the
time—it was right up the road here where I grew up—and it
would take me a day to tell you what all we got into! But after
I learned how to write, that was that. My fingers just naturally
curved to a pencil and I sat down to writing like a ball of fire.
They skipped me up one, two grades in school. When I was
not but eight, I wrote a poem named "God's Garden," which
was published in the church bulletin of the little Methodist
Church we went to then on Hunter's Ridge. Oh, Daddy was
so proud! He gave me a quarter that Sunday, and then I turned
around and gave it straight to God. Put it in the collection plate.
Daddy almost cried he was so proud. I wrote another poem in
school the next year, telling how life is like a maple tree, and
it won a statewide prize.

That's me—I grew up smart as a whip, lively, and naturally
good. Jesus came as easy as breathing did to me. Don't think
I'm putting on airs, though: I'm not. I know what I know. I've
done my share of sinning, too, of which more later.

Anyway, I was smart. It's no telling but what I might have
gone on to school like my own children have and who knows
what all else if Mama hadn't run off with a man. I don't
remember Mama very well, to tell the truth. She was a weak
woman, always laying in the bed having a headache. One day

we all came home from school and she was gone, didn't even bother to make up the bed. Well, that was the end of Mama! None of us ever saw her again, but Daddy told us right before he died that one time he had gotten a postcard from her from Atlanta, Georgia, years and years after that. He showed it to us, all wrinkled and soft from him holding it.

Being the oldest, I took over and raised those little ones, three of them, and then I taught school and then I married Glenn and we had our own children, four of them, and I have raised them too and still have Marshall, of course, poor thing. He is the cross I have to bear and he'll be just like he is now for the rest of his natural life.

I was writing my column for the week of March 17, 1976, when the following events occurred. It was a real coincidence because I had just finished doing the cutest little story named "A Red-Letter Day for Mr. and Mrs. Cardinal" when the phone rang. It rings all the time, of course. Everybody around here knows my number by heart. It was Mrs. Irene Chalmers. She was all torn up. She said that Mr. Biggers was over at Greenville at the hospital very bad off this time, and that he was asking for me and would I please try to get over there today as the doctors were not giving him but a 20 percent chance to make it through the night. Mr. Biggers has always been a fan of mine, and he especially liked Mr. and Mrs. Cardinal. "Well!" I said. "Of course I will! I'll get Glenn on the phone right this minute. And you calm down, Mrs. Chalmers. You go fix yourself a Coke." Mrs. Chalmers said she would, and hung up. I knew what was bothering her, of course. It was that given the natural run of things, she would be the next to go. The next one to be over there dying. Without even putting down the receiver, I dialed the beverage store. Bert answered.

"Good morning," I said. I like to maintain a certain distance with the hired help although Glenn does not. He will talk to anybody, and any time you go in there, you can find half the old men in the county just sitting around that stove in the winter or outside on those wooden drink boxes in the summer, smoking and drinking drinks which I am sure they are getting free out of the cooler although Glenn swears it on the Bible they are not. Anyway, I said good morning.

"Can I speak to Glenn?" I said.

"Well now, Mrs. Newhouse," Bert said in his naturally insolent voice—he is just out of high school and too big for his britches—"he's not here right now. He had to go out for a while."

"Where did he go?" I asked.

"Well, I don't rightly know," Bert said. "He said he'd be back after lunch."

"Thank you very much, there will not be a message," I said sweetly, and hung up. I *knew* where Glenn was. Glenn was over on Caney Creek where his adopted half-sister Margie Kettles lived, having carnal knowledge of her in the trailer. They had been at it for thirty years and anybody would have thought they'd have worn it out by that time. Oh, I knew all about it.

The way it happened in the beginning was that Glenn's father had died of his lungs when Glenn was not but about ten years old, and his mother grieved so hard that she went off her head and began taking up with anybody who would go with her. One of the fellows she took up with was a foreign man out of a carnival, the James H. Drew Exposition, a man named Emilio something. He had this curly-headed dark-skinned little daughter. So Emilio stayed around longer than anybody would have expected, but finally it was clear to all that he never would find any work around here to suit him. The work around here is hard work, all of it, and they say he played a musical instrument. Anyway, in due course this Emilio just up and vanished, leaving that foreign child. Now that was Margie, of course, but her name wasn't Margie then. It was a long foreign name, which ended up as Margie, and that's how Margie ended up here, in these mountains, where she has been up to no good ever since. Glenn's mother did not last too long after Emilio left, and those children grew up wild. Most of them went to foster homes, and to this day Glenn does not know where two of his brothers are! The military was what finally saved Glenn. He stayed with the military for nine years, and when he came back to this area he found me over here teaching school and with something of a nest egg in hand, enabling him to start the beverage store. Glenn says he owes everything to me.

This is true. But I can tell you something else: Glenn is a good man, and he has been a good provider all these years.

He has not ever spoken to me above a regular tone of voice nor raised his hand in anger. He has not been tight with the money. He used to hold the girls in his lap of an evening. Since I got him started, he has been a regular member of the church, and he has not fallen down on it yet. Glenn furthermore has that kind of disposition where he never knows a stranger. So I can count my blessings, too.

Of course I knew about Margie! Glenn's sister Lou-Ann told me about it before she died, that is how I found out about it originally. She thought I *should* know, she said. She said it went on for years and she just wanted me to know before she died. Well! I had had the first two girls by then, and I thought I was so happy. I took to my bed and just cried and cried. I cried for four days and then by gum I got up and started my column, and I have been writing on it ever since. So I was not unprepared when Margie showed up again some years after that, all gap-toothed and wild-looking, but then before you knew it she was gone, off again to Knoxville, then back working as a waitress at that truck stop at the county line, then off again, like that. She led an irregular life. And as for Glenn, I will have to hand it to him, he never darkened her door again until after the birth of Marshall.

Now let me add that I would not have gone on and had Marshall if it was left up to me. I would have practiced more birth control. Because I was old by that time, thirty-seven, and that was too old for more children I felt, even though I had started late of course. I had told Glenn many times, I said three normal girls is enough for anybody. But no, Glenn was like a lot of men, and I don't blame him for it—he just had to try one more time for a boy. So we went on with it, and I must say I had a feeling all along.

I was not a bit surprised at what we got, although after wrestling with it all for many hours in the dark night of the soul, as they say, I do not believe that Marshall is a judgment on me for my sin. I don't believe that. He is one of God's special children, is how I look at it. Of course he looks funny, but he has already lived ten years longer than they said he would. And has a job! He goes to Greenville every day on the Trailways bus, rain or shine, and cleans up the Plaza Mall. He gets to ride on the bus, and he gets to see people. Along about six o'clock he'll come back, walking up the holler and not looking to one side or the other, and then I give him his supper and then he'll watch something on TV like "The Brady Bunch" or "Family Affair," and then he'll go to bed. He would not hurt a flea. But oh, Glenn took it hard when Marshall came! I remember that night so well and the way he just turned his back on the doctor. This is what sent him back to Margie, I am convinced of it, what made him take up right where he had left off all those years before.

So since Glenn was up to his old tricks I called up Lavonne, my daughter, to see if she could take me to the hospital to see Mr. Biggers. Why yes she could, it turned out. As a matter of fact she was going to Greenville herself. As a matter of fact she had something she wanted to talk to me about anyway. Now Lavonne is our youngest girl and the only one that stayed around here. Lavonne is somewhat pop-eyed, and has a weak constitution. She is one of those people that never can make up their minds. That day on the phone, I heard a whine in her voice I didn't like the sound of. Something is up, I thought.

First I powdered my face, so I would be ready to go when Lavonne got there. Then I sat back down to write some more on my column, this paragraph I had been framing in my mind for weeks about how sweet potatoes are not what they used to be. They taste gritty and dry now, compared to how they were. I don't know the cause of it, whether it is man on the moon or pollution in the ecology or what, but it is true. They taste awful.

Then my door came bursting open in a way that Lavonne would never do it and I knew it was Sally Peck from next door. Sally is loud and excitable but she has a good heart. She would do anything for you. "Hold on to your hat, Joline!" she hollered. Sally is so loud because she's deaf. Sally was just huffing and puffing—she is a heavy woman—and she had rollers still up in her hair and her old housecoat on with the buttons off.

"Why, Sally!" I exclaimed. "You are all wrought up!"

Sally sat down in my rocker and spread out her legs and started fanning herself with my *Family Circle* magazine. "If you think I'm wrought up," she said finally, "it is nothing

7

compared to what you are going to be. We have had us a suicide, right here in Salt Lick. Margie Kettles put her head inside her gas oven in the night."

"Margie?" I said. My heart was just pumping.

"Yes, and a little neighbor girl was the one who found her, they say. She went over to borrow some baking soda for her mama's biscuits at seven o'clock A.M." Sally looked real hard at me. "Now wasn't she related to you all?"

"Why," I said just as easily, "why yes, she was Glenn's adopted half-sister of course when they were nothing but a child. But we haven't had anything to do with her for years as you can well imagine."

"Well, they say Glenn is making the burial arrangements," Sally spoke up. She was getting her own back that day, I'll admit it. Usually I'm the one with all the news.

"I have to finish my column now and then Lavonne is taking me to Greenville to see old Mr. Biggers who is breathing his last," I said.

"Well," Sally said, hauling herself out of my chair, "I'll be going along then. I just didn't know if you knew it or not." Now Sally Peck is not a spiteful woman in all truth. I have known her since we were little girls sitting out in the yard looking at a magazine together. It is hard to imagine being as old as I am now, or knowing Sally Peck—who was Sally Bland then—so long.

Of course I couldn't get my mind back on sweet potatoes after she left. I just sat still and fiddled with the pigeonholes in my desk and the whole kitchen seemed like it was moving and rocking back and forth around me. Margie dead! Sooner or later I would have to write it up tastefully in my column. Well, I must say I had never thought of Margie dying. Before God, I never hoped for that in all my life. I didn't know what it would do to *me*, in fact, to me and Glenn and Marshall and the way we live because you know how the habits and the ways of people can build up over the years. It was too much for me to take in at one time. I couldn't see how anybody committing suicide could choose to stick their head in the oven anyway—you can imagine the position you would be found in.

Well, in came Lavonne at that point, sort of hanging back

and stuttering like she always does, and that child of hers Bethy Rose hanging on to her skirt for dear life. I saw no reason at that time to tell Lavonne about the death of Margie Kettles. She would hear it sooner or later, anyway. Instead, I gave her some plant food that I had ordered two for the price of one from Montgomery Ward some days before.

"Are you all ready, Mama?" Lavonne asked in that quavery way she has, and I said indeed I was, as soon as I got my hat, which I did, and we went out and got in Lavonne's Buick Electra and set off on our trip. Bethy Rose sat in the back, coloring in her coloring book. She is a real good child. "How's Ron?" I said. Ron is Lavonne's husband, an electrician, as up and coming a boy as you would want to see. Glenn and I are as proud as punch of Ron, and actually I never have gotten over the shock of Lavonne marrying him in the first place. All through high school she never showed any signs of marrying anybody, and you could have knocked me over with a feather the day she told us she was secretly engaged. I'll tell you, our Lavonne was not the marrying sort! Or so I thought.

But that day in the car she told me, "Mama, I wanted to talk to you and tell you I am thinking of getting a d-i-v-o-r-c-e."

I shot a quick look into the back seat but Bethy Rose wasn't hearing a thing. She was coloring Wonder Woman in her book.

"Now, Lavonne," I said. "What in the world is it? Why, I'll bet you can work it out." Part of me was listening to Lavonne, as you can imagine, but part of me was still stuck in that oven with crazy Margie. I was not myself.

I told her that. "Lavonne," I said, "I am not myself today. But I'll tell you one thing. You give this some careful thought. You don't want to go off half-cocked. What is the problem, anyway?"

"It's a man where I work," Lavonne said. She works in the Welfare Department, part-time, typing. "He is just giving me a fit. I guess you can pray for me, Mama, because I don't know what I'll decide to do."

"Can we get an Icee?" asked Bethy Rose.

"Has anything happened between you?" I asked. You have to get all the facts.

"Why *no*!" Lavonne was shocked. "Why, I wouldn't do

9

anything like that! Mama, for goodness' sakes! We just have coffee together so far."

That's Lavonne all over. She never has been very bright. "Honey," I said, "I would think twice before I threw up a perfectly good marriage and a new brick home for the sake of a cup of coffee. If you don't have enough to keep you busy, go take a course at the community college. Make yourself a new pantsuit. This is just a mood, believe me."

"Well," Lavonne said. Her voice was shaking and her eyes were swimming in tears that just stayed there and never rolled down her cheeks. "Well," she said again.

As for me, I was lost in thought. It was when I was a young married woman like Lavonne that I committed my own great sin. I had the girls, and things were fine with Glenn and all, and there was simply not any reason to ascribe to it. It was just something I did out of loving pure and simple, did because I wanted to do it. I knew and have always known the consequences, yet God is full of grace, I pray and believe, and his mercy is everlasting.

To make a long story short, we had a visiting evangelist from Louisville, Kentucky, for a two-week revival that year. John Marcel Wilkes. If I say it myself, John Marcel Wilkes was a real humdinger! He had the yellowest hair you ever saw, curly, and the finest singing voice available. Oh, he was something, and that very first night he brought two souls into Christ. The next day I went over to the church with a pan of brownies just to tell him how much I personally had received from his message. I thought, of course, that there would be other people around—the Reverend Mr. Clark, or the youth director, or somebody cleaning. But to my surprise that church was totally empty except for John Marcel Wilkes himself reading the Bible in the fellowship hall and making notes on a pad of paper. The sun came in a window on his head. It was early June, I remember, and I had on a blue dress with little white cap sleeves and open-toed sandals. John Marcel Wilkes looked up at me and his face gave off light like the sun.

"Why, Mrs. Newhouse," he said. "What an unexpected pleasure!" His voice echoed out in the empty fellowship hall. He had the most beautiful voice, too—strong and deep, like it had bells in it. Everything he said had a ring to it.

He stood up and came around the table to where I was. I put the brownies down on the table and stood there. We both just stood there, real close without touching each other, for the longest time, looking into each other's eyes. Then he took my hands and brought them up to his mouth and kissed them, which nobody ever did to me before or since, and then he kissed me on the mouth. I thought I would die. After some time of that, we went together out into the hot June day where the bees were all buzzing around the flowers there by the back gate and I couldn't think straight. "Come," said John Marcel Wilkes. We went out in the woods behind the church to the prettiest place, and when it was all over I could look up across his curly yellow head and over the trees and see the white church steeple stuck up against that blue, blue sky like it was pasted there. This was not all. Two more times we went out there during that revival. John Marcel Wilkes left after that and I have never heard a word of him since. I do not know where he is, or what has become of him in all these years. I do know that I never bake a pan of brownies, or hear the church bells ring, but what I think of him. So I have to pity Lavonne and her cup of coffee if you see what I mean, just like I have to spend the rest of my life to live my sinning down. But I'll tell you this: if I had it all to do over, I would do it all over again, and I would not trade it in for anything.

Lavonne drove off to look at fabric and get Bethy Rose an Icee, and I went in the hospital. I hate the way they smell. As soon as I entered Mr. Biggers' room, I could see he was breathing his last. He was so tiny in the bed you almost missed him, a poor little shriveled-up thing. His family sat all around.

"Aren't you sweet to come?" they said. "Looky here, honey, it's Mrs. Newhouse."

He didn't move a muscle, all hooked up to tubes. You could hear him breathing all over the room.

"It's Mrs. Newhouse," they said, louder. "Mrs. Newhouse is here. Last night he was asking for everybody," they said to me. "Now he won't open his eyes. You are real sweet to come," they said. "You certainly did brighten his days." Now I knew this was true because the family had remarked on it before.

"I'm so glad," I said. Then some more people came in the door and everybody was talking at once, and while they were doing that, I went over to the bed and got right up by his ear.

"Mr. Biggers!" I said. "Mr. Biggers, it's Joline Newhouse here."

He opened one little old bleary eye.

"Mr. Biggers!" I said right into his ear. "Mr. Biggers, you know those cardinals in my column? Mr. and Mrs. Cardinal? Well, I made them up! I made them up, Mr. Biggers. They never were real at all." Mr. Biggers closed his eye and a nurse came in and I stood up.

"Thank you so much for coming, Mrs. Newhouse," his daughter said.

"He is one fine old gentleman," I told them all, and then I left.

Outside in the hall, I had to lean against the tile wall for support while I waited for the elevator to come. Imagine, me saying such a thing to a dying man! I was not myself that day.

Lavonne took me to the big Kroger's in north Greenville and we did our shopping, and on the way back in the car she told me she had been giving everything a lot of thought and she guessed I was right after all.

"You're not going to tell anybody, are you?" she asked me anxiously, popping her eyes. "You're not going to tell Daddy, are you?" she said.

"Why, Lord, no honey!" I told her. "It's the farthest thing from my mind."

Sitting in the back seat among all the grocery bags, Bethy Rose sang a little song she had learned at school. "Make new friends but keep the old, some are silver but the other gold," she sang.

"I don't know what I was thinking of," Lavonne said.

Glenn was not home yet when I got there—making his arrangements, I supposed. I took off my hat, made myself a cup of Sanka, and sat down and finished off my column on a high inspirational note, saving Margie and Mr. Biggers for the next week. I cooked up some ham and red-eye gravy, which Glenn just loves, and then I made some biscuits. The time seemed to pass so slow. The phone rang two times while I was fixing supper, but I just let it go. I thought I had received enough news for *that* day. I still couldn't get over Margie putting her head in the oven, or what I had said to poor Mr.

Biggers, which was not at all like me you can be sure. I buzzed around that kitchen doing first one thing, then another. I couldn't keep my mind on anything I did.

After a while Marshall came home and ate, and went in the front room to watch TV. He cannot keep it in his head that watching TV in the dark will ruin your eyes, so I always have to go in there and turn on a light for him. This night, though, I didn't. I just let him sit there in the recliner in the dark, watching his show, and in the pale blue light from that TV set he looked just like anybody else.

I put on a sweater and went out on the front porch and sat in the swing to watch for Glenn. It was nice weather for that time of year, still a little cold but you could smell spring in the air already and I knew it wouldn't be long before the redbud would come out again on the hills. Out in the dark where I couldn't see them, around the front steps, my crocuses were already up. After a while of sitting out there I began to take on a chill, due more to my age no doubt than the weather, but just then some lights came around the bend, two headlights, and I knew it was Glenn coming home.

Glenn parked the truck and came up the steps. He was dog-tired, I could see that. He came over to the swing and put his hand on my shoulder. A little wind came up, and by then it was so dark you could see lights on all the ridges where the people live. "Well, Joline," he said.

"Dinner is waiting on you," I said. "You go on in and wash up and I'll be there directly. I was getting worried about you," I said.

Glenn went on and I sat there swaying on the breeze for a minute before I went after him. Now where will it all end? I ask you. All this pain and loving, mystery and loss. And it just goes on and on, from Glenn's mother taking up with dark-skinned gypsies to my own daddy and his postcard to that silly Lavonne and her cup of coffee to Margie with her head in the oven, to John Marcel Wilkes and myself, God help me, and all of it so long ago out in those holy woods.

Georgia Rose

We met on Halfmoon Island, a small resort off the coast of
South Carolina, during one of those sweet long mysterious
summers of childhood, the year the Harmons bought the "villa"
identical to ours, just next door. In retrospect it seems the
perfect setting for our first encounter, an encounter I have come
to regard as "fateful" because of the strange and disturbing way
in which our lives were to touch over the course of the next
twenty years. Our villas on Halfmoon Island that summer were
old, wind-racked, and weathered to a desolate gray; yet they
were summer houses on a grand scale, with servants' apart-
ments out back, widow's walks atop the third story, and vast
salty screen porches with wicker rockers and the indefinite
smell of sorrow. In those days I loved to pace dramatically
back and forth on the widow's walk at sunset, gazing out at
the huge blue sea, imagining catastrophe, heartbreak, and ruin.
Although our villas had identical floor plans, they had settled
differently into the sand. Our floors appeared to sag somewhat
in the middle of every room, producing a general sense of
depression characteristic of my family. But the Harmons' villa
was off level in a madcap, alluring way, with a rakishly tilted
upstairs screen porch and staircases that careened like carnival
rides. And our families could not have been more different.

The Harmons were already in full swing when we arrived. Unpacking, I was fascinated by their screams, their laughter, their bumps and bangings, and the music that seemed to float visibly out from their dark green propped-up shutters all day long and half the night. Paralyzed by shyness, I avoided them altogether for the next two days—no mean feat, since there were so many of them. Feigning headaches, I holed up in my room and read mysteries. At night I became an outstanding eavesdropper, a stellar spy.

I soon realized that the species of life that went on at the Harmons' villa clearly took its tone from the mother. Mrs. Harmon wore her black hair much longer than anybody else's mother did, and in the evenings she pulled it back on one side and fastened it there with a red silk rose. She wore both eye shadow and mascara *all day long*, which was not done on Halfmoon Island, and her eyebrows had been plucked out and then drawn back on in a long unnatural curve. She wore bright red lipstick (Revlon's "Spanish Harlem," Georgia Rose told me later) and a thin layer of something like Vaseline on top of the lipstick, which gave her a glistening rapacious look. During the day Mrs. Harmon shopped, directed her two aging maids, and tried to keep an eye on the twins. But each evening she disappeared for an hour promptly at five o'clock and reappeared again at six, wearing a long startling dress and high-heeled sandals with skinny straps. I was entranced. Mrs. Harmon was the only person I had ever seen who "dressed for dinner."

In the evening she went to the upright piano and played and sang, her rather remarkable husky voice carrying out across the sand until at last it was lost in the sound of the waves. She sang jazz and love songs. At first, I was profoundly disturbed by her singing. I found something unknown and threatening in the low throbbing notes of her voice, something I couldn't connect with anyone's mother, or with my own life, or with that beach house where my family had been coming since years before I was born. I lay flat on the daybed on our screen porch, listening in the dark until I felt sick at my stomach and had to go inside for an Alka Seltzer and a vanilla Coke.

By the third night, my daring and curiosity had reached such a peak that I actually snuck through the shadowed space that separated our villas, crept into the bougainvillea around the Harmons' front porch, and crawled forward until I was lying flat in the dark crawl space under the porch itself. I lay there half paralyzed with excitement and fright, listening to Mrs. Harmon sing a jazzed-up version of "Frankie and Johnnie" while somebody danced, thump THUMP, right over my head.

"Lauren!" my own mother's voice whined out into the night. "Lau-ren?" She switched on our porch light, and its yellow glow fell short of the Harmons' porch by only a few feet. My mother had a thin nasal voice, eyeglasses with pearlized frames, and pastel linen dresses that buttoned up the front; she carried her needlepoint everywhere. Now she peered out cautiously into the dark, sniffing the wind from the sea. "Lauren?" I shrank into the sand. If discovered, I would die on the spot. My mother began calling my father, who eventually appeared behind her, perplexed and bemused as ever, stroking his natty little moustache. "I'll find her," volunteered my brother, Jesse, three years older than me, and he set off down the beach. The light switched off; my parents disappeared. Thank God! I stayed put beneath the Harmons' house, despite a scuttling noise in the sand which I knew was a crab. Overhead, Mrs. Harmon sang "Summertime" in a slow melancholy fashion with a heavy, rolling bass.

Suddenly I almost died of fright. One of the mysterious Harmons came out and sat down in the sand not twenty feet away: Georgia Rose, the one I had judged to be closest to me in age. Through my assiduous eavesdropping, I even knew her name. I could see her plainly in the light from her family's windows, yet she seemed remote from them, curiously alone. Georgia Rose sat still as a stone with her arms clasped around her thin knees, looking up at the stars and the heat lightning off in the distance, her head bent slightly to one side in an attitude of listening. I held my breath in the crawl space. "Lauren! Lauren!" Jesse's voice echoed faintly from the beach. Georgia Rose stretched out her thin white arms toward the sea in a strange pleading gesture, while her mother's voice rolled out over that whole night: "Hush, little baby, do-on't you cry."

The next morning Jesse went to call on the Harmons and then dragged me back over with him that afternoon in order to be properly introduced. This was typical of Jesse, the only outgoing person in our family. Sometimes, even then, I felt that Mother and Father and I only existed at Jesse's pleasure, to give him a family to come from, a place to come back to, a setting in which to shine. I was a born worshipper. I had always worshipped Jesse; and after he introduced me to the Harmons, I worshipped them, too. Close up, Mrs. Harmon was as volatile and theatrical as ever. She had long red nails and she smoked cigarettes, which she waved recklessly about in the air. She had been "on the stage," she told us, until her husband, George, came along and swept her off her feet. Margaret, Georgia Rose's older sister, older than Jesse even, was dark like her mother, with a pure, almost stern beauty. All that summer long she was out in the bougainvillea, kissing college boys. The seven-year-old twins, Dwight and Roland, were like boys in a cartoon. They immediately turned brown in the sun and never burned and grew two inches apiece that summer. They were always getting in trouble and making the maids cry. Leslie, the fifteen-year-old daughter, made me uncomfortable because I sensed something in her that was too close to something in me. Leslie had a thin, pocked face, dark frizzy hair, and she seemed always to be in the grip of some sensitivity too painful to be borne. She never swam in the ocean. Mr. Harmon only appeared at the weekend, looking very important in his dark, baggy suit. His only concession to the beach was to change into a plaid short-sleeved shirt. Other than that, he sat fully dressed beneath their blue-and-white-striped umbrella, red-faced and satisfied, observing the ocean and the beach through the telescope, which he refused to let any of the children use. He never swam in the ocean, either. I was drawn to the Harmons by their sheer number, by their energy and their variety; yet from the start it was Georgia Rose whom I really loved.

If I had set out to create a best friend for myself, I could not have done any better. Georgia Rose was skinny and freckled, just like me. Her nails were all chewed off. She had straight hair and bangs, bleached pale by the sun. She wanted to be a ballerina or a detective, too. She hated green vegetables. She liked to swim and run and fish and play baseball. She had had two imaginary playmates, remarkably like my own, only two years before. She loved Nancy Drew and George Fayne but hated Bess Marvin as well as Pippi Longstocking and Cherry

Ames, student nurse. She had read *The Secret Garden* six times to my five. Best of all, she was as embarrassed by her own family—by their size, their noise, their sheer noticeability— as I was by the dullness and niceness of my own parents. Of course we formed a detective club; of course we became immediately inseparable; but it was July of that year before I found out that there was something very unusual about Georgia Rose.

Barefooted and brown as Indians by that time, we were walking over the causeway to the mainland to get a Coke at the hardware store on the highway. It was a bright pale day, near noon, and nothing moved in the stagnant marshes beneath us. Far ahead we could see Mr. Murdock, the postman, coming toward us in his van, growing larger and larger as he approached through the iridescent heat shimmering up from the pavement. Mr. Murdock was one of our favorites, a fat ruddy man of about forty, with a blue Bermuda-shorts uniform and a blue cap and a friendly way of squinting up his eyes at the corners. When he reached us, he slowed down and waved. "Hello, girls," he said. "Caught any criminals today?"

"Not yet," I said. "Do you know where any are?"

Mr. Murdock chuckled, shook his head, and drove on. I stubbed my toe on a shell; bending over to examine it, I realized suddenly that Georgia Rose was no longer behind me. She had stopped back where we saw Mr. Murdock and she was sitting down right in the road.

"Georgia Rose!" I called. "Come on! What are you doing?"

She didn't move. Curious, with a sudden, certain sense of something wrong, I went back along the causeway. Georgia Rose's blue eyes were open wide and staring straight ahead, right through me.

"What's the matter?" I shook her by the shoulder, hard.

Finally she looked at me. "Mr. Murdock looked so funny," she said in a wondering, hesitant tone not at all like her regular voice. "He had that awful cloud around his chest. It was so scary and I couldn't breathe I was so scared."

"I don't think this is a good joke," I said severely. "This isn't funny at all." I was furious with her. "Get up!"

"Funny," she echoed in that voice. "No, it's not funny, it's awful, it was terrible, it was moving all around him in the van."

"Georgia Rose, I'm going to get a Coke," I said. "You can sit down out there in the middle of the road and talk about weird stuff all day long if you want to. Goodbye."

I had gone about fifteen or so steps toward the mainland when she screamed. "Lauren!" She had a strange high sound in her voice. "Please don't leave me! Please come back!"

I was scared but I went back and held out my hand and finally she took it, stood up, and we went on to the mainland and bought our Cokes at the hardware store. We didn't mention the incident again that day, yet I remember clearly how strange and hollow I felt later that afternoon, crossing the causeway back to the island, making careful small talk, while large birds wheeled wildly overhead through the white-hot sky.

When my mother came back from the mainland fish market the following morning with the news that Mr. Murdock had died unexpectedly of a heart attack during the night, I felt no surprise at all, but a pounding certainty deep in my chest. After my mother told me the news, she put on her blue-flowered apron and began to unwrap the white paper from around the fish. There was a knock at the back door.

It was Georgia Rose, looking younger somehow and thinner than usual, motioning me to come out. As soon as the screen door slammed behind me, she dragged me into the bougainvillea and grabbed both my hands, pressing them so hard they hurt. She stared straight into my eyes. *"Don't tell,"* she said. Her blue eyes were as hard and bright as marbles; the bougainvillea all around us smelled as strong as spilled perfume.

It was still early morning on Halfmoon Island, which I knew like the back of my hand. I could smell bacon frying somewhere, and yet a new kind of thrill—a sense of the totally unknown—passed through me. I was lost in her wild, bright eyes. Behind her, in the kitchen of her villa, a curtain moved, and I thought I saw her mother's dark eyes looking out. *"Promise,"* Georgia Rose said.

"I promise," I said. "I promise." And I never told.

After this, the summer days passed just as swiftly as before—we swam; we caught great blue crabs from the jetties using lengths of kitchen string with chicken necks for bait; we spied on Margaret and her boyfriends; we adopted a stray cat and named him Colin; we lay on the screen porches reading Reader's Digest Condensed Books (*Dear and Glorious Physician, Raintree County*) while summer storms swept walls of rain across the sand. But it was not the same. A difference existed between us, where previously none had been, and even though we never mentioned it, I knew it was there. And finally I had to bring it out into the open; I had to know.

"Georgia Rose," I whispered one night in August when she was sleeping over at my house. "Have you ever seen anything else like that? like you did with Mr. Murdock? I won't tell anybody, I promise. Honest."

"It's been going on for as long as I can remember," Georgia Rose whispered back in the darkness. "I hate it," she added fiercely.

"But *why*?" I was filled with envy.

"It's so awful," she hissed. "It just is. Sometimes I see things, too."

"What kind of things?"

"I just know what's going to happen."

"How do you know?"

"I don't know. I just do. It's awful. It's really awful, because . . . because . . ."

I could tell that she was crying in the dark. I held my breath, waiting for her to finish.

"Because it's NOT my fault!" she burst out. "I can't help it. I don't want it. I can't help what I see."

"Of course not," I said. "Of course you can't." But it was hard for me to understand.

Next door, Mrs. Harmon was playing the piano and singing "My Blue Heaven." We could barely hear her.

"Does *she* know?" I asked. "Your mother?"

"Yes."

"What does she say about it?"

"She says she didn't give up her glamorous career to raise some peculiar daughter. She says I have to stop it immediately. It makes her furious. She won't even let me talk about it, ever. You're the only one outside of the family who knows. Oh, she's *mean*! She says I do it on purpose to make her crazy.

She's just so mean—" Georgia Rose broke into loud hoarse sobs. I patted her shoulder in the darkness, aghast. She cried for a long time, sobbing so loudly and bitterly, with such adult abandon, that Jesse came and knocked at the door.

"What's the matter?" he said. "Can I help?"

"No, it's OK," I lied, and Jesse left and after a while Georgia Rose quieted down. Finally she want to sleep, but I lay awake in the shadows for a long time, listening to Mrs. Harmon sing "Smoke Gets in Your Eyes" and watching the patterns the moonlight made falling across the foot of my bed.

As soon as we arrived back at our home in the mountains, I went straight downtown to the Rexall drugstore and bought three boxed sets of fancy stationery for a dollar. The yellow stationery featured a little stone cottage in the corner of each sheet, with yellow roses climbing a picket fence. The pink stationery featured an idealized circle of children, dancing on every page. But I decided to use the blue stationery first. It was ice blue, rather than pastel, with a stern navy blue border around each sheet. It looked somber and official. "Like something a mortician would use," Jesse joked, but I was not to be deterred. I sat right down and began my correspondence with Georgia Rose. I had high hopes for this correspondence. Of course I had had pen pals before, obtained through the back pages of young people's magazines, but they had all been unsatisfactory. This was to be the major correspondence of my life.

I told her everything: how boring it was at home, how I wished I could paint my room dark purple but my mother wouldn't hear of it, how Jesse was captain of the Academy football team and had been voted the Best All-Around, how I wasn't sure I believed in the Trinity any more although I thought Jesus was all right, how much I hated math. Once I wrote her a poem about Albert Schweitzer and Harriet Tubman, named "I Need a Cause, Because."

Georgia Rose's return letters were printed on incredibly sophisticated notepaper, beige with her initials in brown script at the top. Although I was thrilled with this notepaper, I was actually disappointed with her letters; but for several months I managed to hide my disappointment from myself. Georgia Rose believed in neither punctuation nor adjectives. All her flat little sentences ran together and often she failed to use up even her relatively small, creamy beige space. She never mentioned what I had come to regard as her "powers." She never answered most of my questions or made any comment about my letters. Instead she wrote about boys, pizza parties, and the Sub-Deb Club of Columbia. She had been elected a junior varsity cheerleader. No, she hadn't read *Rebecca* or anything else lately. In fact she was so busy that she didn't have time to read. She wrote fewer and fewer letters. I formed a friendship with Eugenia Dorton, a myopic classmate whom I had hitherto scorned.

Winter progressed. My father worked long hours at the college, where he was a professor of classics. He walked back and forth through the snow, wearing his green knitted cap. My mother had so many migraine headaches that I began to take over the cooking: exotic things only, such as Hamburger Oriental Surprise for supper. My father and Jesse were complimentary. It snowed. My mother lay under a heating pad, face turned to the wall. Without glasses, her unfocused eyes looked milky and malevolent. Jesse was voted Most Valuable Forward on the basketball team.

It was February when the note arrived. It was written on the familiar notepaper, beige with brown initials, and the stately return address—"Pinetops," 11 Green Meadow Lane, Columbia, S.C.—had been stamped as always on the triangular back flap of the envelope. But there was something wrong with it; I knew this immediately, even as I picked it up from our hall table and turned it over in my hands. The handwriting was all angular, skewed and scrawled, quite unlike Georgia Rose's usual rounded, careful penmanship. I took the letter over to the window seat in our sitting room and settled myself very carefully on the fading violet cushion before I began to read. The note was short and almost indecipherable.

Dear Lauren, I read, *I have been very sick, please do not be so upset about your Father. He will be happier*. That was it. I went cold and clammy all over. Was this some kind of joke? What was all this about my father? I decided to ignore the whole thing. I burned the note in the fireplace, studied biology in a frenzy of concentration for the rest of the afternoon, and then fixed something called "Chicken Orangé" for supper.

The next day was Valentine's Day. My father called Jesse

and me into the kitchen early, before eight, and told us in his normal dispassionate voice that he had fallen in love with the recently widowed Mrs. Winthrop, down the street. My mind went around and around. All I knew about Mrs. Winthrop was that she was a plump lady who wore nubby wool suits and pillbox hats with aqua feathers on them. My father wore his old brown tweed jacket with leather patches on the elbows. He burst into tears and pulled us both to him in a great strong hug. I stared into the close-up pattern of his tie, green mallards on gold silk. My father sobbed some more, straightened his tie, and left, walking out into the cold gray drizzle.

"I'll be damned," Jesse said. His face was caught between tears and laughing.

"You want some coffee?" I asked. When Jesse nodded, I went over to the stove and made some for him, and then on a sudden impulse I poured a cup for myself, too, lavishly adding sugar and cream. It was not bad at all. Jesse came over and put his arm around my waist and we drank our coffee and looked out the kitchen window together, watching the early cardinals around our bird feeder in the dripping, melting snow. My father really ran away with Mrs. Winthrop on Valentine's Day, and it was years before I ever saw him again.

For several summers after that, we rented our villa out to other people. We couldn't have gone to Halfmoon Island anyway, since my mother, much to our surprise, had gotten up out of bed and taken a fulltime job as head of housekeeping for the college where my father had taught. She bought several pantsuits and an assortment of chunky gold costume jewelry. She learned to smoke cigarettes and play bridge. Each day she sat at her desk deploying whole teams of cleaning people, laundry people, repairmen, lawn-cutters, and shrub-trimmers via a CB radio on her desk. I made straight A's in school and wrote a forty-two-page Gothic novel named *Beneath the Bloody Moon*. Jesse graduated from the Academy as valedictorian; he gave a commencement address concerning the necessity of keeping one's finger upon the pulse of the world. My father married Mrs. Winthrop and they bought a pink stucco house in Winterhaven, Florida, with her money. Jesse won a More-head scholarship to the University of North Carolina. My mother began dating a florist, Max Holtsinger, whom she even-

CAKEWALK

tually married. He saw to it that our house was full of curly
ferns in brass pots. He fixed her a fresh arrangement of red
roses every week and addressed her as "my sweet"; although
I rather liked Mr. Holtsinger, I was afraid my friends would
find out about the roses. I had become cynical and poetic. My
mother taught Mr. Holtsinger how to play bridge and they
attended duplicate bridge tournaments in other states.

During those years I dated a boy with a limp and wrote long
tortured poems about shattering mirrors. I wrote to Georgia
Rose several times, but she never answered my letters, so it
was with real shock and a certain anxiety that I spotted her
name on the roster of incoming freshmen at Sweetbriar, my
junior year. She should have been a junior, too, I thought, or
a sophomore at the very least. I wondered what had happened,
suddenly aware that I didn't really want to know.

We ran into each other right away, crossing a broad green
lawn to go to dinner during the first week of school. I had
grown thin and tall and arty, interesting enough in my way,
but Georgia Rose had become impossibly beautiful. While my
hair had darkened and coarsened, hers was shinier and paler
than ever, falling now below her shoulders in the long straight
way that was most fashionable that year. She was tall and lush
and graceful, full-figured, her eyes still that deep bright blue.
Nobody looked like her; she looked like a movie star. As we
crossed the grass, wearing our name tags, I attempted some
small talk. Yes, her mother was still the same. Still singing
every night. Still playing the baby grand. Her father had had
to go to Duke for the rice diet after a mild heart attack; now
he, too, was fine. Margaret had married after her sophomore
year at St. Mary's. Now she lived in Atlanta with two baby
girls and a young doctor for a husband and she was head of
the Charity League. Dwight and Roland had been sent off to
separate military schools. Leslie? Georgia Rose hesitated. Actually Leslie was in a sort of therapeutic home up in the mountains of North Carolina, where she had been for some time.
She sure was improving a lot, though. Georgia Rose had grown
more Southern, had blurred and softened except for her blue
eyes. Her musical voice was measured and distant. Her manner
toward me was obviously bored, yet polite. Instinctively, I
found myself volunteering nothing about my family or myself.

Yet, when we had reached the dining hall, she turned suddenly to me and asked, "Where's Jesse now?" Some kind of fear leaped into my heart. "At UVA," I answered truthfully. "He's in law school."

Standing on the porch of the dining hall, Georgia Rose stretched her manicured hands out toward me in that curious pleading gesture I had seen so long ago, touching me lightly on the shoulder. Beside the old stone column, standing so still in the last of the sun, she looked classical and austere.

"Lauren," she said, looking straight into my eyes. "I'm a new person. Everything has changed." I understood then that she felt toward me the same way I had, upon occasion, felt toward friends of my own to whom I had said "too much": a certain repugnance, a drawing back. I was relieved, realizing that any friendship between us was out of the question. We went into the dining room and sat at one of the large round tables; I introduced her to everyone. Later that night I cried for hours, upsetting my roommate. I cried for the loss of my best friend, for the loss of my father, for the loss of my childhood and the way I was then, and out of a pure nameless future dread.

Of course it happened. Even though Georgia Rose and I moved in such different circles at Sweetbriar, still they met— at a party in Charlottesville, I believe—and very soon it was "serious." Jesse called and told me about it, exuberant as always. He said he couldn't believe his luck. What a girl! His voice filled the miles with hope and love. For some reason, Jesse thought that Georgia Rose and I were friends, and I could not bring myself to disillusion him. What did it matter, anyway? In fact, Georgia Rose never spoke to me about Jesse or anything else, even though she smiled and waved at me often across the campus. Still, through some fluke in planning, we ended up at the same houseparty outside Charlottesville one day that spring. This party was hosted by an immensely rich senior law student, already alcoholic, at his family's hunting lodge. The law student was my date's cousin; he was a classmate of Jesse's.

Jesse and Georgia Rose were obviously in love—in the most dramatic, most grandiloquent, deepest sense of that phrase. Theirs was a grand passion. Even when they were in groups of people, they looked only at each other. And they were both so beautiful! Jesse had let his hair grow a little longer than usual that spring, so that it curled around his neck, around his strong brown face. His gray eyes, always quick and kind, were literally alight with love. I had never seen anything like it. They had to touch each other all the time. The current between them was so powerful, so obvious, that it was somehow embarrassing and even threatening for other people, who tended to make jokes and move away.

My date and I were having a final beer on the long front porch Sunday afternoon when Jesse, flushed and rhapsodic as he had been all that weekend, came up behind us and grabbed us. "Come on!" he said. "Quick! It's Georgia Rose's birthday—we're having a little celebration." Jesse propelled us into one of the numerous parlors inside the house, where Georgia Rose, blushing and obviously delighted, sat on an overstuffed couch before a coffee table with a frozen apple pie on it. Jesse had filled the apple pie with pink birthday candles—nineteen of them. Georgia Rose's roommate was there, plus some friends of Jesse's and their dates. I can't remember who all the people were. Jesse drew me into the circle. He put an arm around Georgia Rose's shoulder, an arm around mine. "And-uh-ONE, and-uh-TWO, and-uh-THREE!" he directed, in imitation of Lawrence Welk. We all sang Happy Birthday and then cheered as Georgia Rose, holding back her hair, leaned forward and blew out every one of her candles.

"And this is from me," Jesse said, reaching underneath the sofa to bring out a plain unwrapped cardboard box. Immediately I knew it would contain another, smaller box, and that the smaller box would contain a ring. I braced myself to smile. No one could have been more surprised than I when Georgia Rose carefully opened the top, giggling and expectant, and the quick green lizard popped out and ran along her arm. I jumped; Georgia Rose's roommate squealed out in fright. But Georgia Rose captured it with her other hand and held it and played with it, letting it run back and forth across her fingers. She seemed to know all about lizards. I remembered for a second—uncomfortably—our tomboy summer on Halfmoon Island.

"Oh," she breathed to Jesse. "Oh, he's so beautiful!" Their eyes locked and held while the lizard, iridescent and strange, ran over and over her hands.

26

This was the only time I actually saw them together. About a month after that, during exams, I was pulling an all-nighter before my European history examination when Georgia Rose knocked on the door of the study room in my dormitory. It was late at night—well after midnight—and I was alone in the study room. I was flustered when I opened the door and saw her there. Pale and sweating, wrapped in an old terry cloth bathrobe, she leaned against the woodwork for support. Georgia Rose pushed the hair out of her eyes and looked at me. She seemed to have something to say, but when she tried to speak, a deep gurgling noise came up from her throat. Already nervous from too little sleep and too much coffee, I burst into tears. Her lips looked swollen. She licked them and tried again. "Jesse," she said. It was not her voice.

I grew cold all over. "Please," I said. "Come in, sit down," I said. "Tell me what you mean." I didn't know what to do. Georgia Rose knotted the tie belt of her bathrobe quickly, nervously, and, without looking at me again, she turned and ran off down the hall. I followed, but she was too quick for me. By the time I reached the outside door, she had disappeared. The campus lawns stretched wide and silver in the moonlight, broken only by dark round bushes and tall black trees. "Georgia Rose!" I called out into the night.

The night watchman appeared. "Anything wrong, miss?" he asked.

"No," I said. I closed the door. I thought of calling Jesse, decided not to. I couldn't imagine what I would say.

Georgia Rose dropped Jesse right after that, without ever telling him why. His heart was broken. He haunted Sweetbriar, haunted me, for days. I couldn't help him. Nobody could help him. Georgia Rose began dating a Deke at Carolina, a tobacco heir. Jesse did poorly on his law boards and moped around the house all summer, getting on Mother and Mr. Holtsinger's nerves. I had a job in the public library, so I saw Jesse seldom and was relieved when he enlisted in the Army in late July.

When I returned to school for my senior year, I was happy to find that Georgia Rose was no longer on campus. She had transferred to Chapel Hill. I felt better and set about editing the school newspaper and writing my senior thesis on W. B. Yeats. I was working on my thesis in the library, in fact, when the dean and two of my best friends came to tell me that Jesse had been killed in a freak accident at Camp Lejeune. I was devastated. We were all devastated—Mother and Mr. Holtsinger, my father in Florida, who retreated into his pink house and did not re-emerge for a year—and Jesse's numerous friends. I cannot remember much about that time now, but I do remember the astonishing number and variety of people who came to his funeral. Friends from college, from law school, from the Army—a barber who used to cut his hair, his Academy tennis coach. "We will not see his like again," intoned the acne-ridden young Reverend Walters. Unfortunately, this was true. My mother notified Georgia Rose of Jesse's death, but she did not show up for the funeral; we heard from someone else, later, that she had recently become engaged to Bama J. Reynolds, the tobacco heir.

I finished my senior year at Sweetbriar in a blur. I didn't eat; I didn't sleep. In June, I went back home to Mother and Mr. Holtsinger while my friends went off to graduate schools or to promising jobs in publishing, in advertising, in TV. Irrationally, I blamed Georgia Rose. But then I heard her voice, that thin remembered wail from childhood, once again: "I hate it . . . I can't help it . . . I don't want it . . . it's not my fault." This was true. My anger passed; I mourned. And after the excess of grief had gone, guilt crept over me like a net. I should have died, not he. He was the talented one; I had no business being still alive; somehow it became *my* fault. I took long walks in the woods and ate a lot of Mr. Holtsinger's lemon chess pie. After a long time I got over it. I found a job in a larger city; Mr. Holtsinger gave me an enormous Boston fern for my apartment. It was years before I heard of Georgia Rose again. One day I got a card announcing the marriage of Georgia Rose Reynolds to Walter J. Breeding. I wrote a guarded note, expressing my good wishes. I found an excellent job; I married a lawyer; we had two sons; we bought a house; we bought a bigger house.

Some years later, my husband, Ben, and I had arranged for a sitter so that we could spend a long weekend together at Kiawah Island for our eighth anniversary. It was cocktail time. We lolled about on white pillow-covered wrought-iron furniture on the patio, sipping our drinks. Boats, decorous and picturesque, plied the Inland Waterway in front of us. Behind us, Spanish moss hung in sheets from the live oak trees. A combo, outfitted in tuxes, played dance music from the ornate gazebo.

"Well now, where we come from, *Columbia* . . ." a woman on my left was saying.

I turned to her. "Do you know—or did you ever know— Georgia Rose Harmon?" I asked. My voice was unnaturally abrupt.

Ben leaned forward.

The woman's tanned face registered surprise, followed by a certain distaste. "*Not really*," she said, with a peculiar emphasis. "Well, just not at all," she said.

"When I knew her she was going with a Reynolds boy from Winston-Salem, but then some years ago we had a wedding announcement saying that she had married someone else," I prompted.

"Walter Breeding, but that didn't last either, and she moved to Atlanta where she married again, and I heard—now, don't repeat me—that it didn't work out either."

"But why not?" I pursued. "What happened?"

"I'll tell you, I only saw her socially, and not very often at that. We've known Walter for years, you see. He was in my sister's wedding, as a matter of fact. So Walter is the one we know, and he's just the sweetest thing. Or *was*, until she up and left him like she did, with no explanation whatsoever. He's never been the same since. It's the saddest thing you ever saw, honestly it is. He's the most eligible man in Columbia right now but you can't even get him to accept a dinner invitation. He's just a wreck, and I've heard . . ."

"*Honey*," her husband interrupted. He stood up.

"But what happened?" I pursued. "Why did she leave? *Where is she now*?" I asked, all the old fear and dread coming back in a rush.

"Well, I'm sure I don't know!" the woman said. She put on her sunglasses, gathered up her purse, and left abruptly with her waiting husband. The conversation was over.

"Lauren," Ben said. He leaned forward and took my hand, the small quizzical frown I love appearing between his eyebrows.

"Let's dance," I said suddenly. I stood up and gripped his

arm so tightly that it must have hurt as he led me to the dance floor; when he took me in his arms I pressed myself close, close. The combo played "Heart and Soul." We held each other, barely moving, as the sun went down and a breeze came up off the water; we swayed to the music and the soft Spanish moss brushed our faces and I was crying.

One more incident remains to be told. Recently we attended a bowl game in Birmingham as guests of a company for which Ben has done some consulting. It was a cool September day and the sky arching overhead was an impossible blue, too blue to be real. Football is one of Ben's major passions. Soon he was pounding away at my knee and yelling at the top of his lungs. I was amused. What I like about football games is the color, the pageantry, the crowds. I was looking around at the people in our section when suddenly I saw Georgia Rose standing by the rail with an usher several rows below me, apparently checking her ticket. I stood up immediately, telling Ben I'd be right back. He was so engrossed in the game that he scarcely noticed. It seemed an eternity before I could navigate my way across the legs of everyone in our row and manage to reach the aisle; below me, Georgia Rose was already on her way down.

"Wait!" I called. "Georgia Rose! Wait!"

My cry was lost in the sound of the crowd.

"Georgia Rose!"

She turned then, shaded her eyes with her hand, and saw me. Recognition appeared in her face, then pain, and she turned and hurried down the endless steps to the ground level, where she was caught and held in a group of latecomers. I was breathless when I reached her.

"Georgia Rose!" I said. "It's me, Lauren. Don't try to pretend you don't know who I am."

"I really don't think we have anything to talk about," she said, and for a moment I was stunned into silence, staring at her face. She had changed drastically. Her hair had lost its sheen and she wore it pulled severely back from her thin, lined face, yet a strand of it had escaped the low round bun and hung, lank and stringy, down by her ear like a ghost of the golden-haired beauty she used to be. Her features were as clear-cut and lovely as they had ever been, but now there were circles like smudges beneath her blue eyes and she seemed skittish, as if she were afraid of me.

"Lauren," she said finally. "I'm trying it again. I have a wonderful new husband; I'm meeting him here today. He doesn't know anything about me, do you understand? I don't want him to know anything. I've been through so much, and I keep thinking maybe this time it will be all right. With Jesse, with the others, there came a time when I could see it all out there before me—illness, or sudden death, infidelity, horrors, scandal—well..." She pushed back the piece of hair with a hand that trembled. "You can't go on, once you know something like that, you simply can't go on. This time I think it's different, perhaps. I hope it's different. I'm not in love with him, you see. But I deserve a life too, a future..." She broke off.

I understood then that she was afraid I would expose her in some way, clearly the farthest thing from my mind.

"Of course you do," I said. "Of course." I grabbed and held her hand. "Goodbye."

Ben patted my knee absently when I returned to my seat. I took his binoculars and focused them to watch Georgia Rose as she made her way through the crowd at the other side of the stadium, checking her ticket again. The crowd yelled with a single roaring voice then and surged to its feet around me. I had to stand up too, with my binoculars, in order to see. Georgia Rose had reached the first level on the other side of the stadium. She stood looking back across the field for a second, gripping the railing so hard that her knuckles went white. I could see them clearly. I could see everything about her clearly. She was still a beautiful woman, in a haggard, dramatic way. While I watched her, she extended one arm tentatively in that gesture I knew so well. Then she withdrew her arm to grip the rail again. She turned her face to the sky. Her eyes were still as limitless, as passionate, as cold and blue as the sky. I wished the best for her. I realized that my fear of her had finally disappeared after all these years. The only thing I felt now was a kind of pity, and relief that I was exempt from whatever it was she had seen—and feared to see again—in that huge and annihilating sky. I lowered the binoculars. Ben pounded on my knee. Georgia Rose shrank to nothing, a mere speck, hurrying up the stairs. Alabama made a touchdown, then got the extra point as well. Ben grabbed me up in a big wet kiss while below us, in the stands, the band began to play.

All the Days of Our Lives

It's been a real bad week for Helen. She drives her big Riviera home from work quickly, carelessly, flipping it around the corners and curves of the town that she has lived in all her life. Almost. Except for the time when she ran away with Joe, a time that seems so long now, all stretched out in a big arch over years and years like a giant rainbow only of course it wasn't long at all, only two months actually, or one month and three weeks to be exact.

Helen recalls the Seascape Inn at Daytona Beach, recalls the day they checked in. She was writing a fake name on the register and the fat man behind the desk started up explaining about the name. He said he owned this place. He said that after careful thought he had named this place the Seascape Inn, which had two meanings. He didn't know if they had noticed that or not. The two meanings were *seascape*, like a painted picture of the ocean, and then *sea-plus-escape*, an escape to the sea, get it? Helen said she got it. She walked up the stairs.

Joe never said they would come to Florida, she didn't even have a bathing suit in her bag. In fact she didn't have a bag. She opened the door of their room, 217, and he was in there, pulling the drapes. He turned around in the shadows and held out his arms. Later she woke up and left him still sleeping in the double bed while she went over and opened the drapes and pushed the sliding door open and went out on the balcony and looked at the beach good for the first time. It was so wide, a mile wide it looked like, all the white sand with dots of bodies on it and then the dark blue ocean, far out beyond the sand. Helen sat out on the balcony in her slip while Joe slept in the room behind her and the night came down like a big slow rain across the beach. When it was completely dark, they turned the underwater lights on in the pool of the Seascape, a bright green rectangle right straight below their balcony. She hadn't noticed it before. It glowed out in the night like a big emerald, green and precious and strange. Helen sat out there looking down at the pool for a long time, letting the wind from the sea lift her hair.

Now she smokes three Salems on the twenty-five-minute drive home from work, pushing them out in the overflowing ash tray in her car. Her lungs are the last thing she's worried about, she's got too much on her mind as it is. If she turned left at this light, she would be only five minutes away from Howard, the man she was married to for thirteen years. Tears well up in her eyes. Right now he is over at his neat little office in the Wright Building adding up columns of numbers, moistening his pencil with the tip of his tongue. Howard is a CPA, a sweet steady man. But Howard has left her now. He has married another woman.

Of course *she* was the one who ran off, *she* was the one who went to Daytona Beach with an insurance claims adjustor, as Howard pointed out in court. Once the children are gone, though, Helen will grow old alone. She will have to cut all the packages of frozen food in two with a carving knife, cooking for one. Helen floats all alone through the world. Suddenly she wishes she was a nurse. She wishes she had a white uniform and a pin with her name on it and some of those creepy white shoes.

Instead she wears a floral polyester pants suit and a lime green blouse which is sticking to her back in this heat and lime green high-heeled sandals with straps. Helen is a big woman with long bleached-blond hair, dark brown eyes, and a hard, strong body. She used to think she was made for love, but she doesn't think that anymore.

Helen pulls into her driveway, gets out, and slams the door. The sun comes down like something solid on her head. The only good thing about Helen's present job, which otherwise is beneath her, is that she gets home around four in the afternoon. Will A. Okun, the pest control man who lives in the other side of the duplex that Helen lives in, pops out of his screen door like a man in a clock.

"*Hi* there," he says. Will A. Okun is a bachelor because he took care of his sick mother for twenty years before she finally died, and all his girlfriends married other people. Now he, like Helen, is loose in the world. Sometimes he makes casseroles and gives her half of them, so her kids will get all the vitamins they need to grow on. He worries about her kids.

"*Hot day*," Will A. Okun remarks, shifting from foot to foot. He has curly red hair that springs out in puffs like a clown's hair behind his ears, and Helen won't give him the time of day.

"What?" she asks now.

"*Hot day!*" Will A. Okun says again. He shuffles his feet.

Helen just looks at him and goes in her side of the duplex, banging the screen door shut. She sits down in front of the air conditioner in the kitchen and lets the cold air flow up over her like water.

"Mama, Denise wouldn't let us go down to Rexall," Billy starts in right away. "I wanted to go spend my allowance and Denise wouldn't let us."

"You said I was the boss," Denise says. Denise is fifteen. "Either I'm the boss or I'm not," she says.

"I don't see why I get an allowance if I can't ever spend it!" Billy hollers. He goes in his room and slams the door. Billy is going on nine.

Helen picks Davey up from the floor and takes the pacifier out of his mouth. "Hi Mama," Davey says. He's so old to have a pacifier that sometimes women grab it out of his mouth in Food Town and then he screams bloody murder, which serves them right in Helen's opinion. He can have that pacifier as long as he wants, in her opinion. In fact sometimes she wouldn't mind having one herself.

"Who's this?" she asks. She points at the little pink dog in Davey's fist.

"That's Baby Pink," he says around the pacifier. He always has something to hold.

"I hate you!" Billy hollers from his room.

"Can I go swimming now?" Denise asks. She is too young to babysit as much as she has to this summer, but in some funny way she is not young at all. She has light blue eyes that go straight through you, and curly light brown hair.

"OK, hon," Helen says. "Have a ball."

"*Mama*," Denise says. Denise will never have a ball in her life, and both of them know it.

Denise puts on her bathing suit and leaves. Helen, still carrying Davey on her hip, goes to the refrigerator and gets a Coke and pops the top off, all with one hand, and sits down on the couch with Davey. She lights a Salem and flicks on the TV. This is Helen's favorite time of the day. She likes the Coke fizz in the roof of her mouth, the drone of the air conditioner, the dim blue flicker of the TV, the way Davey smells musty and sweet like a steamy bathroom after somebody has taken a bubble bath in it. Helen switches to Channel 11.

This part of Helen's show is about Nick, Mike, and Felicity. Felicity is in the labor room having a baby. Pale blue overhead lights glare down on her pale, tired face. Nurses and doctors in face masks cluster around. But is this Nick's baby or Mike's baby? Felicity isn't telling. Felicity is an heiress whose parents died in an airplane crash when she was only three. Felicity tosses her long curly hair back and forth on the pillow—no-o-o! Only her old Spanish nursemaid, Mrs. Belido, knows whose baby it is, but Mrs. Belido is illiterate and has been unable to speak since birth. She makes a strangling noise "Yi-yi-yi!" way back in her throat whenever anybody asks her about Felicity's baby. One thing we all know for sure is that Felicity really loved Nick last year, before he went off to Hollywood to write the screenplay for his novel *The Young Doctors*. This is the famous best-selling novel he wrote while he was in medical school, which he has now quit. Oddly enough one of the main characters in the novel is a lot like Mike, the intern right here in Fernville who has become so fond of Felicity in Nick's absence.

There is Mike now in a face mask, fooling around with some medical tools. Over the top of the face mask, his eyes are filled with concern and love. "Bear down!" instructs the kindly white-haired senior resident, Dr. Godfrey. Felicity screams. "Darling!" Mike says. All this pain and emotion is almost too much for him, you can tell, even though he has seen plenty during his internship. "Forceps!" Dr. Godfrey calls out in a tone of command. Mike wipes Felicity's forehead with a little damp cloth. Felicity moans. "Now!" says Dr. Godfrey. Then the *baby* cries, a thin long wail that fills the emergency room and the tiny living room of Helen's duplex. "Darling," Mike says. "Darling, it's a boy!" He rushes out to the waiting room to give Mrs. Belido the news. Mrs. Belido, wearing a funny black lace handkerchief on her head, is right on the edge of her seat. "It's a boy!" Mike cries, tearing off his face mask and embracing Mrs. Belido. Mike's face is young and sweet. Nick, of course, is somewhere out in California and doesn't know anything about any of this. "Yi-yi-yi!" cries Mrs. Belido.

Helen gets Davey some Hawaiian Punch during the commercial. She can hear Billy in his room, kicking the wall. She sighs. She settles down again with Davey as the scene switches elsewhere in Fernville to Michelle, a real bitch who is trying to break up Sandra and Bland's marriage just for her own amusement. Right now Michelle has tricked Bland into coming over to her penthouse apartment by telling him she has a problem to discuss. Bland has always been a sucker for other people's problems, just a big Boy Scout.

"Hello!" Michelle says in her throaty voice as she opens the door. Helen never gets tired of Michelle's apartment, or of Felicity's house, or of any of the places where any of the people on this show live. They have glass coffee tables, thick wall-to-wall carpeting, ferns on fancy little stands, discreet house-keepers in uniforms back in the kitchen, and everyone is so well dressed. Like Michelle, who does not, however, look like she is dressed to discuss a problem. Helen knows, even if Bland doesn't, exactly why Michelle has gotten him over there. Now Michelle is bringing in two frosty drinks on a little tray, and urging Bland to get comfortable.

"What seems to be the problem?" Bland asks. Michelle is busy removing his tie. Bland looks uncomfortable and puzzled. He is so dumb. Michelle pushes him down on the couch and

37

sits down beside him, too close, showing a lot of leg. A light dawns in Bland's face. He jumps up and goes to look out at the city lights from the high picture window. While his back is turned, Michelle quickly hides his tie pin under the couch. Then she gets up and goes over to him and puts her arm around him from behind. Bland hops away. "I have to be going!" he says. He grabs up his tie and leaves. Michelle is left alone in her penthouse apartment with two full frosty glasses and a terrific view of the city lights. She picks up one glass and drinks it down. She lifts up a sofa cushion and gets the tie pin and stands before the picture window with it, turning it around and around in her hands and smiling a bitchy little smile to herself, while the theme music rises and falls.

Helen stretches and goes in the kitchen to see what she's got for supper. Helen's sister, Judy, comes in like a tornado, hugs Davey, and pours herself some Coke. It seems to Helen that Judy likes her a lot more since Howard left her, but she can't be sure. Judy has always kept secrets, not like Helen who tells everything she knows. Helen remembers when they were little girls and Judy spent all of her allowance on a red imitation leather diary with a little lock and key. Every night after supper Judy used to go in their room and close the door and write in her little diary with a fountain pen. If Helen made up an excuse and went in there, Judy closed the diary and just sat until Helen left, and then she wrote some more. What in the world was she writing about? What words did she think of to put on page after page, when nothing ever happened in their lives except the same old stuff?

"He's really too old for that now," Judy says, drinking her Coke and pointing to Davey, who is building a tower of pans on the floor, his pacifier stuck square in his mouth.

"Well," Helen says.

Judy snorts, her way of laughing.

"No, Judy, really. I swear I can't do a thing with the kids anymore. It's been awful ever since school let out, they haven't got anything to do all day except get after each other. And I get so tired. Sometimes I just don't know. Sometimes I wish I had Howard back, believe me."

This really cracks Judy up. "Listen here," she says. "I can't believe my ears. Don't you remember how you used to complain about Howard? How Howard had to have the sheets changed three times a week? And the kids used to drive him crazy, remember? He used to go in the bathroom and sit for hours with the door locked. You came over to my house to take a bath. Don't you remember that?"

Helen stares at her sister. "I just loved Howard," she says.

"What about when Howard didn't want to go on the honeymoon?" Judy keeps on, wrinkling up her face behind her glasses. "He said let's just stay here and give the house a real good cleaning before we move in. Don't you remember that? You cried and cried."

"We cleaned it too," Helen says, dreamy. "It was just spotless." This was the house on Robinson Street, not where she is now. "Howard could clean all night." Howard stands tall in her mind, pale and serious in his shirtsleeves, wearing a dark narrow tie. His glasses gleam. Howard stands so tall that his head's in the sky.

"Well, I think Howard has some problems," Judy says flatly. "I always thought so, and so did Lawrence." Lawrence is Judy's husband, a dark, heavy electrician, and Judy has been married to him for twenty years. One time on New Year's Eve, Lawrence came in a bathroom where Helen was and tried to kiss her, but Helen has never told Judy. It's the only secret she has ever kept from Judy, all her life, but it's not that important anyway. Lawrence *didn't* kiss her, nothing happened at all except that he broke the soap dish.

"Good riddance is what Lawrence said," Judy reports. "Haven't you got anything around here except Coke?" she asks, and Helen puts some rum in it and fixes one for herself. In the Seascape Inn at Daytona Beach, she and Joe got drunk on Piña Coladas.

Billy comes out of his room whistling. "Hi, Judy," he says. "Mom, I'll be out riding my bike."

"Hello, cutie," Judy says. Billy is really her favorite. "How's Jill?" She loves to hear about Billy's girlfriend.

Billy makes a face. "Oh, I gave her to John," he says. "See you."

"Speaking of Howard," Judy says when he's gone and she

39

finally quits laughing, "what about his *mother*?"

"Oh God!" Even tragic Helen has to laugh. "His *mother*!" she says.

"Lord God!" Judy pours herself another drink.

"Here honey, hush now," Helen says to Davey. She puts him up in his high chair, opens a can of fruit cocktail, and pours it out on his tray.

"Do you remember that time I cut her that piece of cake and she wouldn't eat it because it was too *thick*?" Judy shrieks. "Then I cut her that thin piece and she wouldn't eat it either."

"That was nothing," Helen says, "nothing at all. Listen. That was minor. In the first place she won't eat anything that's not light-colored. Everything has to be white. If you've got any colored food, like meat or green beans or anything, forget it. Then everything has got to be mashed up, but none of the food can be touching any of the other food. I mean it can't even be close."

Judy, who has heard all of this before, loves to hear it again and again. She whoops with laughter. "Real problems," she says. "See what I mean?"

Just in time, Helen remembers her daughter. "Oh, I've got to pick up Denise," she says, fishing around under the kitchen table for her shoes. "She's over at the Y pool. I won't let her walk home by herself in the dark."

"I'll stay here with Davey," Judy says. "Won't I, honey?" She pinches Davey's cheek.

It's not far and Helen drives with all the windows push-buttoned down. The wind on her cheeks is hot and dry, making wrinkles no doubt but who cares now? Thank God for Judy anyway, ditto Lawrence, who have stood by her through thick and thin. Helen shakes her head when she thinks how she almost kissed Lawrence back. Judy and Lawrence will have been married twenty-one years come June, no children. Judy has an inverted ovary. Every night Judy and Lawrence watch TV together from seven P.M. on, and on holidays they drive off in their camper, to a new place every time. So far they have been to thirty-one states. They have stickers all over the back of the van. Helen can't figure out how they've stayed married so long, what they *do*, anyway. *What is the secret of a happy marriage?* One time she asked Judy, but Judy wouldn't tell her. "Just luck," Judy said. Helen didn't believe it.

When they were kids, Judy never even wanted to get married, that's the crazy part. Never even had boyfriends. While all Helen ever wanted to do, for the entire length of their childhood, was grow up. All she ever wanted to be was married. Helen knew how marriage would be, herself all dressed up in a frilly little net apron with appliqués on it, cozy little dinners with burning candles and flowers in cut-glass vases, moments of tenderness, walks in the woods. It didn't much matter who you married, you just had to marry somebody to have all that. Never mind that their own parents fought a lot, never mind that their mother died slowly of uterine cancer before their very eyes and their father married a woman named Lyde who never opened her mouth to talk or smile or anything else. Never mind any of that. Helen had known all about marriage anyway, that it was like a beautiful pastel country out there, waiting for her to walk into.

She pulls into the parking lot and there's Denise all wrapped up in her striped towel, huddled against a phone pole. Some teenage boys stand nearby, pushing and jostling each other and calling out into the night. Denise ignores them. Good for her! Helen thinks. She hopes Denise will grow up to be a nurse and an old maid, an old maid nurse.

"I thought you'd *never* get here!" Denise says. "What took you so long?"

"Judy came by. I just don't know what I'd do without her and Lawrence." Helen begins to cry.

"Mama, come on, what's the matter now?" Denise has a dry, knowing, grownup kind of a voice.

As she pulls back out into the traffic, Helen notices the lighted YMCA pool in her rearview mirror, watches a young boy dive off the high board. His body is caught and held still in the air for a second, and then he flashes down into the water like a knife. This pool reminds her a lot of the pool at the Seascape Inn, only that one was smaller, of course.

"Your father is a wonderful man," Helen sobs.

"My father is a turkey," says Denise.

When they get back, Judy is putting on her lipstick, brushing her bangs down, getting ready to leave. "Oh, honey, now now," she says when she sees Helen's face.

"She'll be OK," says Denise. "Don't worry."

But Helen grabs Judy's sleeve. "Listen," she says. "Don't you remember when you used to write in that red diary all the time?"

Judy stares at her. "What red diary?"

"*You know*," Helen says. "That red one you got with your allowance."

"Oh, that one," Judy says. She pulls Helen's hand off her sleeve. "Well, to tell you the truth, I don't remember."

"What's for supper?" Billy comes in just as Judy is leaving.

Helen stares around her little kitchen, her eyes catching on the stack of pots and pans that Davey has left on the floor.

"Oh no. Not again," says Denise.

But Helen is saved by a knock at the door. It's Will A. Okun wearing orange potholder mitts on both hands. He carries a steaming casserole.

"*Hi there!*" He beams. "Just thought this might come in handy for you." He puts it down on a dish towel on the table and pretends to wrestle with Billy. Both boys like him because

---

Will A. Okun's Sausage-Corn combo

1 lb. sausage
1 can creamed corn
½ c. bread crumbs
4 eggs
1 teas. salt
¼ teas. pepper

Mix up. Bake for 1 hr. at 350.

---

of the way he looks in the mornings when he puts on all his pest control gear to go to work, like a man from Mars.

"I thought you might want the recipe," he says, and hands it to her on an index card.

"Thank you," Helen whispers.

"Anything you need," he says again, backing out the door, "anything at all—"

Helen looks at it while Denise sets the table.

Helen changes Davey, makes a salad, and when they finally sit down to eat, the casserole is delicious.

At work the next day, Helen proofreads brochures for a civic House Tour. These brochures have been ordered by Wells Murdock, a silver-haired businessman with a million-dollar smile who comes in the office sometimes. He and his wife are big in community affairs, and his picture is in the paper all the time. Helen sees that his own house, Blackberry Hill, will be a featured attraction on the House Tour, and she knows without even seeing it that it will be full of Oriental rugs and big jars full of dried stuff on the floor. The brochure is OK. She sends it back to the pressroom, then starts typing letters for Mr. Malone. After that, she files all the new work orders in the outer office where she works, and then she files the completed work orders in Mr. Malone's office.

He's in there behind his desk, smoking and working his calculator. "Oh, Mrs. Long," he says. His voice is old and raspy from smoking.

"Yes sir," Helen says.

"I was just wondering," he says. He looks over his glasses at her. "Whether or not you would be interested in learning a little bit more about the printing business."

"Well, I don't know, sir," Helen says. "I mean, I hadn't really thought about it. What do you mean exactly?"

"I mean becoming a salesman," he says, "like myself, or Bill, or Bob Foxwood, or John Jr. Calling on customers, making estimates on jobs, checking to see that it's done right back there in the pressroom, following through. That kind of thing. We could use a woman on our sales staff, and I can tell you right now that your salary would substantially improve."

It couldn't get any worse, Helen thinks. She stares at Mr. Malone. "I appreciate this a lot," Helen says. "I'll think about it and let you know right away. *Tomorrow*," she adds, as Mr. Malone draws his brows together in a frown. He's old and grouchy. He can't understand why Helen isn't jumping up and down with joy and squealing about her new job. He wants her to. Helen can't understand why she's not, either.

"I sure do appreciate the offer," she adds in a bright voice. "It's really a chance, isn't it?"

"All right, Helen," Mr. Malone says. "You think about it and let me know tomorrow."

Helen backs out the door. Millie and Joyce, at their desks in the outer office where they have sat for ten years, stare up at her with some suspicion in their eyes as she goes back to her desk. They know that something is up. Millie is a secretary/bookkeeper. Joyce is a secretary/file clerk. Helen is a secretary/proofreader. Of all of them, why has Mr. Malone singled her out in this way? Why isn't she happy about it? She's been bitching about this job ever since she got it, $3.35 per hour and no sick pay. In high school, all the teachers thought she was so smart. In fact Mr. Hall almost cried when she told him she was going to marry Harold Long and not go on to school. So? So does she want to grow old in one lousy job, like Millie and Joyce have, get all ingrown and petty so she can't see the forest for the trees? Although their desks are side by side, Millie and Joyce have not spoken directly to each other since an argument they had three years ago over the price of a chair, and whether Joyce had agreed to fix the right front leg before Millie bought it or not. Helen knows she doesn't want her life to be taken up by chair legs. But still.

She thinks about Mr. Malone's offer for the rest of the day, while she files orders, waits on the walk-in customers, punches out for lunch at McDonald's and then back in, proofreads copy for a School of Nursing student manual and an advertising flyer, and answers the phone. "Aesthetic Printers," she says when she answers. Sometimes she just says "Aesthetic."

"Aesthetic *what*?" It's a man's voice, silvery and deep and amused.

"Aesthetic Printers," Helen says. She knows right away who it is: Wells Murdock.

"Who is this?" he asks. "Is this the blonde by the front door?"

"Helen Long," Helen says. "Yes sir."

Wells Murdock chuckles again. He is not in any hurry to

get down to business. Helen thinks he probably has a sunken tub and mirror tiles on the wall in his bathroom, in his house on the House Tour. Helen tells him that all his brochures will be ready by ten A.M..

"I'll see you tomorrow," Wells Murdock says. He manages to sound both important and intimate at the same time. But maybe Helen is making this up. Maybe it's all in her mind. When Joe made a pass at her that first time, she wasn't sure of it either. Sometimes it's hard to tell. Helen wonders where Joe is now, where he went when he left the Seascape Inn, and settles on Texas for no real reason. He probably has another woman in Texas by now.

Helen goes to the ladies' room and cries for Howard. Then she goes out to pick roses, which is another one of her jobs. Mr. Malone grows them in a little garden at the side of the building, and every two days during the summer Helen goes out and cuts some and arranges them in bud vases, one for everybody's desk. Then she proofreads some graduation certificates, finds a mistake, and takes them back to the linotype operator for correction. One of the pressmen, Johnston Rhodes, sits drinking a Coke while the big Heidelburg Press that he runs prints calendars behind him. He squints up at Helen. The press makes a loud, regular, thumping noise.

"You ever go bowling?" Johnston Rhodes asks. Helen chokes back a sob.

Helen pretends like she doesn't hear him over the noise of the press, and the rest of the day she works in a fog, thinking about tomorrow and what she'll say to Mr. Malone, and trying to picture herself as a salesman. For instance, what would she *wear*?

Helen's half of the duplex is too quiet when she gets there and her heart jumps right up in her mouth when nobody answers her yell. Then she remembers that it's Howard's afternoon off and that he and his new wife, Louise, have taken the kids over there for a visit. Actually, Howard won custody of the kids in the first place, but that didn't last long. Louise, a real housekeeper after Howard's own heart, couldn't stand the mess. Even though she keeps all the furniture wrapped up in plastic sheets, according to Denise. It sure is quiet with them gone.

On Helen's show, Felicity continues to keep the baby's father a secret. She names him Everett, for her own father, deceased. But Everett develops jaundice and has to be placed in an incubator. Mike keeps watch over him night and day. Shadows show up under Mike's eyes, above the white mask. Along with flowers and a bunch of cards from well-wishers, Felicity receives a one-line note, written in a familiar hand. "Coming back—see you soon. Nick." *Nick!* Felicity puts the note quickly under her pillow, so Mrs. Belido and Mike won't know. Yet. She has to think.

Now it's early morning in Fernville. Michelle gets all dressed up in a forest green dress with a matching jacket and goes to visit Sandra. Sandra and Bland's house is one of Helen's favorites, a two-story traditional house with dormer windows and shutters and a graceful, winding staircase in the front hall. Bland has just left for work, and Sandra is still wearing a long striped robe that might as well be an evening dress. Michelle rings the doorbell. Sandra yawns as she goes to answer the door, expecting maybe the milkman, or anybody except Michelle in her forest green suit.

"Why, Michelle, what a surprise!" Sandra says. Her eyes narrow, but her good manners win out in the end. "Won't you come in for a cup of coffee?" she asks. Sandra is all heart, a really devoted wife who seems to have overcome the leukemia she had last year.

"Oh, how kind of you," Michelle says in her airy way. "But actually I have to run. I just came by to leave this for Bland." She hands Sandra a plain white envelope, sealed. Then she's gone—her high heels click away down the walk. After only a moment's hesitation, Sandra rips it open. *Bland's tie pin! the one she gave him on their first Christmas together!* She knows there's only one way Michelle could have gotten this. Sandra sobs. She slumps down onto the graceful winding stairway in the front hall of her house.

Elsewhere in Fernville, Lydia stands before the gold-leaf mirror in the front hall of her Tudor home, brushing and brushing her hair. Lydia, like Michelle, is sort of a bitch. But unlike Michelle, she doesn't seem to mean to be bitchy. She acts like she can't help it, like she is driven by a lot of desires that she doesn't have any control over. Like right now, for instance. She is brushing her hair so much because she is getting ready to go back to art school to fulfill herself. That's what she told John and all the kids. They were real nice about it, too. Of course! John said. I understand. By all means. Take all the courses you want! Lydia looks at herself once more in the mirror before she leaves. She wears beige slacks and her short mink coat. Her blond page-boy hair swings down below her ears. Lydia goes out and gets in her car and leaves.

The scene changes to an art studio of some kind, full of hippie-looking young people in blue jeans and dirty shirts, all working away at their easels. A black-haired man prowls like a panther among them, giving suggestions now and then. Sometimes he grabs a student's brush and shows how to do it. He is fiery and intense, with a black beard.

The studio door opens and there is Lydia, already late for her first class at art school, looking out of place to say the least in that mink coat.

"Oh, I—I—" she stutters.

The artist walks toward her.

"I—I'm—" she stutters.

He comes even closer. She falls silent, her mouth in a big O.

"*I know who you are*," he says.

Helen gets up and stretches. It's hot in here. She goes over and fools with the air conditioner but it's quit running and she can't get it to come back on. One more bill to pay. Helen feels like she's asleep this afternoon, or maybe it's only the heat. When Judy comes by, she tells her what Mr. Malone said and Judy says, "Well, you'd be a fool not to take it."

A fool. Helen is so sleepy and so hot. After Judy leaves, she goes in the bedroom and puts on a yellow terrycloth playsuit she bought in Florida. She hasn't worn it since she left there, but in the mirror she doesn't look half bad. The kids come bursting in the door then but before Helen can get to the window for a look at Howard he's gone, gunning it off down the street faster than she ever knew him to drive. The kids are as frisky and shaggy as puppies, with wet hair all in their eyes. Howard and his new wife have taken them swimming. Davey has a new little doll named Baby Red. "What happened to the air conditioning?" Billy asks. "Louise gave me this," says Denise. She hands Helen an index card that reads:

From the kitchen of Louise Long:

Beer Bread

2 c. self-rising flour
3 tbsp. sugar
1 can beer

Mix until blended. Turn into loaf pan. Bake at 375 for 20 to 25 min. or until pick inserted in center comes out clean. Brush with melted butter.

"Did you all eat some of this bread for lunch?" Helen asks.

"I guess so," says Denise. Denise is eating potato chips now.

"Well, was it *good*?" Helen asks. "I mean, how was it?"

"It was all right," Denise says with her mouth full. "I guess I've had better before."

"I'm going out to ride my bike," Billy says.

"How's your father?" Helen asks.

"He's a turkey," says Denise. "Can't we do anything about this heat?"

"Take Davey out in the back and turn on the sprinkler," Helen says. "I'll be out there myself in a minute."

Denise goes out and Helen mixes herself a rum and Coke and lights a Salem off the stove since she's run out of matches. While she waits for the burner to heat up, she thinks about Mr. Malone and his rose food and the job, which she knows by now that she won't even tell Denise about, although so far she isn't sure why. She picks up a piece of paper that the kids have left on the kitchen table where they were coloring, last night. It's a list, in Billy's third-grade writing:

Cool Club Rules
1. Bee cool how you walk
2. Ride your bike ruff
3. Get Donny
4. Fix up your
      room cool
5. Yell loud !
6. jump from high places !

Helen laughs. She gets everything she needs and goes out the back door and positions herself in the lounge chair to face the last of the sun. Denise has turned on the sprinkler and put Davey down at the edge of it so that every time it comes around, he hollers and giggles out loud. Denise sits in the other chair reading a library book, shielding her eyes from the sun. Helen's backyard is closed in by a chain-link fence. Helen lights another cigarette off her first one.

Will A. Okun jumps out of his house like a jack-in-a-box. His hair springs out from his head like cotton, like fluff, like bright angel hair in the sun. He points at the sun, in fact. "*A real scorcher*," he says.

Helen nods agreeably. "And I just don't know what to do. Of all days, my air conditioner just broke down!" she cries.

Denise looks hard at her mother and then back down at her book.

"Why, I'll take a look at that for you!" Will A. Okun beams. "Just a minute." He pops back into his house and then reappears with an olive green toolbox, which he carries by a handle on the top. He opens the chain-link gate and goes in their back door by himself, whistling a little tune.

Helen puts her cigarette out in the grass and leans further back in her chair. Maybe Howard is a turkey, after all. But there are other fish in the sea. Helen can't figure out what has gotten into her, these recent months. She can't figure out why she's been mooning around like she has. The future rises up before her in a flash. She knows she won't take that job. She knows she will have a cup of coffee with Wells Murdock in the morning, she will go on the House Tour, she will change her attitude toward Will A. Okun, she might even go bowling, and who knows what she might do after that? Somebody in the neighborhood is mowing grass. Helen hears the mower and also she smells the grass. She loves how it smells. Somebody else is cooking out, hamburgers or something, and that smells good too across the yards. Suddenly Helen sits straight up. A little breeze comes out of nowhere, lifting her hair. The last rays of the sun, shining through the sprinkler, made a shimmering pastel rainbow across her whole backyard. It's so beautiful that Helen catches her breath. When she leans this way or that, the rainbow moves too. It moves with her. It arcs up over the duplex, over the neighborhood, over the town and all the towns beyond this one, promising everything: another chance, another love, another world.

The Seven Deadly Sins

1. Pride

With rings on my fingers and bells on my toes I make music wherever I go. Now I am seated atop the piano, spinning, I sing "Arrivederci Roma," which I will follow with "Mack the Knife," still spinning, mother-of-pearl and chrome piano propelled by inimitable Pekingese hand-trained by Hector's trainer largely through inbred aversions. Hector is my protector. I spin. Everyone is spellbound in my spell as sinuous as snakes as strong as Emily Dickinson as vast as China. Watch out! Now I am playing "The Moonlight Sonata" on strands of my raven hair. They are throwing their wineglasses into the fireplaces even the Senator is moved. The fireplaces quiver, they bellow, my toes move in the archetypal rhythm of "Jingle Bells" and I switch keys into wind chimes. Inexpressible longings arise. The fireplaces produce large glass sculptures which will be resold at many times their original value. Hector has sent me some caviar mousse. With which I am so pleased I delve into "Ol' Man River" plucking large purple and green frog-like notes from my cleavage lavishly I throw them to the crowd. Bravo, they cry, olé, hold that line! Tonight I am wearing my basic black cape my skin like swans my neck like Egypt my cleavage. I play "Rhapsody in Blue" upon my piano teeth moving my calves in unison, they are bleating, the Pekingeses break training to bark, Hector is delighted, sending me apples, chutney, and pears. The crowd is disrobing now, handing their robes to the trainer, round one. Beneath the robes they are exquisitely attired in the latest fashions. I am exquisitely attired in my body. I sing "Honeycomb, Won't You Be My Baby?" in fifties falsetto, delightful, they are taking off their clothes now, throwing them up to me here as best they can. I put them on, everything as best I can, doing that old soft shoe. I wear many fashionable clothes. I can take them or leave them myself. I can sing forever. Hector assists me up the retractable ladder now to the pedestal, ebony with its octagonal patchwork cushion: I am nothing if not chic.

2. Envy

You have been standing by the door now for some time holding your drink, your coat, your wife. Every party has a pooper that's why we invited you. Not true. I see in your eyes the sea. You turn from me still holding all of that, you walk right into one of Hector's fake doors, silvered glass, all mirror, giving the illusion of space another dimension to this party more people another room. Hector is quite a card. Not true. I see tall masts in your eyes in the mirror, then junks, rafts, sampans. I sing the little-known theme of "Surfside Seven." You put on your wife and leave.

Much later alone in my chamber attired in my veils, I am burning green candles incense frankenstein myrrh summoning my ferocious powers honing my defenses to lethal steel points carving her image in Neutrogena soap, patacake, I will wash her right out of my hair.

3. Wrath

Hector and I are playing Prehistoric Putt-Putt. Hector is cheating again, that card, he moves his ball two clubfoot lengths from the side of the aisle and even though I see it I am supposed to pretend that I do not. I bend tactfully to adjust my knee buckles as Hector takes aim and shoots through the skeleton almost making it but luckily deflected by the brontosaurus' left bicuspid and thereby missing the gaping smile the throat Hole 6. Now it is my turn. Luckily the volcano erupts however affording me an extra shot since I am first mired in the primeval mud then with a clever chip I put it right in there right down that ancient esophageal canal. Par! I am so pleased I sing "My Blue Heaven," double-timing. My cleats ring out nicely on the hardened lava flow. But Hector is miffed. Sometimes he wants me to sing and sometimes not. I don't know when those times are. "Let's call it a day," Hector says. He removes his goggles. "But no!" I cry, for I always par on the salt flats right into the archaeologist's sifter, an easy hole.

"Come on here now don't be difficult," Hector says.

"Difficult! I will show you difficult!" I cry.

I jump high into the air clicking my cleats I descend upon Hector's clubfoot flattening it I attack the pterodactyl tearing off its wings stuffing its rudimentary gill slits with fossils I heave the fishes up from the water hazards onto dry land hastening the process I stone the other golfers who are forced to shelter in the caves behind dripping stalactites, stalagmites, I rip up all the score cards I put out the cavemen's fire.

"Let's have some lunch," says Hector.

"Lunch! I will show you lunch!" I cry stabbing the tyrannosaurus with early tools stomping prehensile toes emptying my pocket flask of Chanel No. 5 on all the ferns producing vacuums which Nature abhors.

"She is young and impulsive," Hector explains to the owner. Hector's men are carrying me away but I am wroth, wroth, piercing their ears with my teeth.

4. Sloth

I hang by my feet from the pewter Williamsburg light fixture in Hector's Early American den, swinging gently in the breeze from the open window eating marzipan occasionally reading the *Ladies' Home Journal* spread out on a Queen Anne table below me. I am up here so as not to disturb Penny the maid, who dusts. I wear some monogrammed pajamas with matching piping matching the monogram as I have not bothered to dress today. A knock it is my friend Marianne who lies upon the sofa Penny brings iced tea Marianne and I discuss the grapefruit diet, whether Lucia and Martin are sleeping together, whether Ernie is gay, cucumber cream, *Apocalypse Now*, silicon jobs, and Sea Island, Georgia. Penny is dusting my limbs. Hector comes through with another tour, pointing me out I wiggle a pinky at them all. Hector beams. "Look at that! "Look at that!" he exults. At his request I sing a few bars of "Melancholy Baby." Marianne giggles, the tour salutes Hector, they leave. Hector says, "Step right this way." Penny is dusting my mind which she hasn't got to in months. "What sort of cleanser is that you're using?" Marianne says. "Why! Glad you asked!" says Penny.

5. Avarice

I want you so badly I watch your house your movements your wife's movements your children. I want your Irish setter, your riding mower, your dogwood trees. I want the gravel in your drive. Your wife nods to me, a friendly woman. She does not really see me since I am disguised as the newsboy of the town, my cute red baseball cap. One day when she is off at noonday Lenten services I go into your house by the carport, sneaking swiftly across your Congoleum kitchen flooring the Oriental rugs in your living room (this is where you *live*!) upstairs. In your room I go through your drawers one by one. I want these drawers, your chest-on-chest (antique). I want your dark socks and your garters, your clean starched shirts and your shoes puffed out by the little trees. I enter the closet and bury my face in your hunting jacket, your three-piece suit, sports jackets, gray wool pants. I want your windbreaker most of all I'd like to give you a piece of my mind. But the sliding door is slid. I cower: I am seen. Evidently you have returned for a halyard or a jib or something you forgot. "Well, well," you say. "How about dinner sometime?" I am so happy I sing "Shrimpboats Are A-Comin'," rattling the hangers in time.

6. Greed

We dine in a restaurant safe from prying eyes. It is so private we are the only persons here actually dining. The rest are mere mannequins placed to put us at our ease, their forks lifted, caught deep in animated conversation. There are many waiters however and they wait upon us hand and foot feeding us crossing our legs transporting cigarettes safely from far ashtrays to our lips. And am I hungry! We start with the vichyssoise I have also oysters Rockefeller pâté campagne salade Niçoise fruit cocktail quiche Lorraine. I devour you with my eyes. Our main course consists of filet Bordelaise petit pois coq au vin surf'n turf red wine, white wine. You tell me a story about when you were a little boy and you had an Alka-Seltzer boat, a sailboat for your bath. It had a secret compartment you say into which you put one Alka-Seltzer and three tablespoons of water and then put the boat into the bath and there it goes. I am a fool for stories like that. For dessert I try chocolate mousse baba au rhum Susan's Blueberry Crumble. After coffee I reach for your hand but the waiter brings it to my lips for me and I nibble your index finger, your thumb. "Check please," you say.

7. Lust

At last we are here, the ancient inevitable rented room the bed the tiny cakes of soap in paper wrappers at the sink. We kiss. Your eyes are as clear as the Gulf Stream with lights deep in them as old as phosphorescent fish. I tell you I love you, you say the same thing, but would you have said it if I hadn't first? We kiss some more. You take off your jacket. I take off my coat. You take off your shirt, I take off my dress, you take off your tie, I take off my shoes. All the time we are kissing between garments I am humming a tune of mindless desire. You take off your belt and pants, I take off my stockings and panties, you take off your shorts, I take off my slip and bra. We kiss. You go to the foot of the bed and hold out your arms. You take off your watch, I take off my body. You have an appointment it seems.

I understand. I know how Hector feels and how you feel. I understand. But if you could possibly assist me with this pedestal please it's hurting my ass. And I'll tell you right now what I really hate more than anything else in the whole world and there it goes again that's it that sound: the closing door.

Gulfport

Debbi—who used to be Deborah and take piano lessons in her other life, when she was a child that is, before she started spelling her name with an "i" and took up with so many boys— Debbi sits on the end of the pier feeling awful, and stares at the flat gray gulf. The Gulf of Mexico. Lord! Love will get you into things: expand your damn horizons as they say. But who ever thought she would end up here, beside such a no-account piece of water in spite of its fancy name, shallow as far out as you can stand to walk in it, all warm and milky-weird and full of slick slimy fish that move against your legs and crap that floats up from New Orleans, plastic glasses that say "HIYA from the Hurricane Room" and other stuff too perverted to mention. Lord. Debbi reaches down and fishes something up from the warm smooth surface with her toe and then she leans over and grabs it. It's a white rubber surgical glove with the ends of the fingers mysteriously cut off, like whoever wore it just leaked out and drained away. Gross. Debbi throws it as hard as she can and when it hits the water it doesn't even splash, it just sinks without a ripple, which makes her feel better. Not good but better. If she just had a cigarette. If she just had a beer. If she hadn't locked herself out of the damn apartment—the *room*, that's more like it, but you can't think

CAKEWALK

of everything all the time and Lord, last night was a lot of fun.
Bobby *is* cute, the way he gets so sweet when he drinks tequila
and those things he thinks up to do.

If they could stay there in number 16 all the time, if he
never went out to his job at the Seaquarium and they could
just stay in that room all the time with the air conditioner
humming and the radio on—one thing Bobby can really do is
dance—with the light coming in through the venetian blinds
and falling in stripes across the Beautyrest mattress in the middle of the room . . . at night it's a pink light, too, from the neon
heron on the Beachview Motel sign outside their window, and
it turns their whole room pink. Debbi smiles. She sighs and
stretches. Lord! Debbi is in love.

A little breeze starts up and blows her hair across her face.
Way out there where the breeze is coming from, beyond the
shallow water, the gulf gets blue and deep. There are things
out there you can't even imagine, Bobby says. Flounders with
two eyes on one side of their bodies. Fish with lights in their
stomachs. Whales. And dolphins, of course, like that damn
Lucille Elizabeth that Bobby is so crazy about, dolphins playing
and leaping in arcs through the long blue waves. Bobby *is*
sweet, but a lot of the time lately it seems to Debbi like most
of that sweetness is saved up for Lucille Elizabeth, the dolphin
he's so crazy about at the Seaquarium. Debbi is real tired of
hearing about Lucille Elizabeth and how smart she is, how she
goes through hoops and squeaks one time for yes and two times
for no. So what? Debbi can do things for Bobby that Lucille
Elizabeth couldn't even dream of in her fishy little brain. Debbi
looks out at the Gulf and while she watches, the sun comes
out from behind a bunch of piled-up white clouds just in time
to set, huge and orange behind the water. It gives her a headache. Debbi's horizons have been expanded just about as much
as she can stand.

"Pretty, isn't it?"

The woman's voice behind her is such a shock she almost
jumps into the crummy gulf.

"Oh, I'm sorry. I didn't mean to startle you." The woman
has a soft-soft voice. She puts her hand on Debbi's shoulder
and Debbi looks at it, manicured with perfect oval nails painted
dusty pink. Her own hands are all dirty and the red nail polish

58

is chipping off, half gone. Debbi puts her hands under her thighs and sits on them.

"It's OK," Debbi says. Her own voice sounds funny to her, but of course she hasn't spoken to a living soul all day. She clears her throat. "It's just me. I'm kind of jumpy, I guess. Hard night." She feels like she has to explain. "You wouldn't happen to have a cigarette, would you?"

The woman removes her hand and steps back. "No, I'm sorry," she says. "I don't smoke."

Which figures. This is a classy woman, a lady, wearing one of those nice shiny bathing suits and a matching jacket with loose, full sleeves. The lady makes like she is going, but Debbi's in the mood to talk now that she's remembered how again. "Where are you staying?" she asks. "Did you just get down here?"

"Ye-es," the lady says. She has pretty, straight blonde hair and no makeup, with those hands that never did one day's work in her life. "We just arrived this afternoon. We're staying at the Seagull Inn."

Which figures, too. The Seagull Inn is a real nice place with a pool and a coffee shop, where Negroes come around bringing you a free cup of coffee and a *Times Picayune* every morning, and you can sit out on gliders under the live oaks to read it. The Seagull Inn is separated from the Beachview Motel by a wide strip of sand where a drive-in theater used to be. Some of the speakers are still there, sticking straight up out of the sand. The same hurricane that tore up the drive-in hit the Beachview too, only Mr. Johnson has never bothered to fix it back up the way they did the Seagull Inn.

"How do you like Gulfport so far?" It's been a long time since Debbi has made conversation with ladies.

The lady looks surprised. "Oh, it's lovely. We've never been to this part of the coast before. It's awfully scenic, isn't it? All these big trees. And of course we can let Frederick come down to the beach by himself here since it's not dangerous, not like it is along the Atlantic."

Debbi shades her eyes with her hand and turns around to find this Frederick, who sure enough is poking along the beach at the edge of the water picking up stuff and putting it into an ice bucket from the Seagull Inn. Frederick is a weird little egghead-looking kid with big glasses and skinny knobby legs as white as a sheet of paper.

"Frederick is very interested in marine life," the lady says.

"My boyfriend, Bobby, works down at the Seaquarium." Debbi is glad to have something to say. "He knows everything there is to know about dolphins, I guess."

"Oh, how *interesting*," the lady breathes. "Frederick!" she calls. "Frederick, come here for a minute. I want to introduce you to someone."

When Frederick gets there, the lady does the introductions and her name turns out to be Mrs. John Temple III from Birmingham, Alabama. "Call me Diane," she breathes.

"OK," Debbi says, but then there's nothing else to say. She wishes she had a cigarette.

"Debbi's friend works at the Seaquarium, where you wanted to go," Diane tells Frederick. "He's a dolphin expert."

Frederick perks up and looks at her. His eyes behind the glasses are about twice as big as they ought to be. "Dolphins have sonar," he says. "I was just reading an article about them. They can listen *through* things. Like they can listen to each other through their bodies, like their teeth and bones, but especially all those parts that have air, like the alimentary passages in the stomach and the breathing passages. One dolphin can listen to another dolphin's stomach, for instance, and tell exactly how that dolphin is feeling. So there is no way"— Frederick looks at his mother, pronouncing each word quite distinctly, like he's clipping it out of his mouth—"there is no way dolphins can lie to each other."

"God almighty," Debbi says.

"Well, we'll have to go to the Seaquarium, won't we?" Diane says finally, in a voice as limp as a rag. This kid would be too much for anybody, Debbi can see that already.

But Frederick is gone then, lickety-split off the pier and back up the beach to see something a surf-caster's reeling in.

"Don't get me wrong," Debbi says to Diane. "Bobby isn't a scientist or anything like that. When we came down here in the first place it was for him to work on one of those oil rigs, see, out of Shreveport. They pay real good money and Bobby used to be a Seabee in the Navy. But then that didn't work out, it was too dangerous and too cold and they want you to stay out there all the time, and so then we came over here and Bobby got this job at the Seaquarium. It's just a job."

"I see," Diane says in a voice like she sees a lot. She fidgets around again like she's fixing to leave.

Debbi stands up and looks straight at her. "Me and Bobby are in love," she tells Diane.

"Oh." Diane pulls in her breath and all the features on her face seem to slide around so that she looks off center, lost, and not so pretty any more. Then she notices Debbi's black eye. Debbi knew this would happen sooner or later.

"Why, what *happened*?" Diane cries.

"I ran into a door." The words come out smooth as you please. "It's about gone now."

"Oh," Diane says again. "Well, we have to be going. Perhaps we'll see you again."

Perhaps. Debbi watches Diane walk back down the pier in her snazzy little canvas shoes with the rope bottoms. "Hey! Diane! Do you believe in ESP?" Debbi hollers, but Diane doesn't hear her or acts like she doesn't and keeps on going. Debbi watches Diane go over and put her arm around Frederick and sees them walk away from the water together. This reminds Debbi of her own mother who is up in Johnson City, Tennessee, having trouble with her back. At least she *said* she was having trouble with her back the last time Debbi called, from a pay phone of course so her mother won't know where she is. Debbi's mother does not understand love: she never has and she never will. All she understands is going to church and hemming skirts. She has hemmed skirts for a living ever since Debbi's father left, all day nine to five at Susan's Smart Shoppe, a job Debbi would rather die than have. But when Debbi thinks about her mother's back, her eyes fill up with tears. This makes the black eye smart. Of course Bobby never meant to do that anyway, and when they made up it was just like the 4th of July with fireworks going off red and blue all over the beach. Debbi watches Diane and Frederick until they are little bitty specks disappearing into the Seagull Inn, and something clicks inside her head.

She can be like that, just like Diane exactly, if she puts her mind to it. If she plays her cards right. Of course she can! Bobby is not taking her seriously, that's the whole problem.

He's got the wrong idea. Well, in fact Debbi can see where he got it since she ran off with him to Gatlinburg right after they barely met at that bar in Johnson City where she was waiting tables. But she can get Bobby to straighten up and quit drinking if she puts her mind to it, she knows she can, and she can get a good job herself someplace and they can get married, that's what! Bobby is plenty smart, he even went to college somewhere before he joined the Navy, she knows that for a fact. Even if he did clam up later and wouldn't tell her where. His folks have got money, too; Debbi can tell from some of the things he says. Why, Bobby would be a good catch! Because Bobby *is* sweet and it's not his fault—not when you think about it—it's not his fault he's got the wrong idea. And it's not like Debbi hasn't got a lot to work with: more than Diane, in fact, whose chest is as flat as Frederick's.

Debbi walks back up the pier and then up the beach, not even noticing where she's going. The first thing she's going to do is get some dusty pink nail polish and the next thing is wash her hair. Debbi thinks she'll go up to the d'Iberville Hotel and get her fortune told too, by that man they had the article about in the paper. That cook with ESP. But Debbi feels like she has ESP herself right now, and she sees it all before her eyes so real she could almost be there: a little yellow kitchen with checkered yellow-and-white linoleum tiles on the floor and yellow-and-white-striped curtains at the windows and plants and spice racks all over the place, just like in a magazine, and her and Bobby sitting at the table drinking Cold Duck out of long-stemmed glasses, her in a turquoise knit dress and high-heeled sandals and Bobby in a three-piece suit. The wind blows off the water harder now, with a fresh sweet smell, as close to cool as it ever gets down here in the summertime, and as Debbi cuts through the wrecked sandy drive-in lot, she imagines everything. *Lord*, she sees it all!

But there's a party in 16 when she gets there, and it's already been going on for a while by the looks of it. Bobby is right in the middle of it like he always is, sitting back on the mattress against the wall drinking a Jax beer and laughing like hell. Bobby looks so cute when he laughs: he throws his head back and really hollers, and his eyes that can get so flat and hard sometimes turn as blue and clear as the sky. Bobby's hair is blond and curly, the kind of hair you'd want your little girl to get. He grins his big wide grin at her and throws his beer can against the wall above the air conditioner. "Hey, baby!" Bobby says. "Debbi! Where you been? Get me another beer, will you, baby," but when Debbi goes into the little kitchenette to get it, she almost trips over Miss Bubbles, the stripper from across the court. Miss Bubbles' real name is Sarajean Pringle and she used to be a coed at Mississippi State College before she switched over to life in the fast lane and broke her mama's heart. Now it looks like Miss Bubbles is drunk, sitting on the floor having a big conversation with Mr. Johnson, who is drunk all the time. Sometimes Mr. Johnson forgets to collect their money and he doesn't pay the light bill and everything gets turned off. The last time that happened, old Mrs. Pugh lost five pounds of hamburger that thawed and then to make up for it, Mr. Johnson bought her a big T-bone steak, which made her so mad she threw it out in the courtyard by the palm tree and a yellow dog ate it. Mr. Johnson is nice, though. It's just that he has had a life of misery and mishap—that's what he told Debbi—and now he doesn't care about anything anymore.

"Then I got this little baby doll for Christmas," Miss Bubbles is saying, "and don't you know my brother was so *mean*, he took it and put it in the stoker so the stoker would feed it to the furnace, and I never could get it back." Miss Bubbles keeps crying and Mr. Johnson keeps talking to her.

Debbi gets Bobby a beer—somebody has put a lot of beer in the refrigerator—and then she sees Lewis, who always makes her nervous, come in through the door and so she opens a new bottle of tequila and pours herself some in a coffee cup. Lewis is a Negro intellectual who is living down here for the climate and the atmosphere or so he says. He's writing a book. In any case he wears spooky jewelry made out of animal teeth.

"Debbi!" Bobby hollers.

"I swear I could smell burning rubber up through those heat vents all winter long," Miss Bubbles weeps.

The Cat Lady, who is also a stripper at the Gaucho Room where Miss Bubbles is the star, is dancing with a fat little sailor in the corner of the room, pushing herself against him. Cat Lady is old and kind of pitiful, but she will give you Valium for nothing, or anything else you want. Bobby says she tries to make people like her by giving it all away. Bobby can be pretty intellectual himself sometimes, which is why he and Lewis are friends. They have these intellectual conversations. Debbi fills her coffee cup with tequila again and then steps over Miss Bubbles and takes Bobby his beer. Bobby pulls her down on the mattress and gets the beer with one hand and reaches up under her shirt with the other.

"Quit that!" Debbi slaps his hand away; Lewis is right there and she doesn't want him to see. But Lewis's dark eyes don't have anything, not anything in them. Debbi doesn't like Negroes anyway, especially Negroes like Lewis who act more white than white people. But Lewis has some dope and they smoke it, even Mr. Johnson, and after a while some more people come in and the party moves half outside on the cracked cement courtyard under the palm tree in the heron's pink light. After a while Debbi just gets the bottle and starts drinking out of it, and then she goes over to Mr. Johnson's room with him to get some Kentucky Fried Chicken he says he has in there, only they can't find it and when she gets back, she can't find Bobby either. "Bobby!" she calls. "Bobby!" But the sailor is the only one in the room, sitting in the single chair with his head rolled over to the side, and he doesn't even look up when she calls. Then Debbi remembers what she was thinking about down at the pier today and she goes in the bathroom to brush her teeth. You've got to start someplace. Ha!

But something's going on in the shower, the baby blue vinyl curtain moving back and forth. It makes Debbi dizzy to watch it. "Oh baby," says Bobby's voice. Debbi sweeps back the shower curtain and catches them at it, Bobby kissing Miss Bubbles like crazy and her leaning back against the mildewed tile wall moaning.

"Oh!" Debbi shrieks. Then she burst into tears.

"Now honey," Bobby says, stepping over the rim of the shower. "Now Debbi," because Debbi has picked up a glass bottle of Prell shampoo like she's going to throw it, which is exactly what she *is* going to do until just in time she remembers.

Very carefully, Debbi puts the bottle back down on the top

of the toilet. "I'm so surprised at you all," she says in a ladylike voice, and she leaves the bathroom with a lot of dignity but not before she sees relief and surprise, a new kind of surprise, move across Bobby's face.

"I don't think I feel very good," Miss Bubbles says just before Debbi closes the door.

Ha! Miss Bubbles can throw up all over Bobby if she wants to, for all Debbi cares. Debbi hopes she *does* throw up all over him: serve him right. But Debbi won't throw up—suddenly, she's not even high. Her head is as clear as a bell. Everybody is gone from their room, but the sailor has left his little black sailor shoes side by side at the foot of the mattress and there's trash all over the place. Old smoke hangs in wispy sheets that wave in the wind from the air conditioner. Debbi walks out the door where she almost stumbles over Lewis, who is lying on a sofa cushion under the palm tree saying to Mr. Johnson, "Borges! I want to write like Borges! He's the Ray Charles of literature, man," but old Mr. Johnson is nodding in his cane-backed chair and Debbi knows he's not hearing a word. He never listens to anybody anyway. Debbi clears her throat.

"I'm going to night school," she says.

"What?" Lewis props himself up on one elbow.

"Night school," Debbi repeats. "I'm going to start in night school right away." She didn't know she was going to say it, but now she knows it's true.

"Oh hell." Bobby comes up behind her and puts his arms around her waist. Miss Bubbles is not with him.

"I am so!" she says.

"You already know all you need to know about the night," Bobby says, and Lewis laughs, and Mr. Johnson tries to say something that nobody understands.

"I bet you went to school yourself, now didn't you, Mr. Johnson?" Debbi asks him, because there has always been something, well, *refined* about him in the sad little slope of his back.

Mr. Johnson looks up. "I went to the school of hard knocks," he says, and smiles and slaps his knees gently. Every move Mr. Johnson makes is halfhearted, like he did it a long time ago.

"Yeah man," Lewis says. "Yeah, we've *all* been there."

But Lewis says this in a way that makes Debbi not believe him, like he thinks he's better than everyone else. He's wearing that fortune in teeth, for instance.

Cat Lady comes out in a white kimono with her red hair pulled straight back from her face. She doesn't look like a cat at all; she just has this old leopardskin costume to dance in. She looks like an old-maid schoolteacher with her hair pulled back that way. "Do you all want some of this?" she says. She's got a big plate of something with bean sprouts on top of it.

"What is it?" Lewis says.

"Health food," Cat Lady answers, and for some reason this tickles Lewis and Bobby so much that they burst out laughing.

"Well, hell," Lewis says, "I better eat some of that," and Cat Lady goes and gets some plates and two spoons and two forks for the rest of them.

"This tastes like shit," Bobby says, and the Cat Lady's tight lined face gets even tighter.

"I think it's real good," Debbi says, elbowing him, and Bobby looks at her again the way he did in the shower. It does taste like shit, though, or at least it's not very good: lima beans and tomatoes and those slimy little sprouts. It's not a thing like the meals Debbi is going to fix for Bobby in that yellow kitchen—she'll cook everything up elegant, with cream sauce. After they finish eating, Cat Lady gets the plates and takes them away, her kimono gleaming pink in the light. Her face looks old in the light. "Thank you," Debbi says again. She feels sorry for Cat Lady who has got two practically grown children somewhere, living with her sister. Mr. Johnson stands up after a couple of tries and says good night and the white of his shirt fades away in the dark. It's real quiet out there in the courtyard. Stars are out, and the wind comes up cool off the gulf. Most of the rooms are dark, the rooms where the electricity even works that is, and even old Mrs. Pugh's light is off so she must be asleep for a change. Mrs. Pugh has trouble sleeping and sometimes she walks the courtyard at night dragging those paper bags and talking in a singsong voice. Mr. Johnson lets her stay there free, Lewis says.

Lewis stretches and sits up, staring at her and Bobby where they sit by the bougainvillea. "Well . . ." he says. He stretches and looks at them.

"Hey, Lewis!" Bobby sits straight up. "Looky there! Get it!"

"Get what?"

"Hush, Bobby," Debbi says. "You'll wake all these people up."

"Lizard," Bobby says. "Get it," and Lewis gets it and holds it up by the tail with one skinny long-fingered black hand.

"Give it here and I'll show you something," Bobby says. He leans over and gets it and flicks it a couple of times, hard, on the white of its quivering throat.

"Bobby, you're hurting it," Debbi says.

"Shut up." He flicks it again. "Now watch here." He brings it up to his ear and the lizard bites on his earlobe and just hangs there swinging, for all the world like a dangle earring.

Lewis whoops with laughter. "How'd you make it do that?" he asks.

"You just hit him right here on the neck," Bobby explains. He takes the lizard off and flicks him on the neck again and then hangs him on his other ear. "If you hit them right, they'll do it every time."

"God almighty," Debbi says but she has to laugh, Bobby is so good-looking anyway and that lizard just swings on his ear. Then Lewis has to make it hang on *his* ear too, and Mrs. Pugh opens her door and says all she wants in this life is a little peace, and Bobby and Lewis are laughing and laughing. Bobby is so cute: who else would know how to hang a lizard on his ear?

Later, though, when they are back in number 16 finally and Bobby has thrown the sailor's shoes out the door toward the palm tree where Mrs. Pugh threw the T-bone steak, when they are finally on the bed, Bobby spoils it all by asking if she would mind if Lewis did it with them sometimes—didn't she think that would be fun? "Well, no I don't," Debbi says. "I don't think it would be fun a bit."

"Oh, come on, Debbi, you know you've always wanted a big—" but Debbi sits right up and puts her hand over his mouth. "I *never*," she says, and then it seems like she might as well say it all right out, right now: "What I want to do is get married, Bobby, so there."

"Shit," Bobby says. "What do you want to do that for?"

67

"I just do," Debbi wails, and then she's crying as hard as Miss Bubbles did.

"Come on, honey," Bobby says. "We couldn't do anything if we were married that we're not going to do right now." He moves on top of her and fucks her, that's all, and he's asleep by the time he's through. Debbi lies under him just thinking for a long time, watching him breathe up and down in the soft pink glow from the window until finally the air conditioner hums her to sleep.

The next day when she wakes up, Bobby's gone—he used to wake her and kiss her before he left—and the room is freezing cold from the air conditioner which is still going full blast and has given Debbi a headache and a sore throat. Debbi wraps herself up in the blanket and turns it off. Then she gets some aspirin for her headache and a beer for her sore throat and opens the door to let some heat in there. The sun is so bright it's awful. But it's hot, all right, a burning hot day already, and in spite of the heat here comes Raymond White all dressed up in his royal blue suit like a tropical bird, going out to save souls. Raymond White is a Mormon on a two-year mission, and every day he takes his pamphlets door to door. Raymond White has a long wobbly neck and a thick gold identification bracelet with an engraved cross on it. When he sees Debbi in her blanket, his whole face splits into a grin as wide as a field of corn. Debbi shuts the door. Lord. It's noon already, and she's got things to do. Debbi shaves her legs and her underarms in the shower, and then she washes her hair. If she had thrown that bottle of Prell at Miss Bubbles last night like she was going to, she wouldn't have had anything to wash it with. Ha! Debbi takes a long time putting on her makeup, getting it right. Then she puts on her pink and white flowered stretch pants and her short-sleeved pink sweater which is her best outfit, and also the only thing clean. Her black eye is almost gone by now, and if Debbi does say so herself, she looks good. She looks so good she doesn't think Bobby will mind if she gets a twenty-dollar bill from the dresser drawer, not when he sees her, so she gets it and then she goes out and sits in the sun with Mrs. Pugh who is knitting a sock by the palm tree.

"This one is for Ernest." Mrs. Pugh holds it up. She knits socks all the time for people you never heard of, people who don't exist anyway, Lewis says, and in fact Ernest would have to be some kind of giant to fit that sock. Nobody else is around. After Debbi finishes drying her hair and drinking her beer, she goes over to the mall where she buys everything to do her nails with and then she does them pink right there on the bench outside Revco. They look good. A lot of kids and their mothers are in the mall, but none of them are as cute as the kids Debbi and Bobby will have. They don't have that curly blond hair. After she does her nails, Debbi goes in Sears to look at draperies. She makes the man show her all the brocade. "I'll think about it," she tells him finally, and then she eats two hot dogs and walks a block up the street to the ritzy d'Iberville to find that cook. Men whistle at her from the passing cars. Once a man in a pickup slows down and bangs on the side of his door. Ha! This one's *sold*, she thinks.

At the d'Iberville, Debbi marches straight through the fancy dining room past all the black-suited waiters and into the kitchen, ignoring the maître d'.

"Where's that cook who has ESP?" she asks a woman whose arms are half gone kneading dough.

"You can't come in here!" The maître d' has followed her. He is little and funny-looking in his black suit, reminding Debbi of a chihuahua her aunt Edna used to have.

"She wants Leon," somebody says, and somebody else says, "Leon's on break," jerking a thumb toward the back of the kitchen.

"You'll have to leave immediately!" screams the little maître d'.

Debbi doesn't even bother to look at him as he follows her yapping all the way past the stoves and the big steel pots and then drops away when she gets to the back of the kitchen. Leon, when she finds him, is a big fat black man smoking a cigarette and reading *Reader's Digest*. Debbi had thought he would be skinny and arty-looking, maybe Hungarian, with a faraway look in his eyes.

"Yas?" Leon says when she sits down on the bench at the table across from him. He blows smoke out in a stream. All around them, people walk by wearing white aprons and grinning.

"I read that story in the paper," Debbi says. "The one where you saw your mother dying in a dream and then she died? and about how you found that man's watch? and I just wondered if you tell fortunes too. If you'd tell my fortune, that is."

"Tell her she's going to have a date with a waiter," a waiter says, going by.

"I do not tell no fortunes, miss," Leon says in a voice that rumbles like a train. "If I knew you, miss, I might have a dream. But I do not tell no fortunes, no, I'm sorry, not like you mean. You'll have to go elsewhere, miss, for that."

"You mean all you do is *dream*?" Debbi is furious. She can't believe she walked over here for this.

"Yas," Leon says. He throws his cigarette down on the floor and stands up, stepping on it, wiping his big black hands on his stomach under the apron. He smells like fish. But he does have something about him, in how purely big he is for one thing, the way he fills up space. Leon is *somebody*: you can tell.

"Listen," Debbi says. "I'm going to write my name down here on this piece of paper, plus Mr. Johnson's phone number, that's how you can call me, and if you ever have a dream about me, you let me know. All right? You call me up and tell me what you dream."

Leon stares at her. He looks very old all of a sudden, like a statue of a big black god. His face is as still as a statue's.

"Yasm," he says. He puts the piece of paper with her name on it into the "Humor in Uniform" section of his *Reader's Digest*.

"OK," Debbi says. "That's it." Crying, she walks back out through the steamy kitchen where they are all laughing at her and then through the long dining room and out the fancy front door of the d'Iberville, but by the time she gets off the bus in front of the Seaquarium her tears are all dry and she's pretty again. So what? Who cares what some fat black Negro has to say? She's playing her own cards anyway, and this time she's playing them right.

The Seaquarium looks like three domes hooked together, the concrete painted aqua blue. It's much bigger than she had imagined, and more expensive too: six bucks just to look at some fish! Debbi pays her money at the little booth and then she spots Bobby, back turned, taking up tickets just outside the door. Ha! His job is not so fine as he lets on.

"Surprise!" She goes up behind him and puts her hands over his eyes.

"Debbi!" Bobby knows who it is right away, but he doesn't look pleased at all. He pushes her hands from his face. "What are you doing here, dammit?" he asks in a fierce hard whisper.

"Well, I've never been here before," Debbi says. She gives him her ticket and he punches it twice as hard as he has to.

"That doesn't mean you have to start now." Bobby is so mean to her, but then he's all smiles when he turns to the next person in the line. *Asshole*. Debbi sighs. But now she's here, she might as well see the sights.

Each one of the aqua domes holds a large round tank of water. With two of them, you walk around inside and look into the water through oval blue windows. But the third and largest tank is outdoors. Rows of seats surround it and flags of all countries fly in the hot open air above it; this is where they have the shows, but it's not time to go in there yet. With the other people in her group, Debbi walks down the damp dim curving hallway to her left, around one of the undersea tanks. She pauses to peer in the windows, but it's weird in there. Clownfish float by in bright schools. A sea turtle looms up at the glass like a freak from the dinosaur days, his scarred shell older than time. Debbi moves on to the next window. She sees coral on the bottom, waving wildly as a shark swims past; this very active coral is really crazy and doesn't look a think like the stiff white stuff you see in the gift shops. Debbi likes it better dead. She moves all around this tank and then all around the other. She sees an octopus, a manta ray, four different kinds of dolphins, every kind of fish you can think of, lots of sharks. The sharks circle by without moving their fins; pure meanness keeps them going. Debbi shivers. The close blue air of the corridors is awful. She feels like she's just left a bad movie when she finally gets back out in the fresh fishy air. Debbi is climbing the concrete steps to get a better seat

71

when she sees somebody waving to her enthusiastically.

It's her friend Diane! With Frederick, talking to a red-faced man in a short-sleeved white shirt. Debbi crosses over to them. Diane is wearing big round sunglasses and a yellow sundress; she looks like a movie star.

"Hello," Diane breathes. "We were just speaking with Dr. Bristol. He's been *so* informative—he's just so good with Frederick."

"That's Dr. Bristol?" Debbi has never met Buddy's boss but she's heard enough about him, that's for sure. He doesn't look so all-fired important and scientific either. He looks just like anybody else, only fatter.

Dr. Bristol is explaining things to Frederick, who has gotten very sunburned now and is all dressed up for this trip to the Seaquarium in shorts and a matching shirt with an alligator on it.

"What do they eat?" Frederick has a high shrill voice.

Dr. Bristol laughs. "A bottlenose dolphin will eat anything, including coins, sunglasses, or anything else that falls in the tank by mistake." Then Dr. Bristol grows more serious and more scientific. "Actually, Frederick, an adult bottlenose may eat twenty-five pounds of fish per day..."

Dr. Bristol goes on and on. Debbi can't even get a word in edgewise, and meanwhile the show has started. There's Bobby all right, wearing a top hat and a uniform like the maître d' at the d'Iberville. Debbi stares. He never told her about his top hat. Bobby blows a silver whistle. It glints in the sun. Then some merry-go-round-type music starts, and six dolphins come into the tank in two little lines, leaping up and down in fast little arcs through the water, just like a dance team on TV. It's amazing. They swim all around in a circle; then half of them turn and start the other way so that there are two circles, one inside the other and both turning in time to the music. They go faster and faster until they make moving wheels in the water. The crowd goes wild. They love it. The flags of all the countries wave in the salty breeze and Bobby's curly hair shines golden underneath his top hat in the sun.

"What happens to the act if one of them gets sick?" Frederick asks.

"Oh, they get sick sometimes," Dr. Bristol says. "But they

can stand in for each other in performing tricks, as long as they've seen the tricks before. They can also show imagination and add to their repertoire of tricks—one of our dolphins here, Lucille Elizabeth, has made up several of her tricks herself."

Diane laughs. "Oh really."

"It's true," Dr. Bristol says. "The human brain weighs fourteen hundred grams, Mrs. Temple, the dolphin brain seventeen hundred, and its cerebral cortex is larger than ours. There's a lot of unexplored territory there, Mrs. Temple. We are working closely with the Navy, who—"

But Debbi can't wait any longer. "Hi," she says, leaning across Diane to Dr. Bristol. "I'm Debbi. I've heard so much about you and I'm real glad to meet you at last."

Dr. Bristol looks confused.

"*Debbi*," Debbi says. "Bobby's girlfriend."

"Oh yes," Dr. Bristol says. "Oh my." He peers at her, across Diane. "Well, it's certainly a pleasure to meet you." Debbi shakes his fleshy pink hand, furious, because it's perfectly clear that he has never heard of her before or if he ever did, he's forgotten.

But Bobby has a red canvas director's chair now and he pretends to be directing two dolphins in a play of some kind in the tank, to dramatic organ music. Only Debbi missed the beginning of it, so she doesn't understand a thing.

"Do they ever get married?" Frederick asks. "Do they ever get divorced?" Frederick's blistery pink face turns white.

"Actually not," Dr. Bristol answers. "There is no permanent pairing. Dolphins exhibit an extremely varied pattern of sexual behavior unconnected with biological productivity. The stimulus can be anything—another dolphin, a turtle, or any other object."

"Goodness," Diane breathes.

Frederick turns a shade pinker again, and the show goes on. It's Lucille Elizabeth's turn. Bobby asks her questions over the microphone and she squeals "yes" or "no." Everybody loves it. Frederick claps and claps, looking like a child for once instead of a weird little grownup.

"A complicating factor in studying the sexual behavior of dolphins is the difficulty of distinguishing between sex and aggression," Dr. Bristol says to Diane. "But we have yet to observe a dolphin becoming fixated on a biologically inadequate sexual partner if a biologically adequate partner is available."

Debbi watches Lucille Elizabeth jump through hoops for fish, through higher hoops, and then through very high flaming hoops. This Dr. Bristol doesn't fool her for a minute: all he wants to do is get into Diane's pants, talking this sexy stuff right out loud to her in the middle of the day. Diane might not know it, but Debbi does. He's just like all the rest of them, she thinks, remembering back to when she was in love with Johnny Malone and then with Richard Jarman. Now Richard Jarman has a TV repair shop all his own, in Nashville, Tennessee. People work for *him*. Debbi sighs. She blew that one, and she blew Johnny Malone too although she was so young then and she did end up with a fifty-pound teddy bear and a real pearl ring. Well.

Debbi watches Bobby put a plastic rose in Lucille Elizabeth's mouth and then watches her swish around in the water to stripper music. Lucille Elizabeth *is* cute. Her mouth looks like it's smiling all the time. Lord she's big, though. Bobby pats her shiny head at the surface of the water just like she's a puppy.

". . . but she'll be back in a couple of days," Dr. Bristol is saying.

Debbi punches Diane. "Who?" she asks.

"This particular dolphin," Diane says. "Apparently the Navy is going to use it for some unusual depth experiments."

"*This* one?" Debbi asks, but Diane says, "Shhh." Diane and Frederick are busy listening to Dr. Bristol explain how Lucille Elizabeth will be picked up in a sling and then taken in a special truck over to the Navy laboratories at Ocean Springs. Although a dolphin can live outside the water for hours, Dr. Bristol explains, its skin dries out very quickly and can literally crack if the dolphin is not kept properly wet down for the length of the trip. But finally the show is over and they all stand up.

Dr. Bristol shakes hands all around. "It's nice to meet you, Miss—"

"*Debbi*," Debbi says.

She's glad to see, when he turns around to go, that no matter

74

how smart he is, he sweats like the rest of us and his shirt is stuck flat to his back.

On her way out, Debbi passes Bobby taking up tickets again at the gate. "I'll see you later, honey," she says. "You were real good."

"Thanks," Bobby drawls. He looks at her in that new way and Debbi knows he's noticed how she looks and who she sat with at the show. Ha! "See you later," Bobby says. His eyes are deep blue and sexy. In fact there is something real sexy about the way they are standing there in the burning hot Gulfport sun with people coming and going all around them. But Debbi's not about to run a good thing in the ground. "Bye," she says, and she can feel Bobby's eyes outlining her hips like black crayon in a coloring book as she goes off through the crowd.

Well! Since she's got ten dollars left, she buys some big round sunglasses in a gift shop and then, since she's already so close to the pier, she decides to take the boat ride out to Ship Island because it's a historical thing to do. Ship Island had a fort in the Civil War. Debbi sits on the top deck and watches through her sunglasses as Gulfport gets smaller and smaller until even the cranes and the biggest ships at the dock look like toys. The boat to Ship Island rolls up and down over the waves. Beyond Ship Island is the big part of the Gulf, real waves and God knows what all: Russian subs, surfers, killer whales. When they dock, most of the people head straight toward the water, on a path across the dunes. They have come here to swim and fish. Some of them have brought picnics—they can stay until the last boat leaves at eleven tonight, if they want to.

The fort looks like an old round brick circular hill, a big doughnut, with grass and stuff growing between the cracks and on the top. It reminds Debbi of the Seaquarium, and it also reminds her of graves. But all the people who died here did it a long time ago: even their bones have turned to sand. The prettiest crape myrtle Debbi has ever seen is growing right in the middle of the fort, on top of all those dead people. It's beautiful—a deep, bright pink, with huge blooms that are inches and inches across. The way it smells is heady, reminding

Debbi suddenly of the summer she spent at her grandmother's farmhouse outside Blacksburg, Virginia, a house she hasn't seen or even thought about for years. She was seven then and her baby brother was with them; that was the summer before he died. *Lord*. Debbi does not read the historical marker. She goes out of the fort and into the little restaurant where she lets a Japanese man buy her two beers. But that's all. Since the next boat back doesn't leave for an hour, she goes over to the beach where the rest of them are all spread out in the burning sun like meat on a barbeque grill. Of course she doesn't have a bathing suit with her. When she takes her shoes off, the sand is so hot it hurts her feet to walk in it. Debbi goes out to where the sand is wet and the waves are coming in. This water is really cold, compared to the stupid gulf at Gulfport. It's deep green here and an even deeper green all the way out, with whitecaps rising. A big wave comes in, drenching the bottoms of her stretch pants. Debbi sits right down in the surf, letting it wash in around her to her waist. Lord. It feels so good that after a while she just lies all the way back in it. Every time a wave comes in, she can hear its roar in her ears before it gets there; then it swirls sand around in her hair. Sand slides in and out under her body, giving Debbi the funniest feeling, like she's floating on top of the earth at the start of the world. She lies back in the surf for a long time, and three different people come over to ask if she's OK. The answer is *yes*, she tells them. Debbi lies there for an hour and lets the waves wash over her body. Then she gets up and walks back to the dock to catch the five P.M. boat back to shore. She does not go back in the fort, and the wind has dried her clothes by the time she's halfway home.

Debbi sits on the top deck, licking salt sometimes from her arms. She feels fine, all dry and hollowed out like driftwood, spare and clean. The waves are bigger now, running against the boat. The boat goes up and down in the wide green troughs of the waves. "Look! Look!" everyone cries, and Debbi moves to the back of the boat to see two dolphins playing in the wake. She lets the Japanese man buy her another beer on the boat and then she lets him take snapshots of her. The sky, which has been flat and white all day, glows orange and strange as the sun goes down. Lights come on along the coast—Gulfport, then Biloxi, Ocean Springs. If you could see that far, that is. Neon winks out beyond Gulfport on the bypass, where Cat Lady is dancing already maybe, where Miss Bubbles waits to go on. The coast is like a long jeweled necklace up and down, the lights twinkling off into the darkness as far as she can see.

Back at the Beachview Motel, Lewis and Mr. Johnson are playing chess outside on a card table, their board lit up by a single bulb hanging down from the palm tree on a single wire that runs out of Mr. Johnson's window. Lewis wears a flowing white shirt with embroidery on it, and a shell necklace. He looks up. "Bobby said to tell you he'll be back in a little while," he says. "He said he was going out to the store."

Mr. Johnson does not look up. He slumps forward lower and lower until his head almost touches the board.

"Mr. Johnson! Your move!" Lewis says.

Debbi goes past them to the door of number 16 but for some reason she's not ready to go in yet. She wants to hold on to the day. Plus she has this hunch—you can call it ESP if you want to—that she might see Diane at the beach.

"Tell Bobby I'll be back in about fifteen minutes," Debbi calls across the courtyard to Lewis and Mr. Johnson. Her own voice sounds low and ladylike, floating over the bougainvillea. They do not look up, seated in their cone of light like actors on a stage. Lord! Debbi will be glad to get out of the Beachview and move on to better things.

Diane *is* there, too, on the end of the pier in the half-light made by the rising moon and the moon's reflection up from the slithery gulf. The wind smells warm and kind of sweet, like fruit about to go bad. Debbi walks out on the pier. Diane sits all hunched up, barefooted. She has her head down on her knees and she's crying.

"Why, what's the matter?" Debbi rushes to kneel beside her, to put her arm around Diane's thin shaking shoulders, because after all they are all such good friends.

Or are they? Diane pulls away. "There's nothing you can do about it, Debbi, it isn't any of your business. It doesn't have a thing to do with you. I'd really like to be alone now if you don't mind." Diane draws herself into a sad tight ball, not touching Debbi, who has never been able to take no for an answer in all her life.

"Is it Frederick?" Debbi asks.

"No."

"Well, what is it, then? Is it your husband?" Debbi has no picture in her head of Mr. John Temple III; he might as well be a ghost.

"Yes," Diane says after a long wait, and then the words just come tumbling out. "He just—it's just—well, you wouldn't understand, you couldn't, I mean, I don't know—our life is so comfortable, so circumscribed. I just want out, that's all. I know it's wrong and I can't help it, but I hate it like it is, like this. I never in my life lived with a boy like you do, for instance, not even when I was young. All I ever did before I got married was make my debut and give Coke parties in my mother's backyard. I mean there's nothing *wrong* with that, of course. Nothing. John went to W&L. There's nothing wrong with that, either. Nothing. I just, that is—" Diane gulps air and starts again. "John just made a major decision. He told me he had made this major decision to simplify his life. I was so excited. I thought he wanted to sell the house or something and move to Alaska or something. But oh no. *Oh no.* Do you know what it was? I'll tell you. He had decided to buy all the same color socks from now on, that was it. That was the whole thing. Then they'll never get mixed up and they'll be easy for the maid to sort out and he'll never be stuck with only one sock. So from now on he's going to buy all one color, charcoal gray. Isn't that a riot? Of course he'd pick charcoal gray."

All this sounds crazy to Debbi. It's so hot down here that Bobby never even wears any socks. "Well," she says after a while, "why don't you just leave him, then?"

Debbi really can't remember seeing *anybody*, ever, cry as hard as Diane is crying right now. "I can't," she wails. "I would, but I can't. It's just so complicated. There's nothing wrong, in the first place, nothing at all, it's just me. John loves me, that's the whole problem. He loves whatever I do. Oh, you'd never understand, you just do whatever you want, it's a different life, I see that. And Frederick's therapist says a divorce would be disastrous, so that's out. That's why we came

down here, to try to work all this out, but we won't. We won't
work anything out." Diane wails in the wind like a cat.

Lord. Debbi's mind is whirling. She scoots closer to Diane
again, to try to comfort her, but Diane leaps up to her feet.
Debbi stands up too. They are almost the same height, she
sees, exactly. The air around them is heavy and ripe now,
sweet-smelling. Heat lightning flashes out over the ocean.

"I really have to go now," Diane says. Her voice is clear
and changed.

"Wait," Debbi says, but Diane is gone like a yellow streak
back over the pier and Debbi knows, all of a sudden, that Diane
will never speak to her again. She has said too much, so she'll
never say anything else. Debbi sits on the end of the pier and
worries.

Later it doesn't seem so important, though, when she and
Bobby have eaten the barbeque he brought back from Winn-
Dixie and she's had some tequila and then some Mateus. She
and Bobby sit on the bed with the white paper boxes from
Winn-Dixie spread out all around them. Bobby's bare chest is
covered with a blond mat of curly hairs like little yellow springs.

"You didn't know what to think when I showed up at the
Seaquarium, did you?" Debbi asks. She pulls one of the little
hairs.

"No," Bobby says. She can't tell a thing from his eyes. He
leans across her and turns off the light and then kisses her.
"You had you a big time today, I guess," he says real sweet
in her ear.

"I did, Bobby, I really did. One thing was, I went on the
boat to Ship Island and it's real nice out there, you ought to
go sometime." Pink light shines over the mattress, and it's
starting to rain outside.

"Maybe I will," Bobby says, "and I'm glad you had such
a good time. You ought to have. You ought to have had yourself
twenty dollars' worth of good time to be exact. It's real nice
the way you feel perfectly free to go tripping off like that but
you can't be bothered to clean this place up or buy groceries
or do any other damn thing around here that really needs doing."

"Well," Debbi says.

"Don't do it again." Bobby is suddenly up kneeling on the
mattress with his knee pressing down on her ribs. He grabs her

79

arm and pulls it behind her back. "You understand?"

Debbi cries some because it hurts, but mainly she's crying about Diane, who will not be her friend anymore. Crying turns Bobby on, so pretty soon they make love and then he falls asleep right before she does, with Bobby's pink arm across her stomach and the roar of the rain in her ears.

Debbi is so tired from her big day that she doesn't wake up when Mr. Johnson comes in the wet gray light of that early morning, six o'clock, with an emergency telephone message for Bobby, and she does not hear Bobby when he leaves.

"He what?" she asks Mr. Johnson later, wrapped in the sheet, drinking coffee in the old man's room. "They said what?"

It looks like Mr. Johnson doesn't feel too good either. "It was about the dolphin," he says. The hairs of his mustache are stuck together with old food or something. "It was that doctor, Bobby's boss. The dolphin is off course, the dolphin is lost, the dolphin this, the dolphin that. A lot of dolphin shit," Mr. Johnson says.

Debbi grins. "I know what you mean," she says. She looks around Mr. Johnson's room and it's so sad: he must have been collecting *National Geographics* for twenty years. *Thirty* years. They're stacked up all along the walls. "Me and Bobby are going to get married," she tells him, but he looks down into his cup. "That's nice," Mr. Johnson says. Debbi looks around his room some more. Poor old thing—Mr. Johnson cooks all his food on a double burner in a skillet and a saucepan missing the handle. He could have a stove if he wanted. He could do a whole lot better than he does. He buys good coffee, for instance; this coffee's real hot and real good. But mostly Mr. Johnson doesn't want to. He wants to stay just like he is. Debbi notices a framed black-and-white picture of a pretty woman, her hair done up like the thirties, on the nightstand beside his bed. "Who's that?" she asks, pointing. Mr. Johnson looks up and then stares back down in his cup. "That's Mrs. Geraldine Molesworth," he says. But he won't say a thing after that.

Debbi leaves with the sheet wrapped around her, holding it up to her knees, and walks back across the courtyard in the rising clouds of steam that the sun makes, drying the rain.

"Well! Good morning!"

Raymond White is such a dope that Debbi doesn't even bother to act like he's there. Lord! She feels awful so she knocks on Cat Lady's door, number 9, and Cat Lady gets up after a while and gives her some pills in an envelope that says "International Harvester" in the left-hand corner. Clutching the envelope and the sheet, Debbi goes back to her room where she takes some of the pills and then sleeps until afternoon.

When she wakes up again she just lies there, with the memory of the dream in her mind. But it wasn't a dream, it was a memory—it had happened to her, in real life—and then she had dreamed it again, a dream like an instant replay on CBS. This dream was about the time she ran off with Bobby and the first night they spent in Gatlinburg, Tennessee. They had stayed at a motel with elks on the wallpaper—Debbi remembers their antlers, branching into a repeated pattern on the walls—and after they had been in the motel for a while, they walked downtown through the crowds of tourists with their arms around each other's waists.

"You've got to see this," Bobby said. What Bobby wanted to show her turned out to be a place where they made candy, and you could stand outside in front of a big window to watch. And it really was *something*, after all. She and Bobby had stood there eating corn dogs and watching them make fudge and then pralines and then candy canes, for what seemed like hours. The candy for the candy canes came out of a big tube, all gross and thick and sticky, and the man grabbed it and stretched it out in lengths as long as his arm, flipping it a couple of times and stretching it out on the flat steel table until it was thin and striped like a barber pole. Then he did another, then another, then another. The soft unformed candy just kept squishing up out of the tube. The man kept grabbing it, twisting it, laying it out perfectly straight. It was amazing. Then when the whole steel table was full of those perfectly regular lengths, he took up a cleaver and chopped them into perfectly regular sticks. Running his hand down the ends of the sticks, he made the candy canes curve last of all. Then he was finished, and the whole watching crowd clapped and whistled. The man took off his chef's hat and bowed to them. He was a wiry black-haired man about thirty years old, with a sticking-out Adam's apple. On the table in front of him were four or five hundred candy canes, all of them just alike, and that was when Bobby said, "Stick with me, honey. You'll see more sights than this, and I'll expand your damn horizons as they say." Then he had bought her a turquoise ring, the one she is wearing right now.

Debbi stretches, remembering. When they get married, she hopes Bobby will get a new job, something more dignified, with no top hats and no fish. Debbi still feels kind of funny but she puts on her bathing suit, a red two-piece Lurex shot through with gold thread, and then she walks down to the beach wearing her new sunglasses. If anybody in this crazy motel tries to talk to her, she's not going to say a word. But nobody does. Debbi takes the bottle of tequila with her, wrapped up in a towel, and when she gets to the beach she sits on the towel and drinks it. There's a strong wind now from the south, which has blown the clouds away, and the rain smell is gone from the air. Far away up the beach she sees a figure on the sand who might or might not be Diane. So what? Fuck her, Debbi thinks. Ha! She drinks some more tequila and when she gets to a certain point as always nothing is crazy or painful any more and nothing is even surprising. She isn't even surprised to see Frederick, standing by her towel.

"My mother told me not to speak to you," Frederick says in his usual high voice.

"She did, huh?" Debbi says. "Well, have a seat."

Frederick sits down. "It was a shame about the dolphin," he says. It's hard to tell because he's naturally so snotty and so weird, but it seems like he's trying to be nice.

Debbi sits up. "What about the dolphin?" she asks.

"It beached itself," Frederick says, looking at her curiously. "It's been in the news all day. Sometimes they just do that, nobody knows why. Dr. Bristol was on the news too. He said it's not unheard of for cetaceans to behave this way. He said it might be related to some kind of refusal or at least reluctance to accept freedom, or maybe to the more primitive instinct that led animals to leave the sea in the first place."

"What first place?" Debbi asks.

"In *evolution*," Frederick explains. "Anyway the dolphin just suddenly began to veer from its course and head straight for the nearest point of land and nobody was able to catch it or head it off although they even got the Coast Guard in on it. The Coast Guard set up barriers at all the wrong places. The dolphin outsmarted them because it didn't go in where it was headed so they couldn't stop it after all, and they couldn't even find it until it was already dead. But what I really wanted to ask you," Frederick goes on pleasantly, "is if you will show me your breasts."

Debbi stands up abruptly and nearly falls. "No," she tells him. "I won't." She leaves him sitting right there with his legs stuck out in front of him like an ugly little toy boy on the beach. It's a hot dry day now, closing in on her head. So the main thing is to walk very slowly and carefully with one foot right in front of the other through the hot powdery sand of the deserted movie lot and then across the flat hot concrete of the courtyard carefully not thinking anything, back to number 16. Which turns out to be unlocked, although she locked it when she left, and even this is not surprising.

"Looky here," Mrs. Pugh is at her elbow, holding up a monstrous red glove.

Debbi pushes her out of the way and goes in the room, where she is not at all surprised to find the dresser drawers pulled out and the closet door flung open, and all of Bobby's things gone. Just like Bobby himself. Well, fuck him, Debbi thinks. Ha! But she throws herself down on the mattress and cries as if her heart will break—which, of course, it has. Sooner or later everybody comes to see her, exactly like she's some ailing royal queen or like she's suffered a terrible accident, which she has. Mr. Johnson and Lewis come in and tell her the rest of it, how Bobby paid up and then left with Miss Bubbles that day around five o'clock. Lewis tells Debbi she's lots better off without him. Lewis says Bobby is a pathological liar with a wife in Richmond, Virginia, and for some reason whether it's true or not, even this comes as no surprise. Mr. Johnson has brought her a cheeseburger; he puts it on top of the dresser. After they leave, Debbi drinks the last of the tequila although she knows there is not any more. Then Raymond White comes by after a while to her complete surprise and asks her if she'd like to go for a walk. Ha! But Debbi says no, not right now, thank you, maybe some other time, and she eats the cheeseburger. Cat Lady comes in offering everything, including a job at the Gaucho Room. No thank you, Debbi says, and then she says maybe she'll think about it.

She goes to bed. Without Bobby the mattress is enormous, stretching out and out to fill up number 16 wall to wall. Debbi thinks Bobby will come back for her, having left Miss Bubbles at a rest stop on the interstate. She thinks this for a long time and then she lets it go, and when it goes the mattress gets even bigger, stretching out forever across the ocean in the night, but the funny thing is that it's comfortable after all. There's lots of room to sleep in, and she sleeps. Mr. Johnson sleeps too, and Lewis, and Raymond White, and Cat Lady with her hair in plastic curlers and her spit-curls Scotch-taped to her forehead. Leon, in his small room behind the d'Iberville, turns massively in sleep and dreams a dream that will soon come true. Bobby drives all night and does not sleep, but beside him Miss Bubbles snores slightly in an unpredictable and totally charming way with her head turned to the side and her nose mashed into the Chevrolet's Naugahyde seat. Mrs. Pugh does not sleep either, but wanders the dark at the courtyard's perimeter, dragging her paper bags. Over at the Seagull Inn, beyond the drive-in movie lot, Frederick stirs in the grip of a nightmare, and John and Diane Temple sleep closely entwined in a way that is profoundly uncomfortable yet romantic—which is, in fact, the best they can do.

Artists

*It is one of those hot Sunday afternoons that seem to stretch
out,* all green and gauzy and golden, over the length of my
childhood; I walk in my grandmother's garden. The others are
back on the porch in the curly wicker chairs, talking. Their
voices come to me in little waves, musical and nonsensical like
the sound of bees in the garden, across the wide green grass.
I hear my mother's laugh. I cannot see her, or the others. They
are cool up there on the porch, I know it; they have iced tea
in the tall skinny glasses, with mint. But I want none of that.
I attain the roses and halt before them, self-consciously. *I am
transfixed by beauty*, I think. In fact I like the names of the
roses perhaps more than I like the roses themselves—Pink
Cloud, Peace, Talisman, Queen Elizabeth—the names unfurl
across my mind like a silken banner, like the banner the children
carry in the processional on Eastern Sunday. I held a corner
of that banner then. My grandmother taught me these names.
I lean forward, conscious of myself leaning forward, to examine
a Peace rose more closely. It is perfect: the pale velvety outer
petals wide and graceful, then turning, curling and closing
inward to its strange deep crimson center. The leaves are pro-
fuse, glossy, and green. There are thorns. I draw back. What
I really prefer is the baby's breath along this border, the riot

85

of pinks by the fountain, the snapdragons like a sassy little army at my feet. But my grandmother has told me that these roses are the pride of her heart. And she grows no common flowers here—no zinnias, no marigolds. This baby's breath is so fragile I can see through it and beyond, to where a lizard flashes shining across a stone and is gone in the phlox. I suck in my breath, feeling dizzy. The sun is so hot on my head and my feet hurt a lot in my patent leather pumps with the straps— because I have nearly outgrown them, I guess, just like my mother says. She says it is time for me to buy some more grown-up shoes, but I have been resisting this, finding excuses not to shop. I like these shoes; I hope that the pain will make me a better person and improve my soul.

For I am all soul these days. I have not missed Sunday School in four years, not even on the occasions when my mother hauls me off to Tucson or Florida and I have to attend strange churches where I ask pastors with funny names to sign affidavits concerning my presence. I mail these documents back to Mr. Beech at the First Methodist Church, so that nothing will mar my record. I have earned so many gold bars for good attendance and special merit that they clink when I walk and Daddy says I look like a major general. I have gone forward to the altar so many times during summer revivals that my mother, embarrassed by my zeal, refuses to let me attend them any more unless I make a solemn pledge that I will not rededicate my life.

"Religious," then, I am also prone to fears and tremblings of a more general nature, and just about anything can set me off: my father when he's in a hurry; my black-headed first cousin Scott who is up in that big old sycamore tree right now, gathering a collection of sycamore balls; anything at all about cripples, puppies, or horses. For instance I had to go to bed for three days after my aunt Dora foolishly read me "The Little Match Girl" a couple of winters ago. I am "sensitive," "artistic," and "delicate," and everybody knows this is how I am, because my grandmother has laid down the law. Rarely does she lay down the law in such definite terms, preferring that her wishes be intuited, but now she has and this is it: *Do not tease Jennifer. Do not cut her hair.*

I wear a white piqué dress in my grandmother's garden this

Sunday, a dress my mother ordered from Miller and Rhoads in Richmond, and I love it because I think it makes me look even thinner than I am. I want to be Peter Pan. I also want to be a ballerina, a detective, a missionary among the savages. My pale blond hair, pulled back by a white velvet bow, hangs down to my waist. My bars for good attendance and special merit jangle ever so slightly when I walk. They are calling me now from the porch. I pretend not to hear them, crossing the grass to where the iron marker has been placed near the thicket of willow trees at the edge of the creek. This marker reads

> *The Scent of the Rose for Pardon*
> *The Song of the Birds for Mirth*
> *I am Closer to God in my Garden*
> *Than Anywhere Else on Earth.*

I stop and run my fingers over the raised iron lettering, hot from the sun. "Rose for Pardon" blazes into my palm, and in the back of my mind I see myself in fifteen years or so on a terrible gory battlefield somewhere or maybe it is a dingy tenement, pardoning a man both elegant and doomed—a *rake*. I think he has tuberculosis.

"Jennifer!" My mother stands beside the rose garden, shading her eyes with her hand. "Come on! Your father is ready to go."

My mother wears a red linen dress and black-and-white spectator shoes. She likes golf, bridge, and dancing to jazz music. She hates these Sunday dinners. I follow her back to the porch, pretending not to see Scott, who throws his sycamore balls down with great skill so that they land silently in the grass just close enough to annoy me, too far away for me to complain. Scott is one of the crosses I have to bear. It's too soon for me to tell whether Sammy, my own little brother, will turn out to be such a cross or not; sometimes he exhibits certain promise, I think. Other times he is awful. When he had a virus, for instance, he threw up all over my diary, eliminating February. Sammy is already in the car when we reach the porch. I can see his blond head bobbing up and down in the rear window. My father stands by the gate in his seersucker suit, waiting for us.

"Let's go!" he calls.

"Hurry and make your manners, now," my mother tells me in an undertone. "I can't wait to get out of this damn dress."

I ignore her vulgarity and head for the porch, as full of relatives as it is every Sunday, where I have to wait for my uncle Carl—my great-uncle, actually—to finish telling a story. The other people on the porch are my cousin Virginia, Scott's pretty older sister, whom I hate; my aunt Lucia, Scott's mother, who holds a certain interest for me because of a nervous breakdown she is rumored to have had in her twenties; Scott's boring father, Bill; my maiden aunts Dora and Fern; my grandfather, sweet and bent over in his chair, whittling; and my grandmother, of course, imperious as a queen in the glider, moving ever so slightly back and forth as if pushed by a personal breeze. My grandmother wears a pink brocade suit and a rhinestone sunburst pin, which I consider beautiful. Her hair, faintly blue, is piled into wispy curls that float above her wide white forehead, above her pale blue milky eyes, which look away from them all and across the river to the mountains where the sun goes down.

"And so I hollered, 'Well, John, start it up,' and John started his up, and I got in and started mine—" My uncle Carl is a famous storyteller even in Richmond, where he is in the Legislature, and he will not be hurried. The story he is telling now is one I've heard about a million times before, but it's one of Grandaddy's favorites, all about how Uncle Carl and Grandaddy were the first people in this county to consider automobiles, how they went to Richmond on the train and bought themselves an automobile apiece and drove them home, and then—the climax of the story—how they, the owners of the only two cars in the county at that time, went out driving with their new young wives one Sunday ("in the springtime of our lives," as my uncle Carl always put it) and had a head-on collision on the hairpin curve at the bend of the Green River.

Grandaddy claps his knees with both hands and doubles over laughing, scattering wood chips all over the porch. He is the best-humored man in town—everybody says so—and everybody loves him. He could have been in politics himself, like Uncle Carl, if he had had the ambition. But he did not. He laughs so hard he coughs, and then he can't stop coughing.

The wood chips fly all over the porch.

"What a display, Mr. Morris," my grandmother says without moving her mouth.

"Daddy, are you all right?" My own father moves from his place at the gate, starts up the concrete walk. My aunt Lucia stands up by her chair.

"Sure, sure," Grandaddy wheezes and laughs. "But do you remember how those cars *looked*, Carl, how they looked all nosed into each other thataway? And old man Rob Pierce asked if we was trying to mate them."

Daddy grins, on the step below, but Grandmother leans forward to examine the undersides of the fern in the pot by her feet.

"Don't you remember that, Mother?" Daddy asks her.

My grandmother sits up very straight. "Oh yes," she says in her whispery voice. "Oh, yes. I was cast into the river," she says, her head turned away from us all. The glider moves back and forth with the slightest of motions so that in her pink brocade suit she appears to shimmer, tiny and iridescent before us, like a rainbow on the verge of disappearing.

"Now, hell, Flo, that didn't happen at all!" Grandaddy says. "We were right there on the curve where Stinson's store is now. Nobody went in the water."

"Cast into the rushing stream," my grandmother says, looking off.

Uncle Carl guffaws, Grandaddy slaps his knee, and everybody else laughs and laughs.

"Come on now, Jenny," my mother calls. She gets in the car.

"Thank you so much for dinner," I say.

"Oh, can't she stay, Roy?" My grandmother suddenly springs to life. "Can't she?"

"Well, sure, I guess so," my daddys says, with an uneasy look back at the car. "That is, if she—"

"Oh please, Daddy, please please please!" I run down the steps and cling to his hand and beg him.

"Have you met my daughter, Sarah Bernhardt?" my mother says to nobody in particular.

"Please," I beg.

"Well, I suppose so, Jenny, but—" my father says.

My mother closes her door.

"I'll bring her home in the morning," Grandaddy calls from the porch. He stands up to wave as they pull off down the long dirt driveway. Sammy sticks his thumbs in his ears and wiggles his fingers, and grins out the car's back window. They round the bend beyond the willows, almost out of sight. I know that right now inside our car, my mother and my father are lighting cigarettes; I know that they will go home and sit on wrought-iron chairs in the yard with gin and tonic, and Sammy will play with the hose. I wave. When the blue Buick has disappeared, I enter my grandmother's house where it is always cool, always fragrant with something like potpourri, where even the air is cool and dense, and the pictures of people I never knew stare out of the gloom at me from the high dark walls.

My grandmother was famous in our town, and her character was widely discussed. Her dedication to what she referred to as the "finer things of life" was admired by many people and ridiculed by others who found her affected or even laughable. I had heard Mrs. Beech, the preacher's wife, refer to her passionately as a "great lady." I had seen my mother's sister Trixie hold her sides laughing as she and my mother recalled incident after incident in which my grandmother played the role of a comic figure, "putting on airs."

In any case everyone knew her. For at least forty years she had been a fixture in the First Methodist Church, taking her place each Sunday in the third row from the front, left hand side, directly beneath a stained glass window that depicted Jesus casting the moneylenders out of the temple in a fury of vermilion and royal blue. She had headed the Methodist Ladies' Auxiliary and the Garden Club until all the ladies died who had voted for her year after year and these groups were overrun by younger women with pantsuits and new ideas. She still wrote long, complicated letters to local newspapers on the subjects of town beautification, historic preservation, and the evils of drink; she wore hats and white gloves on every possible occasion. Her manner of dress had changed so little over the years that even I could recognize its eccentricity. She *dressed up* all the time. I never saw her in my life without her pale voile or silk or brocade dresses, without her stockings, without her feet crammed into elegant shoes at least two sizes two small for her, so that at the end her feet were actually crippled. I never saw her without her makeup or the flashing rhinestone earrings and brooches and bracelets that finally she came to believe— as I believed then—were real.

I never ate dinner in her kitchen, either. Meals were served in the octagonal dining room with its dark blue velvet draperies held back by the golden tassels, its wallpaper featuring gods and goddesses and nymphs. Meals there were interminable and complicated, involving courses intended to be brought in and taken away by that long procession of servants my grandmother hired and then dispensed of, big hardy dough-faced country women who could hoe all day but didn't know what to do next when she rang that silver bell. I was present at the table when one of them, after a fatal error that escapes me now, threw her white apron entirely up over her head crying out "Lord God" in a strangled voice, and fled forever out the back door as fast as her feet would take her. (Some people, my grandmother informed me solemnly after this memorable meal, cannot be taught anything and are best left down in the mire.) Of course I looked up "mire." Of course I remember everything on that table, to this day: the roses in the center, in a silver bowl; the pale pink crystal water goblets, beaded with icy drops, sitting on their cut-glass coasters; pale pink linen napkins and mats or maybe pale green ones and on special occasions the white Irish lace tablecloth; the silver salt and peppers, shaped like swans; the little glass basket, wonderfully wrought, which held pickles or mints or nuts. My grandmother declared the round mahogany table itself to be a family heirloom, then an antique, then a priceless antique from France. In any case it was large, dark, and shining, supported by horrible clawed feet with talons three or four inches long. The knowledge of these cruel taloned feet, right there beneath the table, added greatly to my enjoyment of these meals.

One ate only at the table in that house. Sometimes, though, I let my bestial elements get the best of me and snuck down into the kitchen for a snack after I was sure she was asleep. Once I surprised my grandaddy doing the same thing. The light from the refrigerator turned him light blue in his long flannel nightshirt and he broke into a delighted cackle at the sight of

me. We ate cold fried chicken and strawberry ice cream together at the kitchen table and he told me about how he had
traded a pony for a bicycle one time when he was a boy and
how he tried and tried to get it back after his sprocket chain
broke. We laughed a lot. I washed our dishes and he dried
them and put them away and kissed me goodnight. His moustache tickled my cheek and I loved him so much at that moment;
yet I felt disloyal, too. I climbed up the long stairs in shame.

Grandaddy called my grandmother Flo, but everyone else
called her Florence. "Flo," she said severely, "has connota-
tions." I did not know what those were, nor did I inquire. I
called her Grandmother, as instructed. Grandmother called
Grandaddy "Mr. Morris" in public all her life. Yet despite her
various refinements, my grandmother was a country woman
herself, born right in this county. Her father had started the
First Methodist Church by importing a circuit rider to preach
beneath the big sycamore tree, before the house was built. Her
father had been by all accounts a hard, dangerous kind of a
man, too, who had made a lot of money and had carried a
pistol with him at all times. He had not believed in the education
of women, so my grandmother never went to school. Eventually
he was murdered, but no one ever mentioned this fact in front
of my grandmother. She had married my grandaddy when she
was only fifteen years old, but we didn't mention this fact
either. Grandaddy was a carpenter who refused to elevate himself; he loved his work and he worked only as much as he had
to. At least she had inherited the house.

All her ideas of refinement had come from books and from
the self-improvement courses she took by mail, many of these
deriving from a dubious institution known as the LaGrande
University of Correspondence, which figured largely in my
mother's and Trixie's glee. My grandmother knew all about
these, among other things: Christianity, including particularly
the lives of the saints; Greek mythology; English country houses;
etiquette; Japanese flower arranging; Henry VIII and all his
wives; crewel embroidery; and the Romantic poets. She wrote
poetry herself and locked it away in a silver filigree box. She
made Japanese flower arrangements for everyone, strange flat
affairs usually involving one large dried flower, a considerable
array of sticks, and little porcelain Oriental men with huge

sacks on their backs. She had ordered dozens of these little men for her arrangements. My grandmother had read the entire *Encyclopaedia Britannica* cover to cover, or claimed to have read it; even my mother found this admirable, although Trixie did not.

The primary cross my grandmother had to bear was Grandaddy, who steadfastly refused to be drawn into the rarefied world of the finer things in life. He stayed there, in fact, only long enough to eat. Otherwise he was whittling, smoking cigars out back, cracking jokes, drinking coffee in the Rexall drugstore downtown, building cabinets occasionally. He liked to drink bourbon and go hunting with his friends Mr. J.O. McCorkle and Mr. Petey Branch. My grandmother seemed to amuse him, I would say, more than anything else: he liked to "get her going," as he said. My father did not even like to "get her going"; but he was her son, too, in many ways, consumed by all that ambition my grandfather lacked, a man eaten up with the romance of making money. He made a great deal of money, luckily, since my mother was an expensive wife. Very early in their marriage she developed delicate health and terrible sinus allergies that required her removal, for months at a time, to Tucson, where Trixie lived, or to Coral Gables, Florida, where my father bought her a house. My father encouraged these illnesses, which got us all out of town, and in retrospect I can see that they broadened my horizons considerably. At the time, of course, I never wanted to go. I wanted to stay with my grandmother, and sometimes I was allowed to and sometimes not.

I am alone in the parlor while my grandmother works on a watercolor at her easel in the garden (her newest enthusiasm) and Grandaddy is off to the barber shop. I love this parlor, mine now; I love the gloom. I love the blackish gnarled voluptuous roses in the patterned carpet, the tufted velvet chairs and the horsehair sofa; I don't care how uncomfortable anything is. I love the doilies on the tables and the stiff antimacassars on the arms and the backs of the chairs, the *Leaves of Gold* book of poems on the table. I consider this the most beautiful room in the world. I move from portrait to portrait—mostly old daguerrotypes—along the walls, looking. There is stern-faced old Willie Lloyd Morris, her father, staring down his hatchet nose at me across the years. *Murdered.* A delicious chill travels from the top of my head down the length of my spine. There is my grandmother herself, a young girl with a face like a flower, seated primly in a wing chair before a painted backdrop of mountains and stormy clouds. She wears white. I see countless babies, my father among them, in stiff embroidered dresses and little caps. My aunt Lucia gazes soulfully out of her gold-leaf frame at me with strangely glistening dark eyes, like a movie star. My father stands at attention in high boots and the uniform he had to wear at military school, a wonderful uniform with at least a hundred shiny buttons on it. He looks furious. I pause before a family portrait that must have been taken just after my father finished at the University and swept my mother off her feet at a debutante ball in Richmond: it includes my aunts Dora and Fern, young then; my uncle Carl with a pipe in his mouth; my grandaddy grinning broadly, his thumbs locked in his suspenders; my grandmother standing slightly to one side; my father, young and impossibly dashing; and my mother with her hair all a tangle of curls. Then it hits me: *I am not there.* I am not anywhere at all in this picture. Looking at this picture is like being *dead.*

"Gotcha." Scott gooses me.

I whirl around, absolutely furious, mainly because I don't know how long he's been in this room. I don't know how long he's been watching me. I jump on him and we fall in a tangle onto the rose-figured carpet; I kick him in the nose until it bleeds.

"Hey," Scott keeps saying. "Hey."

We lie on our backs breathing hard.

"What's the matter with you?" Scott says.

"You can't just come in here like this," I say. "You can't." I start to cry.

Emboldened by my weakness, Scott sits up. "What do you do in here all the time?" he asks. He scoots closer. He looks like an Indian, having inherited my aunt Lucia's dark exotic charm.

"Nothing."

"Come on, Jenny," Scott moves closer still. *He exerts a*

94

certain fascination for her, I think. *Jennifer succumbs to his appeal.*

"It's just so pretty," I falter. "I like to look at everything."

"Like what?" His black eyes shine through the shadows, close to mine.

"Well, like that table over there, like all the stuff on it." In my confusion I indicate what is in truth my favorite piece of furniture in the room, a multi-tiered mahogany stand that holds my grandmother's figurine collection, a wondrous array of angels, whistling boys, soldiers, Colonial ladies, cardinals and doves, unicorns—a whole world, in fact, topped by her "*pièce de résistance*" as she calls it, a white porcelain replica of Michelangelo's *David* displayed alone on the top tier. She ordered it from the Metropolitan Museum of Art in New York City. I love the *David* best of all because he seems entirely noble as well as beautiful, his left leg thrust forward in pursuit of justice in some doomed and luminous cause.

"I know why you like that one," Scott sneers.

"What one?"

"That one on the top. That naked guy."

"That's not a naked guy, Scott." I am enraged. "That is Michelangelo's famous statue *David*. It's a work of Art, if you know anything about Art, which you don't, of course." I do not forget to pronounce the statue's name *Daveed*.

"You don't know anything about art either," Scott hollers. "You just like to look at him because he hasn't got any clothes on, that's all."

I stand up shakily. "I'm going to tell Grandmother," I announce.

Scott stands up too. "Go on then. Tell her," he says. "Just go on and tell her. She's even crazier than you are. She's so crazy because Grandaddy has a girlfriend, that's what my mother says. She says it's a good thing Grandmother has an outlet—"

Even in my horror I recognize a certain terrible authenticity in Scott's words; he sounds like his mother, who uses psychological terms with great aplomb—something I have, in fact, admired about my aunt Lucia in the past.

Now I hate her.

"That's a *lie!*" I scream. "Get out of here!"

Instead, Scott grabs me by the shoulders and pulls me to him and kisses me on the mouth until I get my senses together and push him away. "Yuck!" I wipe my mouth with the back of my hand.

Scott is laughing, doubled up with laughing in my grandmother's parlor. "You're crazy, Jenny," he says. "I'm the best kisser in the eighth grade. Everybody says so."

Still laughing he goes out the front door and gets on his bike and rides off down the curving drive. I go upstairs and brush my teeth. Then I go in the bedroom, fling myself down on the bed, and wait to have a nervous breakdown. *In anguish she considers the violation of her person,* I think.

After a while I went out into the garden and asked Grandmother if I could try painting a rose. "Why yes, Jennifer," she said. Her pale blue eyes lit up. She sent me into the house for more paper, a glass of water, and the lap desk, so that my paper might remain, as she told me, absolutely stationary.

"Anything worth doing is worth doing well," she said severely. "Now then." She dipped her brush into the water and I did the same. "Not too much," she cautioned. "There now."

We painted all that afternoon, until the sun was gone. I did three and a half roses. Then we gathered up all our materials and put them away just so. I went ahead of her, carrying the lap desk and the easel into the hall. I came back out to the porch and found that Grandmother had spread my roses out on the glider. She was studying them. I thought they were pretty good, considering. We stood together and looked at them for some time as they glided ever so gently back and forth.

Grandmother turned to me and clasped me violently against her, smashing me into the spiky sunburst brooch on her bosom. "Jennifer, Jennifer," she said. She had grown little and frail by then and we were almost the same size; I couldn't see her face, but I was lost in her lavender perfume. "Jennifer, Jennifer," she was sobbing. "You must live your life, my darling. You must not get caught up in the press of circumstance; you must escape the web of fate."

I couldn't breathe and I had no idea what "web of fate" she referred to, but I felt as though I had received a solemn commission. "I *will*, Grandmother," I said. "I *will*."

"Hello, ladies!" It was my grandaddy, stumbling a bit on the steps. Mr. J.O. McCorkle stood behind him, grinning broadly. They both appeared to be in a wonderful humor.

"Oh, Mr. Morris, you gave me such a turn!" Grandmother whirled around; seeing Mr. J.O. McCorkle, her eyes narrowed. "Well, Mr. Morris!" she said with a certain significance. She swept up my three and a half roses and vanished mysteriously into the house.

"Now Flo, don't you Mr. Morris me!" Grandaddy called after her. He and Mr. McCorkle laughed. Grandaddy came up on the porch and gave me a whiskery kiss. "How about some checkers?" he asked me.

"Not right now." *Jennifer said meaningfully*, I thought. I turned and went into the house.

This was the first indication of my Talent. Spurred on by my grandmother's enthusiasm, I painted more roses and at length a morning glory. I ventured into daisies, then columbine; I mastered Swedish ivy and attempted, at last, a Still Life. This proved somewhat more difficult because Sammy kept eating the apples and spoiling my arrangement. "Never mind," Grandmother told me when I rode my bicycle over to her house to weep after one such disaster. "Never mind. Great art requires great suffering," my grandmother said.

The second indication of my Talent came from school, where I had written a sonnet, which my English teacher, Miss Hilton, praised extravagantly. This sonnet compared life to a carousel ride, in highly symbolic terms. It was named "The Ride of Life." Miss Hilton sent "The Ride of Life" to the local newspaper, which printed it on the book page. My mother drummed her fingers on the tabletop, reading it. "For heaven's sake!" she said, staring at me. My grandmother clipped it and had it framed. I was suddenly so artistic that my only problem came from trying to decide in which direction to focus my Talent. I did not forget to suffer, either, lying on my bed for a while each afternoon in order to do so.

It didn't surprise me at all, consequently, when I came down with a virus, which all turned into bronchitis, then pneumonia. For a long time I was so sick that they thought I might die.

The doctor came every day for a while, and everyone tiptoed. A spirit lamp hissed night and day in my bedroom, casting out a wispy blue jet of steam that formed itself into the camphorous blue haze that still surrounds my entire memory of that illness. Grandaddy came every day, bringing little wooden animals and people carved from pine. Once he brought a little chest of drawers he had made for me. It was incredibly intricate; each drawer opened and shut. I dozed in my blue cloud holding the chest in my hand. Every now and then, when I awakened, I would open and close the drawers. Once when I woke up I saw my mother, in tears, standing beside the bed. This shocked me. I asked for Coca-Cola and drank it; then I sat up and ate some soup; and at the end of that illness it was Grandaddy, not me, who died.

He had a heart attack in the Post Office; after examining him, the hospital doctors said there was nothing they could do and sent him home, where he lived for three more days. During this time, my grandmother's house was filled with people— all our relatives, all his friends—in and out. The kitchen was full of food. My grandmother did not enter his bedroom, as she had not entered mine. Illness made her faint and she had always said so; nobody expected her to. She stayed in the Florida room, painting cardinals and doves, while my aunts sat on the divan and watched her.

From the time they brought Grandaddy home, my own father sat by his bed. I have never, before or since, seen my father as upset—*distraught*, actually, is the word—as he was then. On the morning of the second day, Grandaddy raised his head from the pillow and rolled his eyes around the room. Daddy came forward and bent over him, taking his hand. Grandaddy made a horrible gargling kind of noise in his throat; he was trying to talk. Daddy bent closer. Grandaddy made the noise again. The veins in his forehead stood out, awful and blue. Daddy listened. Then he stood up straight and cleared his own throat.

"By God, I'll do it!" my father announced in a ringing voice, like somebody in a movie. He turned and left the room abruptly, and all of the people remaining looked at one another. My grandfather continued to stare wildly around the room, with his breath rattling down in his throat.

Twenty minutes later my father came back bringing Mollie Crews, the woman who had been my grandaddy's lover for twenty-five years. Mollie Crews was a large, heavy woman with curly and obviously dyed red hair; she was a beautician, with a shop over the Western Auto store downtown. Mollie Crews wore her white beautician's uniform, an orange cardigan sweater, and white lace-up shoes with thick crepe soles. Her hands flew up to her face when she saw Grandaddy, and her big shoulders shook. Then she rushed over to take the chair at the side of his bed, dropping her purse on the floor. "Oh, Buddy," she sobbed. *Buddy?* I was stunned. Grandaddy's eyes fastened on her and an expression like a smile came to his face. He sank back into the pillow, closing his eyes. The rattle of his breathing softened. Still firmly holding his hand, Mollie Crews took off her cardigan—awkwardly, with her free hand— and slung it over the back of the chair. She reached down and fumbled around in her purse and got a cigarette and lit it with a gold lighter. She exhaled, crossing her legs, and settled down into the chair. My father brought her an ashtray. Aunt Lucia stood up abruptly, flashing her black eyes at everyone. She started to speak and then did not. Aunt Lucia exited theatrically, jerking me from the room along with her. My cousin Virginia followed. The hall outside Grandaddy's room was full of people, and Aunt Lucia pulled me straight through them all, sailing out of the house. Scott was in the front yard. "What did I tell you?" he said. "What did I tell you?"

Aunt Lucia never returned to Grandaddy's room, nor did my uncle Bill or my cousin Virginia or my old maid aunts. Uncle Carl came back from Richmond that night and stayed with him until the end. So did my father, and my mother was in and out. The whole family had to take sides. I went in and sat dutifully with Grandmother, working at her easel in the Florida room. "This is a woodpecker," she said once, exhibiting her latest. "Note the pileations." But I couldn't stay away from Grandaddy's room either, where I was mesmerized by Mollie Crews with her generous slack mouth and her increasingly rumpled beautician's uniform. She looked like a nurse. *A fallen woman*, I told myself, and I watched her sit there hour after hour holding his hand, even when he was in coma and no longer knew she was there. *A Jezebel*, I thought, watching her.

I wondered whether she would go to hell.

When my grandfather actually died, everyone left the room except Mollie Crews, and after a long while she came out too, shaking her curls and throwing her head back as she opened the door. We were crowded into the hall. She looked at all of us, and then for some reason she came back to me. "He was a fine man," Mollie Crews said. She was not crying. She looked at everyone again and then she walked out of the house as abruptly as she had come and sat on the front porch until somebody in a battered sky blue Oldsmobile picked her up, and then she was completely and finally gone.

Mollie Crews was the only person in town who did not attend the funeral. Grandmother wore her black silk suit with a hat and a veil. She came in like royalty and sat between Daddy and Aunt Lucia, never lifting her veil, and she stood straight with my mother and me under a black umbrella when they buried Grandaddy in the church cemetery afterward, in a fine gray drizzle that started then and went on for days. Everyone in town paid a call on my grandmother during the week after that, and she sat in her parlor on the tufted sofa beside the tiered table and received them. But her blue eyes had grown mistier, paler than ever, and sometimes the things she said did not connect.

I am walking by the ocean, alone, on the beach near my mother's house in Florida. It is a bright, clear morning. Sometimes I bend down to pick up a shell. Other times I pause and gaze dramatically out to sea, but this Florida sea is not as I would have it: not tempest-tossed, not filled with drowning nobility clutching at shards of ships. This is a shiny blue Florida sea, determinedly cheerful. The waves have all been choreographed. They arch and break like clockwork at my feet, bringing me perfect shells. The weather is perfect, too. Everything in Florida is hot and easy and tropical and I hate it. My mother has yanked Sammy and me out of school and brought us down here to humor her famous allergies, but I can't even see that she has any allergies: all she does in Florida is shop and play bridge. I feel like a deserter from a beautiful sinking ship. I have deserted my grandmother, just when she needs me most.

My mother has arranged for me to have a Cuban tutor who

is supposed to teach me Spanish as well as other things. This Cuban tutor is named Dominica Colindres. She is a plump, dark young woman with greasy hair and big sagging bosoms and pierced ears. She sweats under her arms. I hate Dominica Colindres. I refuse to learn anything she tries to teach me, and I refuse to have anything at all to do with any of the other children my age who try to befriend me on the beach. I walk the shoreline, picking up shells. I think about sin, art, heaven, and hell. Since my arrival in Florida I have written two poems I am rather proud of, although no one else has seen them. One is a poem about the ocean, named "The Sea of Life." The other is named "Artifacts of Existence," about shells.

The sun is hot on my back, even through my long-sleeved shirt, so I pick up one last shell and walk back up the beach to our house. I wear a hat and long pants, too, wet now below the knee: I refuse to get a tan.

My mother is entertaining our next-door neighbors, Mr. and Mrs. Donlevy from Indiana, on the patio. She wears a yellow sundress, looks up and smiles. Mr. and Mrs. Donlevy smile. I do not smile, and my mother raised her eyebrows at Mr. and Mrs. Donlevy in a significant manner. I know they've been talking about me. They are drinking bloody marys and reading the morning paper. The hibiscus around the patio is pink and gaudy in the sun.

I go into my room to work on my shell collection. I have classified my shells as to type, and arranged each type in gradations of hue. This means that every time I find a good shell, I have to move *everything*, in order to put the new shell into its proper place. I take a certain pleasure in the difficulty of this arrangement. I am hard at work when the bells begin to ring, and then, of course, it hits me. *Sunday!* Mother and the Donlevys were reading the Sunday *Times*! It's the first time I've missed Sunday school in four years; my perfect attendance record is broken.

I put my last shell, a *Tellina lineata*, carefully in place. I leave my room. Mother is telling Mr. and Mrs. Donlevy goodbye at the front door. It's already hot; the air conditioner clicks on. I cross the white carpet in the living room, the red tile kitchen floor. Once on the patio, I rush toward the round glass table with its striped umbrella and push it violently, overturning it onto the flagstone. The whole glass top shatters. The umbrella crushes the hibiscus. The frosted bloody mary glasses are flung into the grass, and one of them breaks.

I go back in the kitchen and find Sammy, who has just gotten up, eating Wheaties at the kitchen table. He has made a little mess of his own, fixing his cereal, and this gives me extra satisfaction.

"I had a funny dream," Sammy says.

"What was it about?" I sit down with Sammy at the kitchen table. My mother comes through the kitchen humming and goes out into the patio.

"It was real funny," Sammy says. Milk dribbles down his chin.

"But what was it *about*?" I ask. Out on the patio, my mother has started to shriek.

"I can't remember what it was about." Sammy looks at me with his big blue eyes. "But the name of it was 'The Secret of the Seven Arrows.'"

I get up and hug Sammy as hard as I can, laughing. He *is* cute. Maybe he won't be a cross after all. Then I start to cry. I cry for two hours as hard as I can, and then after that I feel fine and my mother takes Sammy and me out to a fancy restaurant for dinner.

My mother never said a word to me about the broken table, although I knew—in the way children know things, almost like osmosis—that she *knew*. Workmen in overalls came the next day and replaced it. The new umbrella was lime green, with a flowered lining. My mother took me shopping and we bought new bathing suits for both of us; eventually I acquired a tan. I even learned a little Spanish, and on the day before we left, Dominica Colindres pierced my ears.

The day we came back—this was in February—I went straight over to my grandmother's house, of course, riding my bicycle through the falling snow; but even though Daddy had told me how it would be there, I was not prepared. Grandmother had "failed considerably"—those were his words—in the eight weeks we had been gone. Daddy had hired two practical nurses to stay with her, one at night and one in the daytime, and he had turned the dining room into a downstairs bedroom since

Grandmother could no longer manage the steps. When I arrived, Grandmother was sitting in the tufted rose velvet wing chair where she always sat in the winter, but she seemed to have shrunk by one or two feet. Or maybe I had grown. In any case Grandmother was so small that she looked lost in the chair, and her feet dangled above the floor. She was dressed as carefully as always, though, and this reassured me at first as I stood in the dark hall pulling off my gloves, my boots, my coat. Noise from the television blared out into the hall: this was very unusual, since Grandmother hated television and said that it had been invented to amuse those people who needed such amusements. The parlor looked all different somehow, lit primarily by the glow of the TV. A tall thin woman stood up from where she sat in the rocking chair. "You must be Jennifer," she said. "I'm Mrs. Page." Mrs. Page wore her hair in a bun; she was crocheting a brown and white afghan.

"It's so nice to meet you." *Jennifer said mechanically like a windup doll*, I thought as I crossed the flowered carpet to take my grandmother's hand. Her hand was little and frail, her bones like the bones of birds. She would not look at me.

"Grandmother!" I said. "Grandmother! It's me, Jennifer." Grandmother watched the TV. I noticed that she wore three of her huge rhinestone brooches in an uneven row on the front of her dress. "Grandmother," I said.

"Excuse me, miss, but she doesn't know anybody right now. She just doesn't. It takes them that way sometimes." Mrs. Page looked up from her afghan and smiled.

"Well, this is my grandmother and she will know *me*!" I snapped.

But she didn't.

The only response she made came later, in that same awful afternoon. I had been sitting on a footstool beside her while it grew darker outside and more snow fell and the bluish-white light of the television danced off the bones of her face. The program had changed again; this time it was a stock car race, and it seemed to interest her. She leaned forward and said something under her breath.

"Do you like this, Grandmother?" I asked.

"Listen," Mrs. Page said. "She just likes it all. She doesn't even know what she's watching."

This infuriated me. "What are you watching, Grandmother?" I asked. On the television screen, the cars went around and around the track, and one of them turned over and burst into flames.

"Serves him right for driving that thing," Mrs. Page remarked.

"*Grandmother*," I said.

Grandmother turned to face me, fully, for the first time. Her light blue eyes seemed to have grown larger. They shone in the pale bony planes of her face. In front of her, the numbered cars went around a track somewhere in Georgia. Grandmother opened her mouth and stared back and forth from me to the television screen.

"What are you watching, Grandmother?" I asked again.

"Art," she said. "I'm watching art, Jennifer."

The cars went around and around on the television, and after watching them for a while longer I put on all my things and rode my bike home through the snow. The road had been scraped but it was still icy in spots, and a fine mist of snow covered the asphalt. I should have been careful, riding, but I was not. I pedaled as hard as I could, gulping huge mouthfuls of cold air and falling flakes of snow. I was moving so fast that the snow seemed to rush straight at me, giving me an odd sense of weightlessness, as if I were somehow suspended between the earth and the sky.

This feeling of suspension—a kind of not belonging, a sense of marking time—hung on even after my grandmother died, which happened a few weeks after our return. Her house was bought by a young attorney. Everything in the house was parceled out among the relatives, who insisted that I should have all the art supplies and the entire figurine collection, including *David*. These things sat in two cardboard boxes in my room for a long time, while I remained suspended. Then one Saturday morning in early May, I knew exactly what I wanted to do. I hauled both boxes out to the tool shed, placing them neatly beside the garden tools. I closed the tool shed door. I went inside and took the saved-up allowance money out of my jewelry box; then I got on my bike and rode straight downtown, parking my bicycle in front of the Western Auto store. Mollie Crews cut my hair off in a page boy, which curled softly under my ears. It looked terrific. Then I rode my bike over to see Scott, who turned out to be—exactly as he had promised—a good kisser. So I grew up. And I never became an artist, although my own career has certainly had its ups and downs, like most careers. Like most lives. Now I keep my grandmother's figurine collection on a special low table for my own children, who spend long hours arranging and rearranging all the little figures in their play.

Heat Lightning

"It's not supposed to be that way."
—WILLIE NELSON

Geneva moves through a dream these days. Right now she sits in a straightback kitchen chair on the front porch, stringing pole beans on a newspaper on her lap and looking up every now and then at the falling-down sidetrack up on the mountain across the road, at the dusty green leaves the way they curl up in the heat, at nothing. It is real hot. The black hair on Geneva's forehead sticks to her skin and she keeps on pushing it back. She strings the beans and breaks them in two and drops them into the pot by her side without once looking down. She feels a change coming on. Geneva has known that something is up ever since last Wednesday night when she hollered out in church.

She never knew she was going to holler before she did it, she never thought of it one time. Then when she did it, she did it so loud she jumped. "Amen!" she yelled, in a hoarse carrying voice that didn't have anything to do with her at all. "Tell it!" she yelled again, about ten minutes later, and everybody was so surprised and some people turned all the way around to see who it was back there in the back making such a commotion. Her daughter, Tammy, who is nine years old and full of notions anyway, put a hymn book up in front of her face she was so embarrassed. Now there are some regular yellers in Geneva's church but they are mostly old and Geneva is not one of them. Geneva never yelled out before and she has been going to that church ten years. After prayer meeting was over Brother Deskins, the preacher, came up to Geneva outside and said he surely felt the spirit moving in that room.

Geneva pulled her mouth into a bunch. "I reckon," she said. Brother Deskins was little and scrawny and looked like a guinea hen. Geneva looked at him and he went away.

Tammy went ahead of her up the dirt road home from church, sort of bouncing and dancing in that way she had like she was too good to touch the ground. Geneva walked with her hands down at her sides and her back as straight as a board, wondering what meanness Wesley Junior had got into while she was gone. On the way home Geneva did not think once about her hollering but her mind went skitting around and around it, almost getting there a couple of times, like a fly trying to get at a piece of cake and somebody keeps swatting him off.

Now Geneva goes on stringing beans. From where she sits she can see the dirt road in front of her house beyond the fence Wesley put up when Wesley Junior was little, them not realizing then that there never was a fence that could keep Wesley Junior out or in either one, or away from anywhere he wanted to go. Wesley Junior plays in the dirt on the edge of the road and when a car or a truck goes by he throws a rock at it. "You quit that," Geneva calls out sometimes, not thinking about it, knowing already he won't. There is a lot of traffic today because the James H. Drew Exposition is on up the holler, spread out like a crazy-quilt in the bottom at the fork of the road. Dust hangs in the air after every car and truck go by, hangs there solid as you please just like a curtain. This is the dryest spell anybody remembers and Geneva's crape myrtle by the clothes-line has died. She has to haul water from the well to the garden, ten or twelve buckets a day, she never thinks about it when she's doing it and it doesn't do much good.

Tammy prisses out. "I know you're going to say no," she says.

"Say no to what?" Geneva pulls out of her dream, which

is about nothing really, a waiting dream.

"Well, you *are* going to say no, aren't you? You always say no. I'm not even going to say it since I know you're going to say no."

Geneva looks at the road.

"Well, aren't you going to say no?" Tammy keeps it up, pushing her face into Geneva's. Tammy has got Wesley's curly hair, his light coloring and freckles, she looks like she has been dusted all over with gold dust out of a flower. Wesley has spoiled her rotten, Geneva thinks. When she was little, all he did was give her Tootsie Rolls and throw her up in the air.

But when Wesley Junior was born, Wesley was off working on a pipeline in Ohio and nobody was there except Mrs. Goins and some neighbor women and they laid him in the bed right next to Geneva and she was almost scared to breathe he was so little. He was born a long time ahead of when she figured he was due. But Wesley Junior was dark too, as dark as Geneva herself and all her people away off in West Virginia. "Now this is *my* baby," Geneva said to herself, and she still keeps him with her all the time and when he breaks things she hides it from Wesley. When she tells Wesley Junior no, he beats his head on a wall or the floor until it gets all bloody unless she holds him down. He is a cute little thing, though, and anyway Geneva can understand what he says just fine.

"*Mama*," Tammy says again, pushing into her shoulder. "All right, I'll tell you. You don't even care, do you? It's going to the carnival. *Why* can't we go to the carnival? Everybody is going. Everybody I know is going. *Lois Ann* is going," she adds.

"Well, Lois Ann hasn't got any business going," Geneva says.

"You never take us any place." Tammy is getting good and wound up now. She starts crying and then she goes in the house and Geneva can hear her in there, batting things around.

"Well," Geneva says after a while, to nobody. It's so hot that there is a fine gloss on everything and the heat pushes in on her head. Away off in the sky there is thunder but that doesn't mean anything, it thunders all the time in the mountains. Wesley Junior hits the tailgate of a blue Chevy pickup with a rock real hard and the truck slows down but then it goes on and dust hangs in the road. Geneva finishes the beans and wraps up the scraps and the newspaper in a neat pile and sits with it there in her lap.

"Lois Ann says they've got a two-headed pony and a double ferris wheel," Tammy says from behind the screen door.

Geneva gets up and goes in the house and washes out the beans and puts them on to cook with some sidemeat. Geneva is a big woman with a long white body. Her hair is long and black and she wears it pulled straight back in a ponytail low at the back of her neck. Somehow she has gotten to be twenty-eight. She washes up the sink, listening but not listening to Tammy, and Tammy goes on and on. They all talk so much, all of them—Tammy, Wesley, Wesley's Mamaw next door, Wesley's brother, Corbin, that lives with them sometimes. Geneva gets worn out listening.

Oh, there is a change coming on, all right, but Geneva doesn't know what it will be. Three times before in her life Geneva has felt it coming this way. The first time was when her pa died and she was real little, just sitting by the fire up in West Virginia and the dog started to bark outside and it hit her like a rock that her daddy was dead and sure enough, here came somebody before long to tell them and he was. The next time was the first time she saw Wesley, when she was not but sixteen years old and he came up there to work on the interstate. She was in the store buying a loaf of bread for her mama when he came in all dirty from working and that hair red-gold like a flame on his head. "Well, hel-LO there!" he spoke right up and held the door open for her, grinning, and Geneva had felt such a blush start that it went all the way down to her legs. Then he took her to the show and talked a mile a minute and then he married her three weeks later, nobody ever could see why. But when she saw him come in that door that's when she felt it, when she knew. Twelve years, now that's a long time back. The other time was about five years ago when she was carrying the baby that died, the one between Tammy and Wesley Junior, and she knew it was dead as soon as it quit moving and when Wesley took her into the clinic sure enough it was. She was about six months along at the time.

So there. Geneva sits at the table and looks at the pattern on the oil cloth, little yellow lamps in little blue squares with a blue border around them and red stripes running between. Lois Ann comes over, all dolled up, and Geneva hears them with a part of her mind but she is dreaming, then she hears them all fighting out in the front. She looks at the oilcloth and traces a square with her finger, over and over again. Nothing is worth getting up for.

"Mama! Mama!" Tammy comes in the house a while later squealing with her hair flying every which way. "Mama, Mama, come look, it's fixing to rain!"

Geneva gets up and goes to the back door and sure enough, the clouds have moved in close and it's thundering again and a little steady wind has come up and turned the leaves inside out on the shade tree in the back so their silver sides are showing, moving ever so little in the wind. Out in the back Wesley Junior whirls around and around like a top, he loves it when a storm comes up.

"You better go over to Mamaw's," Tammy says, but Geneva knows it and she is already gone out the back door and across the ditch to Wesley's Mamaw's house, a company house just like their own except that Mamaw has a TV.

"What took you so long?" Mamaw is mad as a wet hen, all wrapped up tight in the bed with everything shut down, the windows and doors and the shades pulled down. It's hot as hell and black as night in Mamaw's house. Lightning is the only thing in the world that Mamaw's scared of.

Geneva knows just what to do, she has done it so much before. She gets on the bed in the dark and holds Mamaw like a child on her lap. Mamaw is so old she has shrunk up to almost nothing and she smells like old rags and snuff and something sicky sweet that Geneva can't name. Mamaw has lived in this house in this holler all her life, near about. Geneva feels like she is going to get sick or holler out again, she can't tell which, but she never does either one in the end and she holds Mamaw tight while it thunders loud and Mamaw begins.

"Well, I wasn't but eight or nine years old and I was sitting in the front room and it was storming so hard you could see the rain coming in like waves across the valley and we had this tin roof, it was making the awfulest racket you ever heard. Then all of a sudden a ball of lightning come in the attic and rolled down the stairs, rolled right through the kitchen and on down the hall and through the front room and got me where I was just a-setting in my little chair. Then it rolled on out the door and it was gone.

"I fell right out of the chair on my face and I was passed out for upwards of a hour. I turned black as a cinder, too."

"How do you know you turned black?" Geneva asked. "If you were passed out, I mean." She never has thought to ask it before.

"I turned as black as a cinder, I tell you!" Mamaw hollers out in her thin old voice and twitches on Geneva's lap. Geneva is burning up. She listens awhile longer but the thunder has stopped and she can't hear any rain either so she puts Mamaw back down on the bed and gets up and puts up the shade to let in the light. Mamaw has little old black eyes way back in her yellow face.

"While you're over here I wisht you—" she starts, but Geneva is already gone, walked straight out the back door and over the ditch to her own house. The rain didn't amount to a thing, she sees. Thunder and heat lightning, that's about all.

Geneva goes straight in the house by the back door and won't even answer Tammy, she goes right in her room and locks the door behind her and pulls the suitcase out from under the bed and starts going through all the clothes that Anita, Corbin's wife, left her when she ran off with Bull Hopkins in such a hurry she couldn't even stop to pack her clothes. Anita was a wild thing, Geneva knows she has got halters and short shorts in here. Geneva strips down fast and leaves her own clothes lying in a pile on the floor. Then she pulls on a pair of Anita's red polyester short shorts and puts on a white halter with ruffles on it. It takes her a while to figure out how the halter works. Then Geneva goes over and stands in front of the dresser mirror and looks at herself. She has never worn shorts or a halter, either one, before, and in the mirror she is wavy and full of flesh. Her face is the same it always is, old Indian face Wesley used to say, he likes to say all kind of stuff and try to get a rise out of her.

Now Geneva takes out the sock where she keeps the money she is saving to buy curtain material. Wesley has some silver dollars in there that he has had since he was a kid and she takes those too, along with the money. Then she goes back out in the kitchen and hollers for the kids.

"What is it, Mama?" Tammy asks all big-eyed, seeing Geneva in the shorts, but Wesley Junior doesn't notice anything and he kicks at a kitchen chair until it falls over. Geneva lets it lie. Wesley Junior is small and black-headed, face like a smart little animal. Geneva leans over and kisses him hard on the face and he squirms in her arms. She straightens back up. "Come on," Geneva says. "We're going to the carnival."

Tammy and Wesley Junior both start hollering and jumping but Geneva grabs Wesley Junior tight by the hand and holds on. They go out the front door and she shuts it and looks back once where she planted the caladium bulbs she sent off for, but the dirt is dry and cracked where they never came up. "Goodbye, house," Geneva says all of a sudden, real loud.

"*Mama*," Tammy says, and looks at her funny, and then she closes her mouth but not for long. "Mama, can we take Lois Ann with us?" she says after a while.

"Sure," Geneva says. "Take Lois Ann. Go get her. Take anybody you want."

Tammy runs off and Geneva and Wesley Junior keep walking, her holding on to his hand. In a little while Tammy is back with Lois Ann. Lois Ann is wearing a tacky pink dress and she has pierced ears just like her mother who is on welfare.

A long time before they get there they can hear it, the carnival music and people talking loud, car horns, a lot of noise. Away off in the distance there is still some thunder but it's not as hot as it was. Geneva walks in her dream but when she gets there the dream is gone and all the colors are so bright they hurt her eyes. Tammy and Lois Ann are holding hands and squealing and Wesley Junior pulls first one way and then the other. They fall in with a whole raft of people moving in a steady flow across the old wooden bridge and into the bottom and Geneva loses Wesley Junior and then she grabs him again just in time to keep him from falling off. "You watch where you're going," she tells him, but he acts like he doesn't hear.

The bottom is all changed now, all different, all new. The carnival people have put up their tents everywhere and put streamers all around and set up little stalls all over the place, and the ferris wheel is so high it takes your breath away. All the rides are going. Everything in the carnival is bright and moving. None of this was here Thursday, Geneva thinks, and none of it will be here tomorrow. Every bit of this will be gone. Geneva looks back down at the creek and sees two carnival women down there with their earrings catching the sun, beating out clothes on a rock. Then they are up to the gate and Geneva pays two dollars for herself and a dollar for each of the kids. A carnival man is there just inside the gate. He is dark-faced with long curly hair like a gypsy and he has something in his hand.

"Here you go, sonny," the carnival man says, and holds out his hand to Wesley Junior, and even his voice is different and strange. Geneva thinks to stop him—you can't tell what a carnival man would have in his hand—but she can't move and Wesley Junior sticks his hand right out and gets it, a little green and red plastic snake with sequin eyes. The carnival man grins and his teeth are brown and stained, and when Geneva looks down to get away from his eyes the skin on her legs looks so white.

"Mama, Mama, can I get one of them monkeys?" Tammy grabs at Geneva's hand and points to a monkey that dances on a stick and Geneva buys it for her and buys Lois Ann an American flag and buys Wesley Junior a plastic sword with a gold handle and a black case that hooks on to your belt.

Geneva goes over to the ticket booth and buys a roll of tickets for each kid, a quarter apiece, which doesn't sound bad until you see that each ride costs two tickets or more. Geneva doesn't care. She stares hard at the woman in the ticket booth, a woman who has dyed blond hair and a lot of makeup and shorts Geneva a dollar on change. But Geneva doesn't care. They start riding the rides and Geneva rides every one, the Tilt-A-Whirl, the roller coaster, the merry-go-round, the bumper cars. She squeals as loud as the kids and when they get dizzy and sick from riding they eat cotton candy and popcorn balls and drink warm Cokes because the ice machine broke down. While she is standing in line at the food trailer to buy the food, Geneva sees the carnival people's trailers and tents right behind the carnival, up against the tree line. That's where they live, she thinks. After they all eat, they go down the row of little tents where the games are, and everybody calls out at Geneva. Sometimes she lets the kids play and sometimes she doesn't, then she gets to throwing baseballs herself into a bushel basket and she is so close to winning so many times that the man keeps making special deals for her and finally she wins a big blue Panda bear for Tammy almost as big as Tammy herself.

"Mama." Tammy pulls at her hand. "Mama. Lois Ann has got to go to the bathroom."

"Can't you wait?" Geneva asks Lois Ann, but Lois Ann screws up her face and says she can't. Wesley Junior sets in crying because he wants to ride the silver bullet and finally Geneva says all right and buys another roll of tickets and gives him some and tells him to stay on it until she gets back, and then she takes Lois Ann and Tammy by the hand and goes off to find a bathroom. "No bathrooms!" a carnival woman says loudly, waving her hands, and Geneva backs off from her and goes to ask the old man in the food trailer. "We don't have public bathrooms," he says. "No bathrooms. I'm sorry."

Lois Ann starts crying and twisting her feet around. Geneva stares at the old man in the food trailer until he leans over and jerks a thumb back toward the mountain where the carnival people live and says, "Just go on back that way. Take her somewhere back in there."

"Will you go in the bushes?" Geneva asks Lois Ann.

"*No!*" Lois Ann says, stomping her foot.

"Well, you're going to," Geneva says.

Back in the mess of trailers she sees how they live, sees their underwear strung up to dry, and when they get beyond the last one, Lois Ann squats down finally in the bushes and does it and when she straightens up she screams.

"What's the matter with you?" Tammy says.

Lois Ann puts her hand over her mouth and points, and in the door of the closest trailer a man is standing, just watching them.

"Here, girls, run on now," Geneva says, handing them some tickets, and they giggle and carry on and duck their heads and run.

Geneva stands still and looks at the man. He opens the door of the trailer, an old beat-up blue Airstream, and inside the trailer Geneva can hear a dog yapping until the man comes out and shuts the door behind him. He stands on the trailer steps, squinting in the sunlight. He is the same man who was at the gate when they came into the carnival. Now he has taken off his shirt and his shoes and he is wearing some old work pants down on his hips. He stars at Geneva like he stared at her before and she stands there absolutely still and looks back. "You from around here?" he says finally, but Geneva can't talk and she nods her head yes. The man looks at her some more.

"Why don't you come on in here and visit with me awhile?" he says. "I won't bite you." He grins, a wild carnival grin that doesn't give a damn about anything, and Geneva grins back. Then she runs off as fast as she can go, without another word, and she is out of breath by the time she gets back where the rides are. But Wesley Junior is all right, he is right up there on the silver bullet like she told him, going a hundred miles a minute and screaming all the time.

I could of done that, Geneva thinks suddenly. I could of gone in that Airstream trailer and never come out. I could of moved with them wherever they are going, and stayed every night in a different town. I could of beat out my clothes on every rock in every river in the world. Geneva throws back her head and laughs until tears come up in her eyes and everybody is looking at her. Wesley Junior looks down and sees her and laughs too and his little arms flap like wings in the wind. Different, that's how Wesley Junior is, but there is something about Geneva that is like him and she might as well be up there herself right now, look at him go, like some kind of a crazy bird. Fly away, fly away. Geneva feels good. She sits down and stretches out her legs. I might as well get me some sun, she thinks.

After while Lois Ann and Tammy come along and find her and Geneva gives them two of Wesley's silver dollars to spend on gumball necklaces. Then after Wesley Junior uses up the last of the tickets they start on back. Wesley Junior runs in and out of the traffic and breaks his sword but Geneva doesn't even get after him for doing it. Lois Ann and Tammy take turns carrying the big blue panda bear and when they get close to the house Tammy gets sick. Everything Tammy throws up is pink.

Wesley is sitting in the kitchen drinking a beer. He is fit to be tied. "Where you been?" he starts in, but then he sees the panda bear and the snake and the monkey on a stick. He sits back and watches Geneva while she makes some cornbread and slices tomatoes and sets the table. Wesley Junior gets under the table and rolls around and pulls on his daddy's feet, and Geneva makes Tammy take Mamaw some cornbread.

When Geneva brings the beans over from the stove, Wesley reaches out and makes a big grab at her. "Gotcha!" he says, with his blue eyes jumping, but Geneva slips right by and puts the beans down on the table. "You all come on and eat," she says.

Dear Phil Donahue

I used to be so cute and so gay, I can't tell you. The quote under my picture in the high school yearbook was all about "trodding" and "springtime" and "gay." Sometimes I still trod gaily such as yesterday even, I picked up both babies and danced and danced all over the house to "Boogie Shoes" on Jerry's *Saturday Night Fever* album. While I was doing this Jerry came in to get some more of his stuff, including that album, as it turned out. He turned down the volume and went to the refrigerator and got some yogurt (Jerry never used to eat yogurt) and stood there eating and watching me with this weird expression. It was a party before he came in.

But now I've blown it, Phil. I mean when you opened this letter and saw that first line you probably thought it was from some brilliant bisexual celebrity who wanted to be on your show. Well now you know. This letter is from me: Martha Rasnick, age twenty-eight, currently separated from my husband because I kept a man in our garage for three days. Three days is not a lifetime. I realize I'm writing this letter in a tone of what I would call (from my dim past as an English major before I dropped out) quirky desperation.

You probably wonder why I'm writing to you at all, Phil. Why I picked you out from among the hundreds of celebrities who grace my screen. It's because you talked to me, Phil, all those mornings.

Not only that but you've taught me all kinds of things on your show. I know about child psychology, common sexual myths, investing, acupuncture, birth control, problems of aging, politics, stress, and *anorexia nervosa*. I even know Rosalynn Carter. One thing I love about you, Phil, is that you've kept my brain from drying up. I mean that literally: you kept my head from caving in. Another thing I love about you is the way you look everybody in the eye. It's perfectly clear that if some radical Californian sat down on your show and announced that he had just planted a bomb in the studio you would be so terrific, so cool, you would look him straight in the eye and say, "Now tell us, Mr. Blah, how you first became interested in explosive devices."

As a matter of fact my house is an explosive device. It never goes off, though. It never goes off because I, tricky little dervish that I am, whirl through it every day wielding vacuum cleaner and dust rags, sticking in pacifiers and baby suppositories, watering plants and changing diapers, turning the dials to their proper positions for the specific time of day OFF ON PRE-SOAK BROIL, emptying and consuming, maintaining this equilibrium. But let me tell you that it's barely, just barely, maintained. Chaos is right around the corner in my house and explosions lurk everywhere.

This is what I do, Phil. The thing I'm trying to determine is whether or not it is separate from what I am. And whether either of those things has anything to do with this man I kept in the garage. If I were on your show, Phil, you could ask me pertinent questions and I could give you informative answers and we could get it all worked out before the station break. As it is, you're not here with your questions and I don't know where to start since there's no real beginning to this story at all. People who have been to China are always showing you slides. I've got some slides of my own, Phil, and they're pretty colorful. I'll provide the commentary—and here are some interesting tapes.

Look at our house. Glass and stone, somebody said it "approaches the organic." Approach our organic house. Look at our huge shag-carpeted living room (you rake a shag rug), with its lower "conversation center" around the fireplace. In the conversation center, I've never been able to say a word. Look at our glass coffee table, our mushroom chairs, the little geometric tables that fit together to make a big table, the antique grandfather clock, the carved frog, the split-leaf philodendron tree, the Oriental ashtrays, the fake Calder mobile. In the white kitchen, look at the gleaming espresso coffee maker, which I don't know how to use. You'll notice several things on this tour. One is that the stuff we have is good. The other is that we really don't have very much. You'll notice a lot of long, bare non-organic spaces. This stuff is all new and none of it is paid for.

We never had anything until two years ago when Jerry finally finished graduate school and got this good job. I quit college myself and worked as a secretary while he was an undergraduate, then while he was in the Army, and then while he was in graduate school. Believe me, I was ready to quit when the time came. Now suddenly we have all this stuff because Jerry said we had to have a house where we could "entertain." I don't work anymore and we have two babies because Jerry said he wanted a "family." But I always wanted babies, so that's all right. I wanted a house, too.

It's just that when you get *things*, and they're your things, then they take over. You have to take care of them. You have to dust them and polish them and fix their cords. I was born to do that, however, right here in Nashville. My mother was a home ec teacher for thirty years until she died. And I always knew what I wanted to do: take care of my home and my family. It should be a joy to take care of our things. In fact I enjoyed it. At least I thought I was a snappy little dervish full of joy.

JERRY: Well, we did it.

ME: Did what?

JERRY: Bought the block. The whole damn block. There was this one guy holding out but he finally came across. He finally saw the light.

ME: The what?

JERRY: The *light*, Martha. Christ, are you deaf?

ME: Does anybody live there now? I mean, what happens to the people who live there now?

JERRY: They *move*, baby.

ME: But, Jerry.

JERRY: *What?* Look, come over here, Martha. Give your old man a kiss.

ME: A what?

JERRY: A *kiss*. You're deaf, Martha.

ME: Yes. (I give him that kiss.)

This is an aerial slide, showing our whole neighborhood. Our address is 28 Country Club Circle. Jerry loves our address. A funny thing about the neighborhood, though. The circle is OK. But this circle is surrounded by lowlife. By houses that change hands, houses that different people sleep in, houses with flamingos and hubcaps in the front yards, houses where men sit outside on the steps barechested in summer drinking beer and in the windows behind them you can see women through the slats of the venetian blinds, ironing in their slips, pale strange women with cigarettes hanging out of their mouths.

The country club golf course is laid out so that sometimes the fairways pass close to these houses and the people who live there come out in their dirt yards to stare at the bright golfers. What are they thinking? Some of the golfers have complained.

One of these houses, pretty close to our own house if you cut through the yards and driveways, is run by a widow who lets her rooms only to psychiatric outpatients of the Veterans Administration Hospital. They're allowed to live here and hold jobs in the community while they reorient themselves to the outside world. Let's go in closer for a better look at the crazy veterans. See the fat man with the three-piece suit, sitting Indian fashion in the grass? He must be hot in that suit. See the little dude in the red baseball cap? The doctors must urge them to dress in loud colors. Look at their shirts. The doctors must urge them to walk, too, as a part of their therapy. On Saturday afternoons they walk to town, going to see a movie. I know they're going to see a movie because somebody told me that's what they do. But they walk as though they're not quite sure where they're going or why they're out walking at all. Sometimes they go single file. It upsets me to see them walking and if I have to go someplace on Saturday afternoons I take another street.

Now we have a conversation between me and my mother-in-law, one Tuesday morning when she has unexpectedly dropped by. (I almost wrote *dead* instead of *by*.) Mrs. Rasnick has stopped in on her way home from the beauty shop where they have curled her, sprayed her, massaged her, pedicured her, and filed her nails to silver points. She's wearing some kind of classy pantsuit and silver loafers with Lucite heels. I'm wearing blue jeans (too tight). I'm folding diapers. *Sesame Street* is on. Will is riding his fire engine. Linda is in the playpen chewing up a Metropolitan Museum of Art calendar. Mrs. Rasnick's name is Charlsie and she's always asking me to call her that.

MRS. RASNICK: And anyway I went by Michael Corzine's, just to look, you know, I thought I might pick up a christening present for Louise's new grandson, and they had this marvelous little man down in the basement giving lessons on how to make leather bottles. Incredibly attractive bottles, sort of Spanishy, only the secret is that *they're not leather at all*!

WILL: (screaming) Doose!

ME: Juice, please.

WILL: Doose, pee. (I give him some apple juice.)

MRS. RASNICK: They're just old bottles covered with newspaper! Isn't that the cleverest thing? You take old bottles
and put a layer of newspaper around them and then a
layer of varnish and then a stain and then another layer
of newspaper and so on and it's absolutely amazing, they
look just like leather! They would fool anybody. I can't
wait to try it. I bought all the stuff, doesn't it sound like
fun?

ME: Great!

WILL: (loud) Fruck!

MRS. RASNICK: *What did he say?*

ME: Ha, ha, *truck*, Mrs. Rasnick. He can't say T's yet.

MRS. RASNICK: Oh, isn't that cute? Fruck, I'll have to tell
Louise.

Linda gets her toes caught in the playpen mesh and starts
yelling. I untangle them but she's still yelling so I pick her up
and get a Playtex bottle out of the refrigerator to start running
hot water over it.

MRS. RASNICK: You know dear. (Hesitates.)

ME: What's that, Mrs. Rasnick?

MRS. RASNICK: Well, pardon me if I'm speaking out of turn,
but you really look a little wan this morning. I have
plenty of varnish, why don't I leave a can with you? You
know you really ought to do something with your *hands*.
(Mrs. Rasnick looks at her hands, holding them out so
that I can see them too, making graceful arcs in the air.)

Conversation between me and my old friend Mare, about
two months ago. Mare's real name is Mary but lately she styles
herself "Mare." She sits in her yellow Porsche in our driveway,
sounding the musical horn. I go out carrying Linda, and look

in at Mare who is surrounded by wig boxes and Mark Cross luggage and Kleenex.

MARE: I'm leaving. (Mare is big on drama.)

ME: Oh, are you going on a trip?

MARE: Yes, I'm going to Chicago, but not really—well I *am* going to Chicago but it's only to stay with my sister for a little while. To forget.

OF COURSE I SAY: Forget what?

MARE: Oh, Willis. Willis moved out. He just said he couldn't take it anymore and he wouldn't even say what. He moved out while I was at Kroger's and when I came back I found a note. (She shows me the note. Willis is the man she's been living with.) I'd just bought a leg of lamb and everything. I just had to come by and tell you. I knew you'd want to know. And Martha (leans out, grabs my arm; I almost drop Linda), I might as well tell you, whenever I'm really depressed I come to see you. You and Jerry, well, you're just special people, you know? I mean you're so happy and everything, it gives me faith. Willis was wrong for me anyway, you know that. We never would have had a thing like you and Jerry have, not in a million years. (Mare nibbles her long streaked hair. Linda is getting very heavy and I switch arms.) Well, see you in a week or so. I have to regroup my forces, that's all. Or is it recoup? (Giggles weirdly.) Tell me you're happy, Martha. You and Jerry. Some-body's got to be happy.

ME: I'm happy, Mare. We're very lucky. See you when you get back from Chicago.

A brave wave from Mare. A sad, reckless (she's loving it) smile and she backs out, turns, spinning loose gravel, while I stand in the driveway holding Linda. It's a warm clear day. Oddly enough I do feel happy and lucky and I mean every word I just said, yet I feel strangely fake, too. This air is so clear it's hurting my face.

Jerry at a party, in conversation with a girl in purple velvet pants, overheard by me sliding up behind to get a cigarette.

SHE: What do you do, then?

JERRY: Well, it's hard to describe. I think of myself as an artist, an urban creator, you might say. I'm in the conceptual end of the business, pure thought. On one hand, it's a very intricate process of matching people with places, habitats, filling their little needs. Anticipating their creature comforts. On the other hand, it's like sculpture, dealing with space and form.

SHE: Oh, that must be very exciting.

Jerry sells real estate.

A quick slide of Jerry: you think you've seen him before. He looks like the men who stand beside the cars in car ads: you know the look. Blond, lean, and meaningful as hell. Jerry's looks are deceptive, though. They change. When I started going with Jerry, it was in high school and he had a crewcut and pink shirts. He was a senior, the president of the student government. He went off to college and during the first two years he pledged a fraternity and drank a lot of beer. The last two years he let his hair grow long and protested everything he could think of. Now he has a straight job and straight clothes to fit it but once he gets home—on weekends or when we go out—he looks like he's auditioning for a motorcycle movie. He has all this turquoise jewelry, too. We live in Nashville and there are a lot of music people around and Jerry likes that, he likes to try to hang around with them. Nobody big, though: for instance we know somebody who knows Kris Kristofferson. We go to parties where everyone smokes dope and we also go to straight parties, ornate cocktail suppers with shrimp trees, given by Jerry's business friends. I've always enjoyed being with all our friends but now that this has happened, Phil, nobody much has come around. I thought they were my good friends but I guess they were Jerry's friends and instead of being Martha I was Jerry's wife. I don't know. I mean I'm trying to figure all this out now that it's too late.

But look at the man on the slide: Jerry. My high school honey. I always knew we'd get married and we did, and it was just exactly like I had dreamed it would be, and I've been happy ever since. This is Jerry, ready to go out now: ruffled shirt, leather vest, jeans, boots, a belt with a turquoise buckle. I don't know, I can't seem to get a fix on Jerry even when I show you this slide. Jerry used to say "movie." Then he said "flick." Now he says "film." I mean I've known him so long but there is something I don't know.

Later in October. Late afternoon. Will is running around the yard. Linda is on a blanket on the grass. I'm digging holes in the yard around the cedars, with a spoon. I put a bulb into each hole and then I cover it back up. Will keeps trying to dig up the bulbs but I keep him away by saying "I bet you can't run all the way around the house" and so on. I feel good, the way you feel when you plant something.

Then a man I've seen before walks around the circle and stops in front of our house, on the sidewalk, staring at us. I've never actually noticed him before, but now that he's here I know I've seen him before, walking. I don't know why I say "man." He's just a boy. About nineteen or twenty years old, tall and thin. He has long hair and he wears jeans and an orange windbreaker and I know immediately, from the windbreaker, that he is one of the psychiatric boarders. But the awful thing, Phil, is that he stops walking and stares at me as if I'm somebody he has known very well in the past but has not expected to see again. His hair is feathery and almost white. His eyes are surprisingly dark. They glitter. He stares at me. I move toward Linda on the blanket, thinking *where is Will*? But I can't look away from this boy. His eyes are black and crazy. As I edge toward Linda I feel it, in spite of everything I can do, I feel that answering recognition come into my own face.

"Hiya!" shrieks Will, suddenly at my side, and I grab his hand and jerk Linda up from the blanket and, pulling Will, get inside the house as fast as I can. From the window I see that he's still standing there on the sidewalk for a long time, half an hour, after I have closed and locked the door. I surprise myself. Now I'm concerned that one of the neighbors will notice him there and call the police. When Jerry comes home, I don't tell him about it at all.

The secret madness starts here. But that's the wrong name, Phil. It isn't madness; it's simply something different. Something different starts here. This is when I start being different from what I do. OK: I feed Jerry, I feed the babies. I sleep with Jerry, we go out, the babies are fine, Will starts to catch on to the potty. We have a party. I get a frizzy permanent. Mare comes back from Chicago and starts dating a veterinarian/songwriter.

During all this time it gets worse and worse. I wake up cold and panicked, it's like dying when I wake up. Finally at nine thirty you come on the TV, Phil, and believe me I'm ready for you. I watch as hard as I can. I hoard opinions and facts: what consumers really think, what blacks really think, how Viet Nam veterans really feel. If I listen hard enough, maybe I can collect enough interesting opinions and strong feelings to get me through the day. Getting through the day becomes a major project. I buy a big calendar with spaces for every hour. I know that it's absolutely necessary for me to be as busy as possible at all times. If I slip or relax for even one minute, something horrible will happen. I don't know what. Sometimes I think about it in terms of my head falling apart, caving in or splintering grotesquely outward in all directions. That would frighten the babies. Other times I think about it as something worse: if I relax, if I sit still, something will slip in and take possession. I don't know what. Some sort of insect, creepy.

The things that actually happened during this period are pretty much of a blur, even though it was only two or three weeks ago. Nothing happened, actually. Out of a period of about two weeks there, all you get is a few short tapes.

WILL: Read, read.

ME: OK. Just a minute.

WILL: Read, read, *want*.

ME: OK. Let me get your book.

WILL: Book.

ME: That's right. Now, what's this?

WILL: Airplane in the sky!

ME: Smart boy! Now what's this?

WILL: Airplane in the sky!

ME: No, it's an elephant. El-e-phant. Can you say elephant?

WILL: Efem.

ME: Good. Will, what would you say if Mommy told you she's going crazy?

WILL: Airplane in the sky!

I call my old friend Janice, after staring at the telephone for fifteen minutes. Janice and Mare are my two best friends. Once, years ago, the three of us shared an apartment for the summer. Since then, Mare has gone in one direction and Janice has gone the opposite way and I guess I've just stayed put. Janice is a member of the Junior League. She has three kids and goes to church. I decide to tell her everything.

ME: Janice, this is Martha. Are you busy? I mean, can you talk for a little while?

JANICE: Well, actually, I was just on my way out the door.

ME: Oh, well, I just wondered. This will only take a minute.

JANICE: Yes?

ME: I mean, well it's a little hard to put into words.

JANICE: What is it, Martha? Is something wrong?

ME: No, no, nothing like that. Listen, you go ahead, and we'll talk about it another time. Maybe you can come over for coffee soon.

JANICE: Tell me.

ME: No, it's not anything, really.

JANICE: (relieved) Great. I'll be looking forward to it. (Click. Click. Two very loud clicks. I sit looking at the phone. First I want it to ring and then I don't want it to ring, but in any case, it doesn't.)

The boy walks around our cicle every day now, Phil. He slows down when he passes our house. He wears blue jeans and his windbreaker and tennis shoes. On Tuesday, November 3, he walks up the driveway and into that side of the garage we never use, the side where the junk and the suitcases and tools are stored. He stays in there for about five minutes and then comes out. The next day he goes into the garage again, carrying a cardboard box. On November 5 he goes into the garage again, carrying an airlines bag. This time he doesn't come out.

While the babies are taking their naps, I hold a long excited debate with myself. What should I do? Should I call the police? Should I call Jerry? It would be fun to tell him something exciting, for a change. I haven't had anything exciting to tell him for years. Or should I march right out to the garage and say OK, what are you doing here? Get out.

In the end I do none of these things. I wash my hair and set it (usually I don't set it) and then I cook beef stroganoff for dinner, early. After I feed the babies—Jerry won't be home for an hour—I fix up this little guest tray for the boy in the garage. I'm humming to myself, tra la, a strange operatic humming that I've never done before. I put a plate of beef stroganoff and noodles, two Pepperidge Farm rolls, a nice tossed salad, and some peanut butter cookies and an apple on the tray. I'm not pleased with the peanut butter cookies but I hadn't planned on dessert. I put Will in front of the TV to watch *Misterogers*, go out to the garage, knock on the door of the closed side, and set the tray down right in front of it. I leave immediately. I take the cat inside with me so she won't bother the tray.

Now I'm in suspense. I flit around the kitchen windows, even though I know there's no possible way to see that door from the house. But I keep looking. In fifteen minutes I go back out to check, and the tray has disappeared. As if by magic. No tray, closed door. I'm delighted. I go back into the house, make two martinis, put the pitcher in the refrigerator and continue humming, refining my style.

When Jerry comes in he says, "Hey, great, Martha, what's the occasion?"

"All for you," I tell him. "Have a drink."

The next morning I wake up free of fear. After Jerry leaves, I fix a breakfast tray. It occurs to me that there's no bathroom in there, but I can't be bothered with such details. I fix poached eggs and bacon, and fifteen minutes later the tray is gone. Now both trays are inside the room.

I had thought that he might put the one from supper outside the door, so that I can wash the dishes. Now I imagine dishes stacked up to the low ceiling of the storage room—all my dishes, all my silverware. I'll have to feed my family on paper plates. I start giggling and Will catches it and giggles too. Sooner or later I'll go in there and talk to that boy. I savor it, putting it off. He's mine to talk to and I can go in there and talk to him whenever I want. Whenever I'm ready. I hold long conversations in my head. I tell him everything.

I finally decide to go in later that day, while the babies are asleep. My hand shakes as I brush my hair. Ever since that boy has been in the garage, the fear is gone. As swiftly and as mysteriously as it came. Now I feel weird and light-headed, constantly on the verge of laughter. I take a long time with my hair. When I'm ready the doorbell rings, scaring me to death. It's Janice in a boxy brown suit.

"I thought I'd run over for a minute while Mattie's still at my house to watch Lisa. You're looking good."

I say thanks, holding back the laughter.

Janice lights a Salem and frowns. "What was the matter the

other day?" she asks, looking carefully at my left ear. "You want to talk about it?" She hates conversations like this.

"Oh, nothing," I say. "I mean, just nothing at all. I think my pills are depressing me, some days I really drag around. I've decided to call Dr. Lassiter and see if I can get the sequential kind, isn't that what you call them?"

"Oh *listen*!" Janice says. "You really should. I mean, they can be so dangerous. I had this friend who—" Janice is off and running. She loves a good pill reaction better than anything in the world except an unusual pregnancy. Janice tells me five true case histories involving terrible pill reactions. All through the conversation, I keep thinking Janice would *die* if I told her I have a boy in the garage. She would *die*. At the end of Janice's pill act, Linda wakes up. Janice leaves. I am annoyed yet also relieved, in a funny way, that I haven't spoken to him yet. I have to get my head completely right. I have to save him as long as I can.

I fix roast pork for supper and that night Jerry and I watch Anthony Quinn on Dick Cavett. Anthony Quinn is good. I feel very relaxed, as if I've melted and I'm sloshing around inside my skin. I realize how long it's been since I've relaxed.

Morning. The third day. I call Charlsie, actually calling her Charlsie. She always offers to babysit and I know she never means it; this time she's caught.

ME: Hi, Charlsie. Put your money where your mouth is. (I feel giddy now and out of control. I've just taken him his breakfast; it's going on too long.)

CHARLSIE: What? Is this *Martha*? (This is the first time I've ever called her Charlsie. No wonder she's surprised.)

ME: Yes, it is. Listen, I forgot that I have a doctor's appointment this afternoon and I don't have a sitter and I wondered if you could possibly babysit for about an hour? I can't tell you how much I would appreciate it if you could. (Afterthought:) *Charlsie*.

MRS. RASNICK: Well, let me see, I suppose so. Actually I'm

knee-deep in these bottles...(This vision of Mrs. Rasnick literally knee-deep in bottles nearly cracks me up. But I recover. I give no ground.)

ME: Both the babies will be asleep.

MRS. RASNICK: Well, all right, dear. I suppose I could bring my bottles with me—

ME: Oh, yes. By all means. Bring your bottles. See you about one.

I don't know why I made such an elaborate plan, Phil. I could have walked out to the garage while the babies were asleep. I didn't need a sitter. God knows, I didn't need Mrs. Rasnick. Probably by then I wanted to be found out; I don't know.

I mop the kitchen. Then I get all dressed up, like I'm going to the doctor. Mrs. Rasnick appears, armed with her bottles and goo. She carries everything in a burlap bag covered with seashells. Making seashell bags was her thing two years ago. I sail out of the house, go to the garage, start the car noisily, back out the driveway and park immediately on our side street, cleverly out of view of Mrs. Rasnick. I am so taken with my own cleverness. I sneak through our boxwood and into our garage.

I knock on the door. "It's me," I say.

No response.

"Can I come in?"

No answer.

I knock again: nothing. Now I'm really frightened. What if he's dead in my garage? Somehow that strikes me as funny and then I open the door. I'm still laughing as I open the door.

It doesn't hit me until then, Phil. What I've done. The storage room smells awful; I told you there was no bathroom in there. There are rotten food smells and sweat smells also. It's so bad that I retch at the door. Oddly enough I'm still so conditioned by what I do that I almost go back to get the Lysol spray. But I step inside. It's dark and at first I can't see anything. I remember now that the light in here burned out a month ago and I've been meaning to replace it ever since. There's no window, which means that the boy has been here in the dark for almost exactly three days.

I can't see him. I can't see anything. I wait until my eyes adjust to the darkness and then gradually I see him, curled up in the corner by the lawnmower. I had been staring at him all along. I walk over there, picking my way through the mess. He's curled up, asleep. I realize he doesn't know whether it's night or day. I bend down. He breathes slowly and regularly, as deeply as a child. He has crumpled his orange windbreaker into a sort of pillow and has put it under his head. That windbreaker is the final thing, Phil.

I kneel down and shake his shoulder, gently. I can feel the bones. He murmurs and I keep shaking him and suddenly he bolts up, wild-eyed, like an animal. He tries to stand, loses his footing, and crashes back on some plates and knocks over a tool box. The noise is deafening because it has been so quiet. He hasn't heard any noise at all for three days, remember. He cringes. I cringe. He's breathing hard now, with a sharp sobbing intake of breath.

"Don't be afraid," I say. "I won't hurt you. Don't be afraid." I move a little closer, sort of crawling. I reach out for his hand but touch instead something slimy and wet that he's holding. He makes an unintelligible sound, pulls his hand back and puts it to his mouth. Finally I realize what he has: the piece of chamois that was in the tool box, that Jerry uses to polish the car. He is chewing it. Apparently he has been chewing it for some time.

"Oh, Christ," I say out loud. I feel dead and I can see that I have finally gotten there, dead center. His eyes dart back and forth, back and forth. Looking into them I see how far I've come along the way to where he is. I feel awful so I hold him in my arms and begin rocking slightly back and forth. He goes limp and I hold him, saying things that are meant to comfort him, all lies, like "That's all right," and I hold him for a long time. Looking around I see all the mess and the filth, and the door blows open more and the bright fall sunlight is coming in a straight path from the door and falling short of us by a few feet. I hold him until the sunlight is blocked by Mrs.

Rasnick, black avenging angel silhouetted in her too-young pantsuit against the door frame. This is the last slide: Mrs. Rasnick's silhouette.

MRS. RASNICK: I thought I heard—

MRS. RASNICK: (rising pitch) Martha, are you all right?

MRS. RASNICK: My God.

Mrs. Rasnick starts to scream.

That just about wraps it up, Phil, except for one painful interview with Jerry. You don't want to hear the whole thing, it's repetitive. I'll start about the middle.

JERRY: Martha, Christ, Martha, why did you have to get my mother to babysit for Christ's sake? That's what I can't understand. My mother. She's been in bed ever since, you know that? She's never been so upset in her life. The least, the very least you could have done would be to have said he raped you or something.

ME: But he didn't rape me.

JERRY: I know that, Martha. We both know that. But couldn't you have said that, just to soften the blow a little? I mean, she's got chest pains.

ME: Well, look, Jerry, I'm sorry that your mother has got chest pains but that's hardly the point of this whole discussion. Don't you want to hear my side of it?

JERRY: You haven't got a side of it. Martha, I told you, I'm arranging for you to see a doctor. That's all I can do. We'll discuss this whole thing some other time. (I forgot to tell you, Phil, Jerry is packing. He's folding his cowboy shirt.)

ME: Well, if you think I'm so crazy, how come you're willing to leave the babies with me? (Not that I would ever let him take them, of course; I'm merely testing.)

JERRY: I can't take care of them, I have to work. My mother can't take care of them, she's sick. That's one thing I'll say for you, Martha, at least you didn't lock the babies up out there too.

ME: I keep telling you, I didn't lock *anyone* up out there. That boy went into the storage room himself and all I did was take him some food. That's all—I mean, that's hardly a capital crime, is it? The door was open the whole time. Three lousy little days. I didn't even go in there until the third day when I went in to talk to him and your mother came in and that's all that happened. That's *all*, Jerry.

JERRY: Sure it is.

ME: Jerry, I don't like what you're insinuating. All I did was take him some food and then try to talk to him.

JERRY: That's a real nice, normal thing to do, Martha.

ME: I don't see why you're leaving.

JERRY: Look, I said I don't want to talk about it anymore, Martha. I'm upset, I don't know what I might say to you right now. All along, you've been right there, I could depend on you. This is really a shock.

ME: Do you mean you think I've been a good wife or something? Wow, Jer, that's real nice. That's real touching. (Long silence.) Jerry, I've been a *bore*! a horrible, lousy bore!

JERRY: I just don't understand how you could do it. You endangered the children, my mother, me, my job, everything. You don't know anything about that guy. He could be an ax murderer for all you know.

ME: He's not.

JERRY: You *don't know*, Martha. You don't know anything about him. You still don't. And whatever he is, you've retarded his progress about a million percent. They're probably going to file charges, you know that? *File charges*. That's what the doctor who came with the ambulance said. The Veterans Administration versus Mrs. Martha Rasnick, how's that? Really great, huh? You've outdone yourself.

ME: I don't care about all that stuff.

JERRY: Well just what exactly do you care about? You obviously don't give a damn about me or the children or anything else I can think of. It's more than a little embarrassing, Martha, what you've done.

ME: Jerry. Jerry, please listen to me.

JERRY: You haven't got anything to say that I want to hear right now, Martha.

So that's the way it is, Phil. That's why I'm writing to you. I didn't have anything to say for a long time, and now that I'm ready to talk, no one is here to listen. That's my fault. I've done these things: closed my mind, failed to grow or change, failed to understand Jerry, used my job and then my babies as shields, and—worst of all, last of all—used that boy. Some of it is not my fault, however. A lot of it is not my fault. Anyway it's all done: water under the bridge. I'm sorry, really sorry, about the boy—if I hurt him, that is. If I made him worse. I'm not so sure I did, though. Anyway I am so sorry about the boy. But I'm not sorry about anything else. If Jerry was inconvenienced, if the neighbors were embarrassed by the scene, if Mrs. Rasnick has chest pains, those are their problems. I would do it again. No, I wouldn't, actually. I wouldn't need to do it now. See what I've learned, Phil, from my "experience." See what fine conclusions I've reached. The only thing is that it doesn't do me much good right now, does it, if you're still the only one I have to talk to?

Mrs. Darcy Meets the Blue-Eyed Stranger at the Beach

It was cocktail time. The sun, which had been in and out all day, now found a crack in the piles of gray cloud and shone brilliantly, falsely, down the length of the beach, even though thunder rolled on in the distance. The ocean was full of whitecaps. Its color went from a mean gray, far out near the horizon under those clouds, to steely blue patches closer in where the sun hit it. The tide was coming in, running about a foot higher than usual, eating up the beach, bunching the people on the beach closer and closer together. It was unreliable, irritating weather, typical of August. A strong wind had come up after the most recent shower, blowing straight in from the ocean over the waves. This wind was perfect for kites and kites had sprung up everywhere, flown mostly by grandchildren who tangled their strings or let them get caught on TV antennas and then had to have another one, immediately, from El's Hardware Store on the mainland. It was this day, August 25, nearing sunset, cocktail time in kite weather, when Mrs. Darcy received her first vision.

Below the house, Mrs. Darcy's daughters had arranged themselves together on the beach. Tall, graceful women like flowers, they leaned delicately toward one another and sipped their gin and tonics and shouted into the wind. Their family resemblance was noticeable, if not particularly striking: the narrow forehead, the high cheekbones, the dark eyes set a fraction of an inch too close together: the long straight nose, rather imperious, aristocratic, and prone to sinus. They were good-looking women.

Yet try as she might—and she *had* tried, all their years of growing up—Mrs. Darcy was unable to find anything of herself in them. Mrs. Darcy was short, blond, and overweight, with folds of flesh that dangled like dewlaps from her upper arms. She had been a pretty girl once, but she had never been a thin girl, or a fashionable girl, or a fashionable young woman. These girls took after their father; they had his long, thin hands. Inside the house, Mrs. Darcy leafed through the pile of craft books that Trixie had brought her, and looked down at her daughters on the beach. Craft books! Mrs. Darcy thought. Craft books. What does she know? Wrapping her robe about her, Mrs. Darcy moved to stand at the door.

"What was she doing when you came out?" Trixie asked. Trixie was the oldest, with three teenagers of her own. Her close-cut hair was streaked with gray, and her horn-rimmed glasses sat squarely on her nose. "What was she *doing*?" Trixie asked again, over the wind.

Maria, the middle sister, shifted her position on the quilt. "Not much, I think. Puttering around the kitchen."

"Well, there's nothing to do for supper," Trixie pointed out. "It's already done."

"I don't know," said Maria, who always deliberated, or gave the impression of deliberating, before she spoke. "I think some of the children had come in and gotten a drink or something."

"I tried to get her to help cook," Trixie said. "Remember how she used to cook?"

"You know what really drove me mad?" Ginny said suddenly. "I was telling my shrink this the other day. I mean, whenever I think of Mama, you know what I think of her doing? I think of her putting leftovers in a smaller container. Like, say, we've had a roast, right? and if it were *me*, I'd leave the roast in the pan it was in. But oh no. After dinner, she had to find a smaller pan, right? for the refrigerator. Tupperware or something. The Tupper post-roast container. Then somebody makes a sandwich maybe, and one inch of the roast is gone, so she had to find another container. Then another, then another, then another. She must have gone through about fifteen containers for every major thing she fixed. That's all I can remember of childhood." Ginny had been leaning forward intensely, sucking on a Salem in the wind. Now she stabbed the cigarette out in the sand and flung herself back flat and her long black hair fanned out on the quilt.

"You're feeling very angry about this," Maria said in her precise, well-modulated voice. Maria was a psychologist, married to another psychologist, Mark, who sat some thirty yards behind the sisters on the deck at the back of the house, observing things through his binoculars. "Your anger seems oddly out of proportion to the event," Maria remarked.

"No kidding," Ginny said.

One of Maria's children, Andrew, came up to get his shoe tied. "*Why* can't we buy any firecrackers?" he wailed, and then ran off, a blur of blue jean legs, without waiting for the answer.

"Now, then," Trixie said. The wind had died down, it was possible to talk, and Trixie liked to get right to the heart of the matter. "It does seem to me, as I wrote to both of you, that a certain amount of—er—*aimlessness* is understandable under the circumstances. But as I said before, when I went to Raleigh last month, I just couldn't believe it. I couldn't believe the way she was living. Dust on everything, and you know how she always was about dust. She was drinking Coca-Colas. Hawaiian Punch. Frozen pizza in the refrigerator—*pizza*, can you imagine?"

Maria smiled at the idea of pizza, the mere mention of it so incongruous with their childhood dinners in Raleigh. She remembered the long shining expanse of mahogany, the silver, the peacocks on the wallpaper, the crimson-flowered Oriental rug. "Pizza!" Maria said softly. "Pop would have died."

"He did," Ginny pointed out.

"Really!" Trixie said.

"I think there has to be a natural period of mourning," Maria said, not meaning to lecture. "It's absolutely essential in the cycle of regeneration."

"But it's not mourning, exactly," Trixie said. "It's just being not interested. Not interested in anything, that's the only way

I can describe it. Lack of interest in life."

"I can understand that," Ginny said.

"That could be a form of mourning," Maria said. "No two people mourn alike, of course."

"Different strokes for different folks," Ginny said. They ignored her.

"But you know how she used to keep herself so busy all the time," Trixie said. "She always had some craft project going, always. She was always doing volunteer work, playing bridge, you know how she was."

"She wore spectator heels and stockings every day," Ginny said in a passing-judgment voice.

"Yes, well, that's what I mean," Trixie went on. "And now what is she wearing? Rubber flip-flops from Woolco. She's let Lorene go, too. Lorene only comes in once a week now and does the bathrooms and the floors."

"I can't imagine that house without Lorene," Maria said. Lorene had been a central figure in their girlhood, skinny as Olive Oyl in her starched white uniform.

"Well, Lorene is just as worried about Mama as she can be," Trixie said. "As you might well imagine. I went over to see her in the projects and gave her some money and I wrote down my number for her, at home, and told her to call me up any time. Any time she goes over there to clean and anything worries her."

"That's a good idea, Trixie," Maria said.

"Well," Trixie said. Trixie saw her two daughters, tan leggy Richmond girls, far down the beach, walking toward them in the foaming line of surf. "I'll tell you what I told Mother," Trixie continued. "I said, 'Why don't you start going to church again? Why don't you join one of these retirement clubs in town? They have all sorts of them now, you wouldn't believe .it. They go to the mountains and they go to New York to see plays and everything is all arranged for them ahead of time. Why, we saw a group of them at Disney World in Florida, having a perfectly wonderful time!'"

"I can't see that," Ginny said.

"Of course you can't, you're twenty-seven years old," Trixie snapped. Sometimes she felt as though Ginny were her daughter instead of her sister.

"Still, she did show some interest in coming down here," Maria pointed out. "Surely that's something."

"Interest but no initiative," Trixie said. "I suggested it, I picked her up."

"Aren't you something?" Ginny said.

"Ginny, I realize that you're going through a difficult period of adjustment yourself, but that is no excuse, no excuse at all for childish behavior. I think we have to start thinking in terms of a nursing home, is what I think. Caswell agrees, incidentally. Of course that would involve selling the Raleigh house: it would all be quite complicated. But I do see that as a distinct possibility."

"There's Margaret, why don't you ask her what she thinks?" Maria said. "She came over to see Mama this morning."

"When?" Trixie asked sharply.

"Oh, about ten o'clock. You were at the Hammock Shop, I think."

"Gotcha!" Ginny said.

Margaret Dale Whitted, who had divorced one husband and buried two, made her slow majestic way across the sand. A white caftan billowed about her and she carried a martini balanced carefully in one hand. "Cheers!" Margaret said when she reached them, steadying herself with a hand on Trixie's shoulder. "My God, dears, it's not worth it, is it? Nature, I mean." Margaret's voice was raspy and decisive, the voice of someone who has always had money. She had known their mother for forty summers more or less, since the time when Lolly and Pop had built their house, the Lollipop, next to Margaret's Sand Castle. There had been nothing, almost nothing, on the south end of the island then. They had been pioneers.

"Margaret, how are you?" Ginny asked. Ginny had always liked Margaret.

"Oh, there's some life in the old girl yet." Margaret gave her famous wink. "I'm having some trouble, though, just between us girls, with this shoulder. I fell, you know, in March."

They didn't know.

Margaret sipped her martini and stared out to sea, breathing heavily. Ginny stood up and dusted the sand off her jeans. Margaret's gold medallion winked in the fitful sun.

"We wanted to ask you about Mama. What you think, I

mean," Trixie said. Trixie noticed how her own daughters had seated themselves just far enough away so that no one could connect them with her at all.

"Mama, Mama, it's all tangled up," wailed Christy, Maria's six-year-old daughter.

"Take it to Daddy," Maria said. "He'll have to cut some string."

Trixie and Maria stood up.

"Well," Margaret rasped. "I'll tell you what, girls. It's hell to get old." Margaret laughed and steadied herself on Trixie's elbow. The wind blew Margaret's huge white skirt about their legs, entwining them. Suddenly Ginny dashed off after a Frisbee, got it, and threw it back to Bill, Trixie's son. Maria picked up the quilt, shook it, and walked back up toward the Lollipop, the deck, her husband. Through the binoculars, he stared toward the ocean, with his red beard curled around his pipe. The screen door of the Lollipop opened and Mrs. Darcy came slowly out, blinking in the sun.

Down on the beach, Margaret raised her silver cup aloft. "Cheers, honey," she said to Trixie.

"Look, Mama, look!" Christy and Andrew started up a howl. "Look, Mama, a rainbow, a rainbow!"

Maria nodded to them, with exaggerated gestures, from the deck.

"How's it going, honey?" Mark asked without lowering the binoculars. "Getting everything worked out?"

"Oh, it's just so difficult." Maria put the quilt over the rail and sat down in a chair. "Ginny is so difficult, for one thing. I hate these whole-family things, I always have. There are so many things to work through. So many layers of meaning to sort out."

"Actually there's a great deal to be said for the nuclear family structure," said Mark, focusing his binoculars on the sight he had been viewing for some time now, Ginny's breasts moving beneath her pink T-shirt as she played Frisbee with his nephew.

But Ginny stopped playing Frisbee then and turned to stare out at the ocean and Bill did too, as all movement stopped along the beach.

"Mama, Mama, Mama!" Christy screamed.

"I'll be damned," Mark said, putting the binoculars down. "A double rainbow." Mark put an arm around his wife and they stood together on the deck, nuclear and whole, like a piece of architecture against the wind.

"All the summers we've been here, I've never seen one of those," Trixie remarked to Margaret.

A giant rainbow shimmered above the horizon, pink and blue and yellow and blue again, above the mass of clouds, and as they all watched, the clouds parted and a second rainbow— almost iridescent at first, the merest hint of color—arced across the sky beneath the first, spreading color until the rainbows seemed to fill the sky. The children on the beach, caught in motion as definitely as if they had been playing Statues, broke up with a whoop and began to cavort madly, whirling around and around in all directions. Sand and Frisbees flew. Up on the porch, behind Maria and her son-in-law, Mrs. Darcy moved hesitantly at first, in an oddly sidewise, crablike fashion, further out into the afternoon. Mrs. Darcy wore her flip-flops and a flowered housecoat. She raised her arms suddenly, stretching them up and out toward the rainbows. "Ai-yi-yi!" she wailed loudly. "Yi-yi-yi!" Mrs. Darcy stood transfixed, then fell forward onto the sandy deck in a dead faint.

The next morning dawned clear and beautiful. The joggers were at it early, pounding the road from one end of the island to the other. Fishermen lined the bridge over the sound to the mainland, dropping their lines straight down into the outgoing tide. Marsh grass waved in the wind and strange South Carolina birds flew overhead. Somebody caught a blowfish. Along the road beside the biggest houses, white uniformed maids came out to dump the bottles and trash from the night before, getting their houses ready for the day, lingering to gossip in the sun. Children ran out onto the piers that protruded far into the marsh, checking crab traps, squealing at the catch.

At the far south end of the island, Ginny prowled the beach for sand dollars, watching the shifting tide pools as the tide rushed out to sea. She remembered getting on her raft in the sound at about the middle of the island, drifting lazily through the marsh grass past all the piers, gaining speed as the tide picked up, rocketing around the south end of the island finally, right here, jetting out to sea to be knocked back at last by the waves. Ginny remembered the final, absolute panic each time in the rush to the sea, how strong the current was. In this memory she seemed to be always alone. Maria never wanted to do it, Trixie had been too old, off at school or something. But there had been friends every summer. Ginny remembered the Mitchells from Columbia, whose house had been sold five years ago. Johnny Bridgely, her first beau. The Padgetts who always had birthday parties with piñatas. Ginny sat in a tide pool and played with the hermit crabs. The water was so clear you couldn't tell it was there sometimes. She could feel the sun, already hot on her shoulders, and nothing seemed worth the effort it took.

At the Lollipop, Mrs. Darcy lay back on a daybed in the big rustic living room, surrounded by children and friends who urged her back each time she attempted to rise.

"I still think, Mama, that it would be very silly—I repeat, very silly—for you not to let us take you right up to the doctor in Myrtle Beach. Or down to Georgetown if you prefer. But you cannot just ignore an attack like this," Trixie said.

"I wonder if this might not be some sort of ploy," Maria whispered to Mark in the kitchen. "An attention-getting thing. Unconscious, of course."

"It's possible," Mark said. "Or she might have had a slight stroke."

"A stroke!" Maria said. "Do you think so?"

"No, but it's possible," Mark said. Mark got a cup of coffee and went out onto the beach. His nieces, already oiled, lay on their stomachs reading books from their summer book list. His own children were making a castle in the wet sand farther out.

"I think I'll scramble some eggs," Mrs. Darcy said, but the lady from across the street, Susie Reynolds, jumped up and began doing it for her.

There was something new about Mrs. Darcy, something ethereal, this morning. Had she had a brush with death? a simple fall? or what? Why did she refuse to see the doctor? Mrs. Darcy looked absurdly small lying there on the rather large daybed, surrounded by pillows. She still wore the flow-ered housecoat. Her small fat ankles stuck out at the bottom, the bare feet plump and blue-veined, with a splotch or two of old red nail polish on the yellowed toenails. Her arms were folded over her stomach, the hands clasped. Her hair curled white and blond in all directions; but beneath the wild hair, her wrinkled face had taken on a new, luminous quality, so that it appeared to shine.

Trixie, looking at her mother, grew more and more annoyed. Trixie remembered her mother's careful makeup, her conservative dress. Why couldn't she be reasonable, dress up a little, like the other old ladies out in the beach? Even Margaret, with her martinis and her bossiness, was better than this. *Life does go on*, Trixie thought.

Mrs. Darcy smiled suddenly, a beatific smile that traveled the room like a searchlight, directed at no one in particular.

"She seems a little better, don't you think?" Mrs. Reynolds said to Trixie from the kitchen door. Mrs. Reynolds brought in the plate of scrambled eggs and toast.

"Oh, I don't know," Trixie said. "I've been so worried, I just can't tell."

"Well, I think she looks just fine," Mrs. Reynolds said. "I'll go on back now. Call me if you need me, honey."

Mrs. Darcy sat up and began to eat. Maria, book in hand, watched her silently from the wicker armchair. Morning sun came in the glass doors, and a crossbreeze ruffled the pages of the magazines on the table. Bill came back for his flippers and mask. The volume of children rose from the beach. "How do you feel now?" Maria asked carefully.

Mrs. Darcy's watery blue eyes seemed to darken in color as she looked at her middle daughter. "When I saw the rainbow," she said in her soft Southern voice, "why, it was the strangest thing! All of a sudden I felt this, this *presence*, I can't tell you what it was like, it just filled me up until I was floating. Then I saw him."

"Saw *who*?" Maria put down the book and leaned forward in her chair. In the kitchen, Trixie dropped a coffee cup with a clatter and came to sit at the end of the daybed.

"Why, I don't know!" Mrs. Darcy said in a wondering sort of way. "I just don't know!" She began to eat heartily.

"Mother, I don't believe I quite understand," Maria said calmly. "Do you mean that you saw a stranger, some strange man, on the deck? Or did he come into the house from the front?"

"Oh no," Mrs. Darcy said airily, waving her fork. "Oh no, nothing like that. I went out on the porch, I was looking at the rainbow, I felt this overwhelming presence everywhere, oh, I just can't tell you what it was like! Then I saw him." She beamed at them. "Trixie, honey, could you bring me some salt?" she asked.

Trixie rose automatically, was stopped by the sight of her son Bill standing in the kitchen door, flippers and mask in hand, staring at his grandmother. "Go on down to the beach," Trixie said to him. "Go!" He went. Trixie got the salt, came back and gave it to her mother who sat placidly munching toast and dropping crumbs all down the front of her housecoat.

"Could you be a little clearer, Mother?" Maria asked. "I'm still not sure who this man was."

"But I don't *know*!" Mrs. Darcy said. "Thank you, dear," she said to Trixie, and sprinkled salt liberally on her eggs. "He had long hair, he wore a long white thing, sort of like Margaret's dress as a matter of fact, you know the one I mean, and he had the most beautiful blue eyes. He looked at me and stretched out his arms and said, 'Lolly.' Just like that, just my name."

"Then what?" Maria said.

"Then I went to him, of course." Mrs. Darcy finished her breakfast and stood up. "I may have a swim," she said.

"Oh, I wouldn't," Trixie said quickly.

Mrs. Darcy seemed not to hear. Training her new smile upon each of them in turn, she went into her bedroom and softly closed the door. The sisters stared at each other.

"That beats everything I've ever heard!" Trixie said. "You see why I brought up the nursing home?" Under the brown thatch of her hair, Trixie's face looked nearly triumphant, causing Maria to reflect fleetingly upon the strange accident of birth, the fact that if the woman facing her had not happened to be her sister, they would have had nothing in common at all. Nothing! Maria thought.

"I think we have to proceed very carefully here," she told Trixie. "Let me go and discuss this with Mark."

Trixie went upstairs to lie down, thinking, as she climbed the stairs, that Caswell had been right after all. They should have gone to Sea Island by themselves.

Ginny had joined the others on the beach, standing with Mark at the water's edge to watch the children swim.

"Let me put some of this on your back," Mark said, holding up a bottle of suntan oil.

"No, thanks," Ginny said. "Please. Not any more."

Mark put the top back on the bottle. "Well, what happened with Don, then?" he asked. "You want to talk about it?"

"No," Ginny said. "I don't."

"Mark, Mark!" Maria came running toward them. She arrived; she told them everything. Ginny began to laugh.

Bill came dripping up out of the water, followed by the girls. "There's a real strong undertow," he yelled to everybody. When they didn't answer he came closer, pushing the face mask up. "Grandma's going batty, isn't she?" he said to his uncle and aunts.

"Is that true?" the girls demanded. "Is she going to go in a nut house?"

"Of course not," Ginny said.

"What's a nut house?" Christy asked.

Ginny was laughing and laughing.

"This will take some thought," Mark said, pulling at his beard.

Slowly and daintily, Mrs. Darcy made her way past the whole group of them and stood at the edge of the ocean to adjust her red rubber bathing cap. Her skin was so white that she looked startling among the sun-browned children in the surf. She turned once, waved, before she walked straight out into the waves until they were hip-high. Then she raised her hands and dove.

"You know I don't believe I've ever seen your mother swim before," Mark said to Maria.

Maria stood open-mouthed. "She doesn't," she finally said. In years past, her mother's beach routine had never varied: up around nine, a walk perhaps, some shopping, drinks with friends, but never—never—had she actually gone for a swim. Maria burst into tears. "She needs help," Maria said.

"Oh, come on," Ginny said. "We all do. Look, I'll drive

all the kids up to the trampoline for a while, OK?"

Before them, just beyond the breakers, Mrs. Darcy's red bathing cap bobbed like a cork in the rise and fall of the waves.

Three days passed, all of them sunny and blue, calm and idyllic. Caswell arrived. The Lollipop settled into the old routine of summers past. Plans were made and carried out, menus were planned, groceries were bought and cooked. Caswell and Mark chartered a boat out of Murrell's Inlet and took Bill fishing. Maria was always amazed at how well Caswell and Mark got along; she couldn't imagine what they had to say to each other. Trixie's girls found nice boys from Charleston to date. Old friends came and went. Margaret took Mrs. Darcy to lunch at Litchfield Plantation. Pop was mentioned often, casually and affectionately, and Mrs. Darcy seemed not to mind. She did not mention the "presence" or the blue-eyed stranger again. She continued to pad about the house in her flip-flops and housecoat, but she showed some interest in the cooking and she played checkers with Christy and Andrew.

By Thursday morning, Trixie had begun to relax. She thought it was time to interest her mother in Shrink-Art. Trixie had brought all the materials with her, and now she unpacked them and brought them into the kitchen and spread them out. The others had gone crabbing up at Huntington Beach State Park. "Now Mother," Trixie said, "let's do a little bit of this. It's really fun, really easy, and you'll just be amazed at what you can make."

"Maybe a little later, dear," Mrs. Darcy said. Mrs. Darcy sat in the wicker armchair, looking out at the beach.

"No," Trixie said firmly. "Now is the time. They'll be back before long, then we'll have to make sandwiches. Now look, Mother, all you do is trace designs onto this clear plastic, using these permanent markers. Or you can make your own designs, of course. Then you cut them out and bake them for three minutes and—"

"*Bake* them?" Mrs. Darcy echoed faintly.

"Sure!" Trixie said. "Then they turn into something exactly like stained glass. They're really lovely. You can make jewelry, Christmas ornaments, whatever. They make lovely Christmas ornaments."

"But how would you hang them up?" Mrs. Darcy came to stand beside her daughter at the table.

"Oh, you punch a little hole before you put them in the oven," she said. "I've got the hole-puncher right here."

Trixie spread out the plastic sheets, the designs, the permanent pens. She turned the oven on to three hundred degrees. "OK," she said. "All set. Which one do you want to try?"

"Maybe this," Mrs. Darcy said. She placed a sheet of the clear plastic over a design involving a bunch of tulips stuck into a wooden shoe. Trixie was mildly surprised by the choice, more surprised by her mother's easy acquiescence. Everything seemed so much better since the weather had cleared. Perhaps things were not so complicated, so serious as they had thought. Still, it was reassuring that Mark and Maria had arranged treatment for Mother, back in Raleigh. A most competent doctor by all accounts, highly recommended. Trixie felt sure that Mother would agree to see him. The teakettle began to whistle. Trixie got up to make the iced tea. This pitcher, old heavy brown pottery, had been at the beach house ever since she could remember. Out of the corner of her eye, Trixie watched Mother biting her tongue a bit and gripping her marker tightly, like a small, pudgy, dutiful child. Trixie added lemon and sugar to the tea.

"There now," Mrs. Darcy said, sitting back in the chair, her round wrinkled face rather flushed. She looked at Trixie hopefully. "Now what?"

"Now you cut it out," Trixie said, "and punch a hole, and we put it in the oven for three minutes."

Mrs. Darcy cut the design out carefully, using some old round-tipped scissors that Trixie had found way back in a kitchen drawer. Trixie took the design from her, somewhat distressed to find that Mother had colored the tulips blue. Still, it would not do to appear disparaging. "This is so pretty, Mother," Trixie said. "Now you can watch it shrink if you want to." Mrs. Darcy turned her chair, so that she could peer through the oven's glass door.

The kitchen door burst open at that moment and there they were suddenly, all of the rest of them, with two coolers full of scrambling crabs and the children all talking at once.

"Just leave those on the porch," Trixie directed. "Go on,

take them right back out this instant. Right now. Go on. Bill, what do you mean, tracking in here this way? Go take off those shoes on the porch."

"Bill fell in, Bill fell in!" Andrew danced up and down, still holding his piece of twine with the rock and the chicken neck tied to the end.

"You're so excited, darling," Maria said.

"Well, I'm starving." Still wearing her black bikini, Ginny came barefooted into the kitchen, so that she was the closest one to her mother, the only one who actually saw Mrs. Darcy's face as she watched her tulips shrink, and shrink, and shrink before her eyes. Ginny stopped, caught in the oddest sensation: it might have been her face before her, it might have been her own voice that began to scream.

A fine drizzle fell all day Sunday, jeweling the surface of things. They left for hours, it seemed, and their leavetaking took up most of the day. Lolly knew that they had been up far into the night, deciding what to do about her. She realized that she had created a problem by her refusal to leave. But she did not *want* to leave yet, and she had never created a problem before—not ever, for anyone. So. She remained stubborn and went to bed early, leaving them to deal with her as best they could.

As they told themselves over and over, the others had to go. There was no question. Caswell had to fly straight up to Washington for a conference. The children's schools were beginning again, and Trixie had to buy school clothes for the girls. Maria and Mark had faculty meetings, workshops, classes. It was hard to believe that Christy would be in the first grade.

"Look," Ginny had surprised them all by saying. "Look, I'll stick around for a week or so. OK? You all go on. I'll bring her back to Raleigh before long." It was so unlike Ginny to be responsible that Maria had stared at her with considerable interest.

"I'd like to know why you're doing this," Maria said.

"Why not?" Ginny had answered.

And they had left, Trixie and Caswell and their large children in the long sleek car, Maria and Mark in their van. Christy and Andrew waved madly from the rear window as long as they stayed in sight. Lolly stood on the rainswept back porch, looking across the road to see the rising mist over the marsh. She traced designs in the drops of water that clung to the sides of the water heater. Each little drop seemed singular and profound, seemed to hold some iridescence of its own, or perhaps it was just the reflection from passing cars.

"Mama," Ginny said for the third time. Ginny stood in the kitchen door wearing white slacks, a windbreaker. She looked Lolly in the eye. "Listen, Mama, I'm driving up to Long Beach to have dinner with a friend, OK? The number is by the telephone. I might be back tonight, or I might be back tomorrow. There's a pizza in the freezer. OK?"

"OK." Lolly smiled at Ginny and watched her leave too, running lightly down the steps, slamming into her little car.

Lolly went back in the house. The silence wrapped her up like soft cotton. She got a Coke from the refrigerator, poured it, and sucked off the foam. She smiled to herself, turned on some lights. After a while she went to the telephone and called Margaret and in a little while Margaret came, bringing the friend she'd told Lolly about.

This friend was a wealthy widow of their own age, from Norfolk. "The doctor can't seem to find any explanation for it," she said. "Some sort of damaged nerve. It's just this intense pain, right here." She lifted her forearm so that the heavy bracelets jangled like wind chimes. "Sometimes the pain is so intense I just can't seem to go out at all. I can't even get out of bed."

"I know," said Lolly. Her pale eyes darkened and focused; she smiled. "Lie down," Lolly said, indicating the daybed, and she took the stringy manicured hand of Margaret's friend in her own soft white ringless fingers.

"That's right, dear," Margaret rasped from the wicker armchair. "Don't be nervous, dear. This is exactly the way she fixed my shoulder. I was lying just like that on my own chaise longue. The green one. Remarkable. Now just do exactly what Lolly says. Close your eyes, dear. Relax. That's right. Relax."

Later, healed and radiant, Margaret's friend wanted to pay Lolly, to make some contribution at least to the charity of her choice. Lolly declined, and they all had a glass of sherry.

"Really, how do you do it?" Margaret's friend asked. "Really, if you only knew how much money I've spent on doctors. Why, I even tried a chiropractor at Virginia Beach."

"It's nothing," Lolly said.

"Listen to that!" Margaret hooted. "Ha!" Margaret blew out a great puff of smoke that hung blue in the comfortable glow of the lamps.

"It's not me at all," Lolly told them. "I'm just an agent, you might say. An intermediary."

"Do you do much work with arthritis?" Margaret's friend asked. "I have a friend who's in the most terrible pain."

"I could give it a try," Lolly said.

When they had gone, she heated up the pizza and drank a glass of milk, leaving all her dishes in the sink. She took a bath. She put on a faded terry housecoat. Opening the doors to the ocean, Lolly went out on the deck. Out here everything was cold and clean-smelling and a sharpness bit through the air, signaling summer's end. There were few lights along the beach; most of the summer people and renters had gone. Beyond Lolly, out in the darkness, waves crashed onto the sand. She could taste their salt on her lips. Lolly was not even cold. She seated herself in a damp deck chair, and leaned back. "Now," she said into the night.

Not Pictured

I'm certain those scrapbooks still exist, put away somewhere in my mother's house as meticulously as everything else she has saved over all these years. It's possible, of course, that they are still in the cabinet in the den. But I prefer to imagine each one wrapped in plastic, arranged chronologically in a box that has been taped shut. I imagine this box in the attic or in the basement, more likely, next to other boxes filled with mildewed shoes; with old wrapping paper painstakingly salvaged from our Christmas gifts each year; with all the wrinkled and yellowing papers Sarah and I ever brought home from elementary school, junior high, or high school; with peanut butter jars and jelly jars and fruit jars. I see these boxes beside piles of old magazines and newspapers stacked so high they reach the ceiling along all the dark, damp walls. I shudder. But I'd like to see those scrapbooks again, actually. Perhaps on our next visit I'll search them out, show them to my wife, Katherine, and to our daughters. I am curious to assess the degree of pain those old photographs can produce in me now—or to test the degree of elation. For I am no longer that child: the earlier tormented Michael who pored over the scrapbooks almost daily, looking again and again at the flat gray images to assure himself he was real.

The scrapbooks are bound in black leather, with the date embossed at the center of each in grandiose gold script and "Mr. and Mrs. Michael D. Brooks and Family" similarly engraved at the bottom. As I remember it, the scrapbooks begin in 1944, the year of my parents' marriage, and continue in a formidable black and gold parade right up through 1962, when everything—thank God—fell apart. There is a marked deterioration, as I recall, in the quality of relentless togetherness depicted in those snapshots dating from 1955 on: this was the year they put Lily away, the year when everything changed. And even though it has been nearly twenty years since I saw them, some of those early photographs remain indelibly etched in my mind's eye or—to be more accurate—in my heart.

Nineteen forty-four. Here they are on their wedding day, Mr. and Mrs. Michael D. Brooks, both of them looking somewhat flustered as they bend to slice the precarious three-tiered cake. Beneath the veil, my mother's hair is drawn back so severely that her eyes are slanted in an almost Oriental effect as she stares solemnly into the years of responsible married life ahead. My father grins like the country boy he used to be, one eyebrow arched skeptically, his Adam's apple protruding. They smile for the camera. Actually they are flabbergasted, both of them. Circumstances have produced this event; circumstances have caught them up and whirled them around and set them down plunk at the altar.

Mike Brooks is twenty-nine, a man's man, a poor boy who has "pulled himself up by his bootstraps"—as he would tell us, years later—to a position of a certain prominence in this town. After working fourteen hours a day for the last ten years, he sat down for a breather and saw that the world had changed. There was only one clear course for a man's man in those troubled times, as he saw it: he enlisted; he took a wife. Elizabeth Kinney, my mother, was as shocked as anybody in town by his choice. Pegged as an old maid, she had been teaching English at the high school for the past six or seven years, ever since her graduation from the Women's College. She had recently been appointed assistant principal. But she recognized her duty. She said yes, resigned her teaching position to become a "full-time homemaker"—this is how she put it—assumed the reins of leadership in the Junior Woman's Club, sewed curtains and cultivated roses although she enjoyed neither activity, and produced—nine months later—my sister, Sarah.

Sarah appears momentously in the 1945 album; her appearances increase throughout the ensuing years. Frequently Sarah holds an object she has just won: a ribbon, a cup, a certificate. My mother, too, holds objects—a rose, an arrangement of roses, a plaque from the Hospital League for Outstanding Service in 1951, a silver bowl. I remember one photograph in which she wears white gloves and spectator shoes and holds a pointed shovel with which she will plant a peach tree in a planter in front of the First National Bank. At the upper right hand corner of this photograph can be glimpsed the gaslight on the street corner, one of a whole downtown-full of gaslights that Mother was instrumental in installing as part of a massive restoration effort. Eventually, a park would be named in her honor. It would have a fountain.

But I have gotten ahead of myself. In 1952, my father stands in front of his store. MIKE BROOKS, the sign says. MERCHANDISE. Actually this is the understatement of that or any other year. My father sells hardware of all kinds, electrical appliances, clothes, shoes, kitchen items, dry goods, toys—you name it. Since he began his business in the back of a pickup truck when he was sixteen, he has moved it innumerable times. Since he bought this brick building, he has expanded it twice. Eighteen people work for him now. My father wears a light-colored suit, a striped tie, a straw hat, white shoes, and holds a cigar at a rakish angle to his lips. He is big and fleshy and enormously successful; he goes on hunting trips "with the boys" and returns home grinning, his canvas sack full of doves.

Group snapshots abound. Mother and Father and little Sarah, all dressed up, at a cousin's wedding. Mother and Father and little Sarah wearing rubber-soled shoes, white socks, and bermuda shorts, posed happily with the "Little Old Lady Who Lived in a Shoe" at Rock City, Tennessee. Mother and Father looking happily on—beaming, I suppose, is the word—as little Sarah is awarded a gold necklace with a picture of Jesus on it for some exemplary act at Sunday School.

But where is Michael? Ah, yes. He appears in 1947 as a stern skinny baby in an embroidered christening gown. In 1952 he can be found, by careful scrutiny, among his first-grade peers, having been put on the first row because he's so short, looking at something beyond the picture. He's always doing this: staring away from the group, dreaming. He makes things up in his head. They are all so worried about him. It has been suggested that perhaps he "takes after" Lily, my mother's younger sister, who is never mentioned aloud. In all these childhood pictures, Michael's face is thin and drawn; his eyes are huge.

But now let's forget the albums and examine the times not pictured.

I am in my bed, alone, I am so scared to get up in the terrible blackness of night that finally I wet the bed, again and again, although my father spanks me with a hairbrush every morning and it makes so much more work for Selena, the maid. At day camp I sneak away from the others and lie on a warm flat rock by the river, completely happy, making up names for all the faces I see in the high white clouds. In second grade I can be found up in a tree with Bevan Malone, my best friend. But then I am forbidden to play with him any more because all we do is draw pictures and refuse to join the Midget League baseball team coached by my father. Bevan ("Helluva name for a boy!" my father snorts) is labeled a "bad influence" and I am put into a little red uniform anyway and forced to sit on the bench in hopes I'll develop an interest. I do not. I hate every minute of it.

During all this time I see myself as slight and insubstantial, a shadow boy, while my parents and my sister grow rounder and taller, dauntingly full-dimensional, taking up all the space in our house. No wonder I stare at my picture in the albums in the den. No wonder my fantasies grow more and more complex. I love my parents, but I know I have let them down. I am not like I should be; I am not like them. Sarah is not perfect, either, but I am the only person around who appears to realize it. Secretly, I hate her. I hate my whole life, and I can't imagine how any of this would have turned out if Aunt Lily had never come, if we had not made that trip through the mountains to put her away.

There is, as I recall, a series of snapshots detailing this trip in the album for 1955—I had just turned nine; Sarah was twelve. The photo I remember most clearly was taken by the porter (Father paid him a quarter and showed him how to do it) and shows us all standing on the steps of the Green Park Hotel squinting into the dying sun. Trailing geraniums fill the planters on either side of the step, spilling over; the porch columns are suitably Southern. There were striped awnings, too, as I recall, although these are not in the picture. Lily is in the picture, as beautiful as a fashion model, with one hand on my shoulder.

"*Must* we do this, Elizabeth?" she was complaining, but then it was over and we all went into the hotel (a lobby like a cave, with potted palms and overhead fans and old men playing checkers in the gloom) with the porter pushing our bags in front of us on the cart, and when we got to our room, the first thing I did was to check very carefully for anything white. My chief fantasy that year was both horrific and useful; it had enabled me, at last, to quit wetting the bed. Nineteen fifty-five was the year I invented the Black Barbarians, a tribe of night spirits clothed in long black robes and hoods (they had no faces) who would keep me from all harm as long as I did their bidding. And their bidding was simple: all I had to do was make sure I slept in a room containing at least three white things, in case I had to get up in the night. White counteracted their power; it kept them in thrall (although I was not completely certain what *thrall* meant). If I built up a pretty good record with the Black Barbarians—which, needless to say, I *had*—they would come to do my bidding if any peril should strike. They would show their faces. The Black Barbarians were terrible and fearsome and you didn't call them unless you were at your Wit's End, a phrase I had heard Mother use over and over with reference most often to me, but lately to Lily as well.

This room was fine: the wallpaper was white, sprigged with violets, the woodwork was white, the chairs were green-and-white striped, and even the bathroom fixtures were white. It was OK. Our family had three rooms on the ground floor and ours was the last in the row: one for Mother and Father, one for Aunt Lily, one for Sarah and me.

Sarah went over to the mirror and brushed her hair, which looked like the wood shavings the carpenters had left when they added the new wing onto our house that spring. Sarah was snotty, I thought—big and fat and ugly.

She turned from the mirror and pushed her face into mine. "Aunt Lily is crazy," she said. "We're going tomorrow to put her away."

I knew that. I looked out the French doors at the green trees.

Sarah came over to me. "How do you like that?" she said. "They'll shut her up behind bars."

Mother came into our room still wearing her suit and her high-heeled shoes. She dressed up for a trip the way she did to go to the Hospital Board or the Altar Guild.

"What's he crying about now?" she asked Sarah.

"Beats me." Sarah sounded happy. "You know how he is." Sarah went into the bathroom.

"He's still weak, aren't you, darling?" Mother came and got me and I made myself stiff all over but it didn't help and she took me and made me lie down on the bed. Then she leaned over me and kissed me and her powder smelled so strong I couldn't breathe. I had had pneumonia that year and I had missed so much school that Mother had kept me home for the rest of the year to get well. "Now you just lie still," she said. "There's my good little boy." I couldn't breathe at all but when she went away it was better. Mother turned off the air conditioner and opened the long French doors to the outside. She rearranged everything—the lamp, the chairs, the table, the covers on my bed. I pretended to be asleep. Then Mother dusted everything in the room with a Kleenex and turned off the light and left.

Sarah came out of the bathroom. "Crazy people are a danger to society," she said. "You have to shut them up."

Sarah went out the way Mother had gone. I opened my eyes. Sarah had left the door open behind her so that light from the adjoining room spilled across the floor, and after a while Aunt Lily came in on the path of light.

Aunt Lily sat on the edge of the bed in her pink pants and white blouse. She lit a cigarette and let me blow out the match.

"Do you feel bad or something?" she asked.

"I feel fine," I told her.

Aunt Lily was very beautiful, with her yellow hair falling down over her shirt. She had been married and divorced and Mother said she had done countless other things too awful to mention, so I didn't know what they were. Sarah and I had never met Aunt Lily until she came back to our town that year and stayed with us, and then in the hospital, and then back at our house for a while. I had loved it when she was there. We used to sit out on the porch playing games—Monopoly, Chinese checkers, gin rummy, Scrabble—and other games more elaborate, which we made up with the cards as we went along. Now Aunt Lily made blue smoke, which hung in clouds over my bed.

"Have you got enough white in here?" she asked. I told secrets to Aunt Lily that I had never told anyone else.

"I've got plenty," I said.

"Tell me some more about your ghosts." Her voice was low and lately it shook when she spoke.

"They're not ghosts," I corrected her. "They are Black Barbarians and they speak a separate language all their own. I mean they use the same words, but all of them have different meanings."

"How do they say hello?" Aunt Lily asked. She bent over my bed through the smoke.

"Puma."

"Wow! How do they say goodbye?"

"Chartreuse."

Aunt Lily was laughing and laughing. "Wherever did you get those words?"

"I got them from the Black Barbarians, that's where," I said. "I have to know their language so I can talk to them. You have to say special things to them at night—they keep you really busy."

"I bet they do," Aunt Lily said.

I didn't get a chance to tell her the other thing, which was that you *do not* mess around with the Black Barbarians. They're too powerful. You don't ask for anything unless you are at your Wit's End. They are serious, deadly—Aunt Lily should not have laughed.

"What's the word for goodbye again?" She leaned over the bed and kissed me and I held on around her soft shirt.

"Chartreuse," I said, and then she started laughing again and holding me but she couldn't stop laughing. She laughed and laughed and after a while Mother came back in and said, "Oh honestly, Lily!" and took her back in her room.

The long door was gray with light, the time when night has really come but if you go outside it will still be light even though it looks dark from inside. Father came and filled up the whole doorway. "Anybody for a little dip in the pool?" he asked in his loud voice.

"Michael is resting," Mother said from the other room. "And you know perfectly well he shouldn't go swimming anyway, Mike, he's still recuperating. And I have a strong suspicion he's developing asthma, too. In fact I've written a note to myself to call Dr. Lacock about it as soon as we get back home."

"Nonsense," Father said. "Nothing like a little dip in the pool."

Father went to the Health Club and worked out three times a week and in the mornings he ran around and around our block.

"Mike, I know what I'm talking about!" Mother said. "Didn't I nurse Mama those last five years without any help from anyone? Didn't I nurse Michael all winter long? Didn't I? I think I know whereof I speak."

"You're a real Florence Nightingale, Elizabeth," Aunt Lily said from behind the wall of her room.

I knew who Florence Nightingale was.

"Up and at 'em, son," said Father.

I got up and we went to the pool, which was bright blue and all lit up and heated like a bath. Father swam thirty laps and tried to make me swim laps too, but I wouldn't. I went under the water and looked at everything with my eyes wide open. It was nice under there and I didn't want to come up. Then I stood up in the shallow end and looked down at my legs all short and wavy underneath the water in the pool. Father dried himself off hard with the towel and snapped it three times in the air. He said it was time to go in.

Mother said, "If that child has a relapse I will know the cause, Mike!" when we got back. Aunt Lily wasn't anywhere around. Mother put Mentholatum on my chest.

"Please be quiet, Michael," Sarah said when I went in our room. She was sitting in bed with her glasses on reading the Bible, not the one that came with the room but her own white one with her name on it in gold, the one she had brought from home. Sarah was the president of the Methodist Youth Fellowship.

I got ready and got in my bed and thought the song for the Black Barbarians. Sarah was still reading with the light on. I didn't think I could go to sleep but then I started thinking I was underwater, swimming down and down into a pool with no bottom at all. Everything down there was silver and blue and I could breathe just fine even though I was underwater, and if anybody took a picture of me now, I wouldn't even show up.

Later I awoke and the room was solid black and still, and cool because we were up in the mountains. I thought I heard people talking. After I went to the bathroom, I stood in the door and listened, but all I heard was Sarah's breathing. Then I heard them again, and this time I knew who one of them was. *Aunt Lily.* I went over to the French doors and sat on the floor in the dark.

"Hold me, Mike. Just for a little while." Aunt Lily's voice was crying.

"We'd better go in," Father said.

"Like that."

"Don't, Lily." Father's voice was so different.

"Do you want me to tell you what it's like?"

"No." Now Father's voice was louder.

"You don't want to know, do you, Mike?"

"That's right. I don't want to know."

I could feel the Black Barbarians at my back but I stayed put.

"Look, Lily," Father said. "You don't have to go to Green Mountain tomorrow. Not if you don't want to. There are other places. Elizabeth has checked into all this."

"Elizabeth!" Aunt Lily said. Her voice went up and down.

"A man in my position—" Father said.

Aunt Lily said a bad word.

Then they were quiet and after a while Aunt Lily said, "I want to go, Mike. I'm tired of fighting and fighting. I don't want to fight anymore. I can't. I'm too tired. I want to let it all go."

"You realize that this will be hard on me too, of course, but I feel you've come to the right decision."

"Oh, you'll make it, Mike." Aunt Lily laughed a high laugh like glass breaking.

I scooted across the floor closer to the long door and looked around the curtain and I could see them sitting like that on the bench and Father kissing her hard on the mouth. They kissed each other for a long time and then Father put his face in his hands and cried. Father! I couldn't believe it. I had never in my whole life seen him cry.

I went back to bed and said the words I had never said before, the words for the Black Barbarians. I said the words over and over. I was at my Wit's End. I said them until I fell asleep and then suddenly it was morning and Father, dressed already, opened our door and said, "Up and at 'em, Tiger!" His face was red and shaved and his hair looked wet like it did every morning, but I knew: I knew he had cried in the dark.

I took a shower and said the words for the Black Barbarians. When I was ready, I knocked on my parents' door and Mother came and felt my head and cried, "Feverish and hollow-eyed! Look what you've done now, Mike!" She went back in their room and I could hear her saying, "I don't know how much more I can take. First Mama, poor thing, and then Lily, and now poor little Michael as white as a sheet." I closed the door and walked down the hall and went back in our room.

Sarah yelled, "Don't you *dare* look at me!" and ran into the bathroom and closed that door, too. Who wanted to look at old Sarah, anyway? I went to the French doors and looked out. It was raining. I said the words.

On the way to the dining room for breakfast, Father asked the lady at the desk to take our picture with the huge stuffed bear beside the elevators. This bear seemed to grin, stretching out his paws like he expected a hug. He was not scary at all, even though the sign said his name was "Ol' Devil." He smelled like mothballs. We stood in a group beside Ol' Devil but the lady didn't know how to work the flash attachment, so Father had to step out and show her. Then he came back to his spot, put one arm around Mother and the other arm around Lily. Mother and Father and Sarah are smiling, as I remember the picture; and to the side, behind me, so is that bear.

While we stood waiting for the lady to give us a table at

breakfast, I looked hard at Aunt Lily. She wore a green dress and a green scarf in her hair, and her eyes were as flat and as blue as the TVA lakes we had passed on our trip. She turned to the rest of us, all of a sudden, and said in a very loud voice, "You know what I call this place? I call it the Time's Up Hotel." She laughed that laugh.

"Please try not to embarrass us here, Lily. We'd like to have a civilized meal," Mother said.

I wasn't hungry and Sarah ended up eating all the food Mother had made me order. Father ate pancakes. Mother had two poached eggs. Aunt Lily smoked cigarettes and sometimes she held my hand.

All the way there in the car, I thought the words for the Black Barbarians. The rain came down on our car in waves and it was like driving into the water. The words went along with the windshield wipers, over and over again. I knew it was going to happen. We drove through the tall white gates with the iron things standing straight up in the rain. I knew it would happen. I thought the words. Then we were in front of the main building and Mother said, "Let us know if you need anything," and Father got out of the car and put up the umbrella and stood there.

"Goodbye, Michael," Aunt Lily said. She leaned across Sarah and kissed me but her eyes were flat. She had already gone away from her eyes. I thought the words as hard as I could but it didn't happen. They didn't come. What happened instead was that my father's strong red face crumpled up like wastepaper and although he didn't cry again, he looked a lot like he might. "Oh hell," he said. He dropped Aunt Lily's canvas suitcase in the mud and then he picked it up and put his arm around her waist. "Well, come on, honey," he said, and clinging tightly together, they went inside the building in the rain.

Mother sat up straight in the front seat all by herself and clutched her monogrammed purse so hard that her fingers went white. "For heaven's sake!" she said out loud, to nobody in particular. Rain drummed on the top of the car. Sarah worked a crossword puzzle on her lap and picked food out of her braces now and then. Father came back out, started the car with a jolt, and exceeded the speed limit all the way to Gatlinburg, where we were to spend the weekend.

We stayed that night in a modern motel with nothing white in our room, but I didn't even care. I didn't care about anything in Gatlinburg. I ripped a page out of Sarah's Bible accidentally-on-purpose; talked back to Mother; refused to swim with my father. I spent all my saved-up allowance on carnival rides, mystifying my entire family. "Michael is so unlike himself," Mother said several times. I didn't care.

We spent two days in Gatlinburg and then we went home. That was the end of our trip and—in a curious way—that was the end of the family we had tried for so long to be. Father and Mother kept up elaborate pretenses for several more years, but finally they separated and in 1962 the divorce was final. Putting Lily away proved to have the salutary effect of setting me down firmly, if somewhat roughly, in the real world. For my father, putting Lily away seemed to release many things that he had forced down inside when he determined to pull himself up by his bootstraps, years before. Eventually he sold his business, bought a small farm, and lives there today in a dowdy and comfortable way with his plain, plump wife. Her name is Susie, and she's a giggler. My mother completed a business training program and let up on us after she assumed the first of several increasingly important positions in hospital administration. She relaxes and takes her shoes off now when she comes home; we enjoy our visits together. And Lily? Lily didn't stay put away forever, of course, any more than the rest of us stayed put in order in those albums. She recovered; she remarried; she had kids. She lives in Atlanta now, not far from Sarah and her husband. We all stay in touch.

The real reason I've never looked for those albums on our visits to my mother, I suppose, is that the photograph I'd really like to see was never taken. It was in Gatlinburg, the day we left; my father insisted on accompanying me to the carnival. I didn't want him to come—why wasn't he off playing golf as usual? I was furious, wouldn't look at him. I walked along kicking a rock. "Which one?" he asked when we reached the midway; and I, vindictively, chose the Silver Bullet, the only ride I had never dared to try. I got in and clamped myself into the seat. My father followed, his bulk causing our Silver Bullet to buckle and rock. *Adulterer!* I thought. *Crybaby!* Then I grinned. As the great wheel began to grind and our bullet began its upward trajectory, our hands met and we rushed off through the screaming air into that moment of upside down I cherished, when all the world below turned strange and different and new, when I jangled with magic and the midway lights blurred golden in my eyes like Lily's hair; "Whoopee!" I yelled, holding on to his hand for dear life.

Saint Paul

It all started so far back—way before my daddy died, or Danny, and before I got myself in trouble as they say—when I was still playing jacks and paper dolls and skipping rocks in that still place at the bend of Dawson's Creek, back when I was a little girl in our house, which looked just exactly like all the others in the bottom where we lived, and the Honeycutts lived on the hill. Mr. Honeycutt owned the mine, Consolidated Coal Inc., where my daddy and the other men worked, and he owned our house too because we rented it from the company, only I didn't know that then. All I knew was that the Honeycutts' house was different from all of ours, big and white and crazy-looking, with towers that poked up all over the place, and porches that stuck right out where you never thought a porch ought to be, and woodwork all over it like lace on a wedding dress. It sat a good ways back from the road, with a stone wall around the yard, and in summertime these red rambler roses grew all over the wall. The Honeycutts had lots of grass, too, and a man they hired to come and cut it, and big old shade trees, one of which had a rope swing hanging down from it that I liked to swing on better than anything. The Honeycutts used to let me swing whenever I wanted to, whether Marlene was out in the yard or not. But usually she was, and so we swang on that swing, or played in a lean-to we made out back in the woods behind the garden, or else we played with her dolls—and Marlene had dolls from all over the world, like a little doll with slanty eyes from China and a doll from Holland with wooden shoes. I can't even remember what all we did. Now this is Marlene Honeycutt, who was exactly four days apart from me in age, and we were best friends. We stuck our fingers with needles and mixed our blood to prove it.

Marlene's mother, Mrs. Honeycutt, wore high-heel shoes every day of the week. But she let Marlene and Paul play with the rest of us, from the time we were all big enough to cross the road—if you could ever get Paul to play, that is. Mostly we never could. Marlene had long curly yellow hair and freckles and a smile that showed all of her teeth. Paul had yellow hair too, but his was light-colored and thin and flyaway, like a dandelion going to seed, and it seemed like he never smiled. He wasn't mean or anything, just serious—Paul was serious all the time. He stared hard at everything with these big old blue eyes of his that always looked soft, somehow, the way cow eyes do.

Buddy Lipscomb and Merle Rainey and the other boys in the bottom used to tease him and be real mean to him, like one time they tied him up to a tree and left him there all afternoon, and another time I remember Buddy acted like Paul had said something bad about him, and he knocked him down on the mine road and Paul's head bled like crazy when it hit a rock. Only Paul never said a word about it to anybody, never told on Buddy whose daddy would have whipped him good if he knew, and of course Paul never had said anything to Buddy Lipscomb in the first place, anyway. So after a while all the boys just left him alone, since he wouldn't fight back, and Paul stayed pretty much to himself as I recall. He used to lay up there in their yard on a hammock all summer long, reading big old books. Marlene and I went back and forth, all around the yard, playing—she had a poodle puppy then—but we didn't pay Paul any more mind than we would have if he had been a book himself. One time Mr. Honeycutt bought him the fanciest bike you ever saw, but Paul didn't ride it at all and it just sat up there in the shed. I would have died to have a bike like that but I never did ask to ride, not one time. I wouldn't have asked for the world.

I stayed clear of Paul, like all the rest of the kids from the bottom. Paul was a genius, Marlene said. I didn't know about that, but we were all glad when the Honeycutts sent him off to school because he never did anything in the schoolroom anyway but make a hundred and draw plans of buildings and airplanes and machines, mumbling numbers to himself. At lunchtime he used to eat all alone on the back steps or have a big discussion with Mr. Boling, a fat little man from Wheeling, which was the closest big town, who came three days a week to teach advanced math and science. Mr. Boling smelled funny and blinked his eyes a lot. Paul talked to Mr. Boling in a real high voice, and waved his hands in the air. Lord! I was glad when Paul was gone.

And what I want you to understand here is that I never thought about Paul for one minute after he left. I was too busy at home, which I have not even said one word about so far. Of course our house was not like the Honeycutts'—they had tall dark rooms and thick rugs, and it smelled like furniture polish all the time. We had five rooms—mine and Danny's, Mama and Daddy's, the kitchen and the front room and the bathroom, if that counts—and it smelled like whatever we were having for supper that night. We had a nice green living room suite in the front room with see-through plastic on it so it would last, and linoleum on the floors, and yellow flowers on the wallpaper in the room where I stayed with Danny. At least the flowers used to be yellow.

I don't remember my daddy much before he got hurt, except that he was a big man with a loud laugh and a real pretty singing voice. The first Christmas after the accident, I recall that Mrs. Honeycutt sent us a whole baked ham, but my mama wouldn't touch a bite! and Daddy just laid in a recliner chair back in the kitchen, near the stove, from then until the time he died. It seemed to me like he shrank up before he died.

Now my mama, who was a worrier from the word go anyway, really started in worrying then, even though the company said we could stay in the house as long as we wanted, and we had Daddy's insurance money too from the union. But Mama used to sit in the front room shriveling up Kleenex and saying "Lord! Lord!" in that way she had. This left me to do the cooking and the washing and the taking care of Danny, which I did. I didn't mind that either—he was always the sweetest child. Danny had brown eyes like Daddy's, and a happy disposition as they say. I took him everyplace with me. I was glad to have him along.

I remember one time we all took him swimming, the summer after Daddy died. Marlene went, and my first cousins Ruthie and Loretta, and Buddy and Merle and a whole bunch of us. We used to go in that hole at the bend of Dawson's Creek, where the water came off the rocks in a big rush and then it got real deep and you could swing out on a rope right over the deepest part. I can still see Danny swinging through the air on that long rope, how he went swooping out through the sun and then the shade in his little red bathing suit, and came up squealing to beat the band. He could swim real good for his age. Marlene and I laid out on a big flat rock and listened to her radio and watched him. We listened to Elvis Presley, who was just catching on then. I had a two-piece bathing suit and I was already getting breasts, ahead of Marlene who was still flat as a pancake, and I was feeling so good laying there in the sun that when Paul showed up all of a sudden on the bank—he was home from school for the summer—I sat up and hollered at him. "Hey, Paul," I said—I think I waved—"come on and go swimming with us." But Paul said he had some things to do. Only he didn't leave for a while. He stood right there on the bank and watched us for a long time before he left. Danny was swinging out on the rope and Merle kept splashing water on Marlene and me.

I guess I remember this whole day so good because of what happened three years later, when Danny drowned. Not in Dawson's Creek but out on the lake where he had gone fishing with some bigger boys from Ajax. This was when Danny was eleven and I was turning sixteen. I cried my eyes out, of course—it was like Danny had been *my* baby, in a way, and as I said he was always so sweet.

But if I thought my mama was bad *before*, it was nothing compared to the way she got then. She laid in the bed for three weeks solid, until the nurse from the County Health came in and gave her glucose in her veins. She wouldn't do a thing. Now here I am trying to go to high school, remember, and take care of Mama too. Finally she got up, but she wasn't the same after that.

I remember she had this calendar she had gotten from the hardward store in Ajax, and it was up over the kitchen sink to hide a hole in the wall where a pipe or something used to go— anyway, we had this pretty calendar from the hardware store with a big full-color picture of four baby deer on it, drinking out of a spring. Now Mama got a thing about those deer. "Billie Jean," she used to tell me, "I wish you would look at that little deer to the right, there. I wish you'd just look in his eyes. Don't they look like Danny's eyes, honey? Don't they?" Then she started saying, "Danny has come back from the grave, Billie Jean, to be with us right here and now. He is looking out at me through those deer eyes, I can feel it every time I come in the kitchen, and when I walk back and forth, I tell you, his eyes just follow me wherever I go."

Now a person can only take so much of *that*, and I got to the point where I didn't know whether I was coming or going. Finally I thought OK, Billie Jean, you've got two choices: you can either moon around here and go crazy too, or else you can go out and have some fun. So I went. This is when I got wild, I'll make no bones about it, but I'll tell you one thing: there is only so much to do on a date in a place like that where the movie over in Ajax didn't change but once a week, and I was not the only one that did it, either. I was real pretty, though— I looked like an Indian, people said I took after my daddy that way—and when you're real pretty, everybody just naturally notices what you do, and there is always somebody going to start something about you behind your back.

Oh, I did it all! First I started wearing makeup, then I started smoking cigarettes, then I used to take a drink of liquor if one of the boys just happened to bring it along, then I started letting them feel of my breasts when they kissed me good-night. I didn't give a damn, either! I *wanted* them to touch me like they did. Well, Billie Jean, you've got to do *something*, is what I thought. Marlene used to ask me questions about all of it—where I went and what I did—since the Honeycutts wouldn't let her date anybody, thinking, I guess, that she was too good for all of the boys in the bottom, and I told her everything. I used to go over to her house to spend the night and we made pizza from a mix and smoked cigarettes out the window, so her mother wouldn't find out. Except she did, finally, and after that Marlene couldn't see me anymore except in school and then she went away, too, her senior year, like Paul had.

Now, Paul—I never set eyes on him but once or twice in all those years. One summer I was kissing a boy from Ajax, Cord Parsons I think it was, in the glider on my front porch and all of a sudden I heard somebody clear their throat and say my name in the funniest voice, and when I looked up there was Paul not fifteen feet away from where we sat. Paul had gotten tall and skinny, I guess he must have been in college by then. I didn't know how long he'd been standing there before he said my name. Cord Parsons stood right up and said, "Now you listen here," but by that time, Paul was gone. He had faded right off in the dark.

This was the same summer he went off hitchhiking for one solid month without a dime in his pockets in order to "find himself," according to his father, who got drunk at the 4th of July company picnic and told some men about it. He said Paul had taken a vow of silence and it was all a bunch of foolishness and he said he wished Paul would get a decent job. Mrs. Honeycutt left the picnic by herself, she was so mad at her husband I guess, and she lost about fifteen pounds that month worrying before finally Paul came home. They talked it all up and down the bottom, how Paul had gone off hitchhiking and made his mother lose so much weight, but I didn't see him again myself until one time late that August, when I was walking up the road to the company store where the P.O. is, to mail some bills for Mama, and I saw Paul sitting out in the middle of the Honeycutts' yard cross-legged, staring straight up at the sun.

"Hi, Paul," I said, but he didn't move a muscle and I don't think he even knew I was there. So I hurried right on by— Marlene had gotten stuck up by then, whenever she was home, and we weren't friends anymore and it always made me sad to see those roses on their wall. At the P.O. I told Mr. Looney, the postmaster, about Paul sitting out in the yard, and Mr. Looney said that in his opinion Paul had always had a screw loose someplace, anyway. He said he knew about cross-legged sitting, though—that was meditating, he said, like religion. He said he guessed Paul was going to turn into a saint next, ha ha! Mr. Looney winked at me. He was a smart man who could have really gone places, everybody said, if he hadn't stayed at home for twenty years to take care of his mother.

Which was *not* what I planned to do! So when Jimmy Bell Dean, Jr., started asking me out while I was still a senior, I was just tickled to death—first because I guess I was flattered, him being so much older and a doctor's son, and then because he was so good-looking, a big blond boy like Troy Donahue in *A Summer Place*, which I had seen two or three times. Everybody said we made the cutest couple, which we did. Johnny Bell took me to motels outside of Wheeling for the weekend, where we spent all day in those big beds and then drank bourbon and Coke in the bars at night, and I didn't give a damn what anybody thought. I was in love! I even hoped I'd get pregnant so Johnny Bell would have to marry me, but when I did, he wouldn't.

I remember when I told him I was pregnant: we were sitting up on the ridge in his red Chevrolet one winter day after he had picked me up from school, just splitting a beer and looking out at all the mountains, which had snow on them as I recall, and smoke was coming out of all the chimneys everywhere, and I had on this electric blue mohair sweater he had given me not one week before, under my coat—well, I told him, and Johnny Bell liked to have choked on his beer, so I told him again, and he put his head down on the steering wheel for a while and then he said he'd take me over to Wheeling for a rabbit test, and if I was telling the truth, we'd get rid of it. He said somebody like me wasn't going to force him into anything.

"Take me home, Johnny Bell," I said, and I slammed that door as hard as I could when I got out. And then I went ahead and had the baby in spite of them all. In spite of Dr. Johnny Bell, Sr., coming over to see my mama, wearing a hat, and saying his son would accept no responsibility, and in spite of the principal making me quit school when I started to show. Mrs. Lucas gave me a waitress job at the Ben Franklin Cafe, over in Ajax, and I remember I had gone back to the kitchen to get some french fries when my water broke. So Mrs. Lucas drove me to the hospital in Ajax herself, and I still had my waitress smock on.

Listen: I have not ever regretted it, not for one minute, having that baby. Now this is Betsy, who has been one of the biggest joys of my life, and she has children of her own today. A baby is a baby, is the way I see it, and they're all made exactly the same way, and the amount of paperwork involved—or not involved—does not amount to a hill of beans. Anyway I had Betsy, who was the prettiest little child right from the start. And one day when Betsy was not but about three weeks old, the funniest thing happened. I went out to get the mail and there was this white envelope in the box. Typed, with no return address. I took it in the house and opened it up, and it had six one-hundred dollar bills, folded up in a sheet of plain white paper. Not a word on that sheet! When I showed all this to Mama, she liked to have died. She dropped a pan right in the floor as I recall.

"Well, I guess it's from the Deans," she said finally, and I said if it was, then I was going to throw every bit of it straight in the fire.

"Now, Billie Jean," my mama said, but I went right over to the phone and called up Dr. Dean at his office. Not in, they said. I told them who I was and said it was an emergency, and of course he came to the phone right away.

"Certainly not!" Dr. Dean said when I asked him if he or Johnny Bell had sent me that money in the mail. "As far as we are concerned, young lady, any connection we have had with you is at an end."

"Well, that suits me just fine!" I said, and hung up on him.

That money came in handy, too—I called it the mystery money—and we lived on it until Betsy was three or four months old and I went back to work for Mrs. Lucas at the cafe, and then when she retired, I took over as manager of it. It was long hours but I didn't mind it, the pay was OK and the people were nice, and I had Betsy to come home to every night. I couldn't for the life of me remember exactly why it was that I used to like to run around so much. As for Mama, she had perked up considerably having Betsy around, to the point of her being almost a normal person again.

It was about two years later that I married Loyd Raymond,

a druggist in Ajax who came in the cafe for about thirty cups of coffee every day for a month and a half before he ever got up nerve to ask me out. Loyd was shy but he was sweet, and he was just crazy about Betsy: he used to play hide and seek with her out in the yard, just like a kid. He used to get down in the woodpile and then jump out. We built us a new brick home around the bend from the bottom where we had lived all those years, and we had another baby, Loyd Junior, and my mama lived with us until she died. So I was married to Loyd Raymond for eighteen years in all, and I couldn't complain of a thing. Loyd was an easy man to get along with, and a good man, and I have to say it—he was just crazy about me, too. If he knew I wanted something, he'd go right out and get it before I even opened my mouth. We were both of us funny that way—a lot of times we'd be thinking the same thing, and then we'd say it out loud together. Loyd bought me a diamond dinner ring for our tenth anniversary, and every summer we went to Myrtle Beach. I never looked at another man while he was alive, even though Loyd himself wasn't much to look at—but he was one good man to live with, I'll say that. It was such an awful shame when he died so young, but a bad heart runs in his family, and after I got over the shock of it I went back to the community college and got my CPA license, and turned what used to be the den into my office. So I have made a decent living, and the kids have turned out good if I do say so myself, and I can't say I spent much time thinking about the Honeycutts even though I passed their house at least two times a day, coming or going to the P.O. up at the store, or maybe over to Ajax.

I did go by there right after Mr. Honeycutt died, to tell Mrs. Honeycutt I was sorry and to take her some potato salad, because I believe in letting bygones be bygones and she was a good woman in her way.

"Thank you so much, Billie Jean," she said in this wavery voice, and she said how cute Loyd Junior was. I had brought him along, too. I asked after Marlene and she said Marlene had been married previously, and then divorced, but that now she had remarried and seemed quite happy. Mrs. Honeycutt's voice went up and down on the "happy," and tears welled up in her eyes. She was all bent over in one of those big ugly armchairs that I used to think were so beautiful—now, you can give me French Provincial any day!—and I could see that she herself was not long for this world either. So then I asked after Paul, too, just to be polite, and Mrs. Honeycutt said that Paul was a professor of philosophy and religion at one of those big famous Eastern universities—I forget which one she said, but you would have heard of it. She said Paul had never married much to her dismay, and so she had no grandchildren at all since Marlene had never had any children, either. Then she started to cry again.

"There's one of the books Paul wrote," she said, pointing to a big thick book lying there on the coffee table in with all the sympathy cards and little figurines and things she kept around. "But you can't read it," she said.

I picked it up. "Why can't I read it?" I asked.

"Well, I mean you wouldn't *want* to," Mrs. Honeycutt said, and she smiled for the first time since I had been there. "It's all about the nature of God as different people have thought of it through the ages, or at least that's what it says in the introduction, but you couldn't prove it by me. I tell you, it's dry as a bone."

I laughed and put the book back down on the coffee table. "Paul always was a brain," I said.

"He certainly was!" Mrs. Honeycutt said. "He . . ." but then I guess she forgot what she was going to say next because she let her voice trail off into thin air and just sat there, staring through me like I had already left. So I did, and as soon as we got in the car, Loyd Junior said he was glad to get out of there. He said that house gave him the creeps.

I was not surprised when Betsy came home from work about a month later with the news that Mrs. Honeycutt had passed away in her sleep, and I went over there again, to see if I could help, when I heard that Marlene had come home to clean out the house.

"Oh, Billy Jean!" Marlene said when she opened the door and saw me standing there. "Look at you! You're just the same, I'm so glad to see you, oh *look at you!*" she said, and hugged me, and for a minute it was almost like it had been before we smoked those cigarettes out the window and she had to go off to school. Almost. But I was a widow with a grown daughter

and a nice big son and a business of my own by then and I'll
admit it—I have filled out some, you might say. And I've got
these streaks of gray in my hair that I won't let Neva at the
Clip 'N Curl touch up—"I *earned* that gray hair!" I tell her,
"and you just let it alone!"—and anyway I guess I look a good
ten years older than Marlene. Marlene had spent a lot of those
years—you can always tell it—holding onto her looks, and
she was thin as a rail with her hair all frizzed out in one of
those fashionable new hairdos they wear now. Marlene looked
like a model out of *Cosmopolitan* magazine, and every piece
of jewelry she had on was solid gold. She smoked a lot, though,
and picked at things with her nails. "Can I help you with the
house?" I asked, and she said maybe I could help her supervise
it, but the company had hired a bunch of women for her and
they were already packing everything up. And they were, too—
you never saw so much carrying on and packing in your life.
So we just sat down in the middle of it all and had us a long
heart-to-heart, and that was when Marlene said the strangest
thing:

"You know," she told me, and then she laughed and said,
'Well, you *don't* know, I know you don't, how much I envied
you when we were teenagers."

"Oh, come on Marlene," I said, but Marlene swore that it
was true.

"I wanted to be just like you, I even wanted to *look* just
like you, and I wanted to do everything you did. I was just so
bored with my life . . ." and she went on about how her boredom
had gotten her into her first impossible marriage, which is what
she called it, but she said that now at least she was getting her
feet on the ground, and again I had that funny feeling that she
had somehow gotten years and years younger than me—but
then she dropped the bombshell.

"I'll tell you something else you never knew," she said. By
then we had found two little green glasses and we were drinking
some sherry wine. "My brother, Paul, was always in love with
you, too. We were *both* kind of in love with you, if you know
what I mean, only I believe that Paul was really in love and
he never got over you, either."

"Why Paul never even asked me out!" I said, and she said
it was probably because I used to be so wild and all, and Paul

knew he couldn't compete. But she said she always thought he wouldn't have loved me, either, if I hadn't been so wild, and I said this was all hogwash in my opinion, and then we got to giggling and giggling and finally we went upstairs to see how the women were coming along in the linen closets and the cedar closet and the bedrooms. They were almost through. Everything was stripped and your voice echoed out in all the rooms. Except for one—Paul's—because Marlene said Paul had asked expressly that she leave it alone since he was coming back here to spend the fall semester and write another book before they sold the house, and so the women had not been in there at all.

Now this is something I would not ordinarily have done, I'll admit it, but I was so confounded by what Marlene had just told me, and I had drunk that sherry wine—anyway, I went in Paul's room and—I'll come right out and say it— *snooped* around, while Marlene was down in the front hall writing all those women a check. At first I found exactly what you'd think—books and books, lots of stuff like chemistry sets and little old scale model kits of buildings, like cathedrals for instance, instead of airplanes which you would normally expect to find in what had been a boy's room, only of course that boy was *Paul*. But then in a closet, on a shelf with a lot of other boxes holding collections of various sorts, I saw this fancy wooden box with initials carved in the top, BJL, and those were *my* initials, you know, before I married. Mine! Well, I didn't have much time. I could hear Marlene's voice and the women's voices in the downstairs hall, all of them going up like voices do when people are saying goodbye. But I opened the box anyway—I would have died if I hadn't opened it— and sure enough, it was full of things about me, such as that red velvet bow I used to wear in my hair, and my initial ankle chain I lost the year I was fourteen, pictures the Honeycutts had taken of us all in their front yard, and weird little dried-up flowers and stuff like that. All of a sudden I felt like I was going to get sick to my stomach. Also I heard the door close down there in the front hall, so I took one picture out of the box, to keep—Marlene and me and Paul by the rope swing, grinning into the sun—and then I closed the box back tight and shoved it to the back of the shelf. It made me sick, as I said. In fact my heart was beating so bad I thought I was going to have a cardiac arrest, which I did not. In fact I hugged Marlene goodbye, and told her how good it was to see her—this was true—and then I drove straight home and never said a word to anybody, not even my first cousin Ruthie who is divorced and lives next door now, about what Marlene had said or what I'd seen.

But I did stick that picture of us three children up in the corner of the mirror in my bedroom, don't ask me why. I wasn't about to put it in a frame or anything, like I keep all the pictures of Loyd and Betsy and Loyd Junior and so on, but I stuck it up there in my mirror just the same, while I went on about my life. I started to date a little bit, just for companionship primarily, and also I made some money that year on a piece of land I'd bought earlier, and so that summer I took the kids to Disney World even though I thought Betsy was too old to enjoy it—but you're not ever too old for Disney World, as we found out. We all had a fine time. I never thought for a minute, all during that summer, about what I must have known, someplace deep down inside of me, what I was going to do when Paul Honeycutt came back to live in their house that fall.

I wasn't even nervous, knocking on the door. This was early September, marigolds still blooming, overgrown, along the walk. Nobody came and I knocked again. I knew he was in there, and sure enough, after another minute or so, he opened the door just a crack.

"Yes?" he said. Then he said, "Billie Jean?" His voice still went up at the end.

"It's me, all right," I said. "Aren't you going to open up and let me in?" and so he did, and in I went.

Age had been good for Paul Honeycutt, I saw right away, like it sometimes is for a man. He was still tall, still skinny, and his blond flyaway hair had thinned to a kind of adorable fuzz around his ears. Anyway, it struck me as adorable right then. He had big thick glasses, which looked good. The glasses seemed to hold his features in the right place on his face. Paul Honeycutt looked exactly like what he was, a brainy professor who didn't have anybody to take care of him. And this was obvious, too, by the shape the house was in—dusty, and what little furniture was left was mostly covered up with old white cloths. It looked spooky.

"Now you know me and you know I have never believed in beating around the bush," I told him, and I took off my red cardigan sweater and dropped it over a wingchair and went straight up to him and put my arms around his waist. "I know everything!" I said. "I know how you sent me that money right after I had Betsy, and I know how you have felt about me all my life. So don't try to deny it, Paul Honeycutt, I *know*! And I'll tell you something else"—I was holding him so close that I could hear his heart just beating like a bird batting around inside of his chest—"we are not *old* people right now, either one of us, and it's never too late to make up for lost time."

But Paul Honeycutt pushed me away. Shoved me, so hard I turned my ankle, almost fell. "No," he said. "No, Billie Jean, you don't understand—" and he fluttered his hands in the air, back and forth, like he used to do when he talked about math with Mr. Boling, back in school. He acted like he was scared to death, like a man who has seen a ghost. "It wasn't you, it wasn't ever really you, it was the *idea* of you, which made possible the necessary—" and he went on, and then I started noticing some other things about him that I hadn't seen at first when I came in, how his eyes rolled back and forth, and he wore his pants so high, and the corners of his mouth jerked when he talked. "I couldn't possibly," he said. "I could never actually—"

But I had heard enough. "Well," I said. "OK. If you're so dumb you'd rather have the idea of me than the real me in the flesh, as they say, then you can keep it. Goodbye!" I said, and walked right out and slammed the door. My ankle hurt but I kept walking and even when I remembered my sweater I wasn't about to go back and get it, I'll tell you that! So I left my sweater in that house, and it's there to this day, only he's probably put it up in a wooden box or something, in his room. Who knows?

And I don't care. I've got my own business to think about and also I am considering marrying this Preston P. Diggers, who I met at a CPA convention in Wheeling, and who has got serious intentions, it looks like, in my direction. He's a real nice man. I'd have to be a fool not to snap him up when he pops the question, which I am sure he will. As for Paul Honeycutt, poor thing, he never went back to the university, or wrote his book, and so they never sold the house and he's still there. He doesn't come out except to walk to the company store for groceries, I hear, and his hair is wild and white and he talks to himself on the road as he goes. My grandchildren, Betsy's girls, run when they see him coming, that's a fact. All the children do. It's been six or seven years now since he came back. But here's a funny thing: as much as I love Preston Diggers, which I do, I have never yet taken down that little picture of Marlene and Paul and me which I stuck up in the corner of the mirror so long ago. And sometimes late at night when I'm brushing my hair before I go to bed, or I get up early and look in the mirror before it gets really light outside, you know, when the bedroom is still fuzzy gray, why it seems to me that Paul Honeycutt is looking right out at me from his little-boy face, staring straight into my eyes, and I know what my mama, bless her heart, meant about my little brother Danny and that deer—and all of it strikes me, for a minute, as so sad.

Horses

How the Indian Got the Horse

Once I turned the television on and here came a weary Indian, walking across the plains. The plains stretched in every direction as far as the eye could see. From one corner of the plains a horse came galloping, tossing his mane. He was not tired at all. The Indian was weary and footsore. The horse came galloping across the plains. The Indian had an idea! He snapped his fingers. He quickly gathered a handful of something horses love. He held it out toward the horse. The horse came galloping across the plains, jerked it from the Indian's hand, and ate it all up. Then he galloped away. The Indian stomped his foot. Then he gathered some more. This scene was repeated several times. At last the Indian grabbed the horse's pure white mane, swung up, clamped himself around the horse, and they went galloping across the plains. This did not last long. The horse began to rear and snort. He tossed the Indian far up into the clouds. He whinnied and galloped away. The Indian lay on the ground and wept. He got up and looked around, but the plains were empty and stretched in every direction as far as the eye could see. The Indian sighed. It was night. The Indian ate some jerky and went to sleep. There was a commercial. Did the Indian dream of horses?

It was early morning. A white, ghostly mist drifted across the plains. Out of this mist galloped the horse, tossing his white mane, straight up to where the Indian slept on the ground. It bent down and nuzzled him. The Indian leaped up. He patted the horse. The horse nuzzled him and pushed at him with its nose. There was some horseplay. Then the Indian sprang up on the horse's back and they galloped away through the fine white mist together across the plains, flying, the horse's hooves above strange vegetation, fennel and artichokes and larkspur, together over the unimaginable plains.

My Actual Experience with Horses

My actual experience with horses has been slight. When I was small I was sent every year to a camp, although I was homesick and scared of bugs. At the camp we had a Wish Day. On Wish Day we could do anything that we had not signed up for. My specialty at that point was the making of lanyards.

On Wish Day I stopped making lanyards and walked up the hill to the riding ring. It was hot there and the riding counselors had circles of sweat beneath their arms in the Oxford cloth shirts. They were chewing gum.

We went on a trail ride. My horse was named Martini. He kicked, they said, and so they put me at the end of the line. We entered the woods where it was even hotter and the leaves were a dark, dusty green and they brushed our faces as we went past at a Walk. Crossing a clearing, we attempted the Trot. The Trot was bouncy. We became exhilarated. The counselors passed it back to Walk again.

Once when someone fell off her horse we all stopped and the horses began to eat the leaves. I looked around. Then I thought: I will remember this for the rest of my life. I have, too. Yet it is a completely unremarkable memory: how hot it was, the way the leaves looked, the green fly buzzing around Martini's black neck as he leaned forward, eating the leaves.

The next year, on Wish Day, I took Dramatics.

I am married to John of John's Body Shops, otherwise known as the King of Rock and Roll. He is becoming rich. He owns six Body Shops, two in the city and four in outlying areas. The Body Shops sell records and clothes. The Body Shops have mirrored walls, black light, incense, and periodic art shows. Before my father died, he said, "Martha, your husband is a dingbat." I am not sure this is true. To work, John wears jeans, boots, a vest and a serape. John has a ponytail. To relax, he sometimes wears a tie. John is thirty-eight.

The Horse Family Includes the Horse, the Ass, and the Zebra

The horse family (*Equidae*) is now represented by one genus only (*Equus*), which includes the horse, the ass, and the zebra. The *Quagga*, of this genus, became extinct in 1872. The horse family, the rhinoceros family, and the tapir family are believed to be descended from a common ancestor with five toes on each foot and with the middle toe in line with the axis of the leg. In the horse genus, the other toes have disappeared or have become vestigial, the foot being now what was once the middle one of five toes. The horse's hoof corresponds to the nail of man's big finger or third toe. The horse genus is descended from the Eohippus genus of the Eocene epoch, about forty-five million years ago. The Eohippus (Gr: dawn horse) was about eleven inches high, or about the size of a fox. It had four toes on each front foot and three toes on each hind foot. Its home was the region that is now the Great Plains of North America. Similar animals of the horse family lived in the Old World at the same time. These became extinct.

The Horses in Our House

We had three children in a row. When they were small, it was difficult to eat dinner. Whenever we sat down to eat dinner, a catastrophe occurred. At last I worked out a solution. Johnny was four; Libby was three; the baby was very small. I put the baby in her carriage and wheeled it into the dining room. I put the two rocking horses in the dining room. We ate by candlelight. At the edge of the candlelight we could see their faces, back and forth or up and down, and the creaking of the springs put the baby to sleep.

I think that is the only real solution I have ever made. Unfortunately, it did not last.

The Olive versus the Horse

The city of Athens, having as yet no name, held a contest. The city would take the name of the god or goddess who gave it the most valuable gift. Poseidon struck a stone with his trident and out popped a horse. The people cheered. The goddess Athena came bearing a shrub. "What is that shrub you've got there?" they asked. "This is no shrub! This is an olive tree," explained Athena. "It will make you rich." The people cheered even louder. Athena won the contest and the olive tree took root.

My Mother's Friend

When my mother was young, she lived on the Eastern Shore of Maryland. My mother's best girlfriend's name was Lydia. Lydia's family raised trotters and one of the trotters, Dan Cord, won many races and became famous all over the Eastern Shore. Lydia was famous too, later on. But when they were young girls, my mother and Lydia and Lydia's father took a load of bricks on a boat somewhere and were becalmed for three days. Later, Lydia became incredibly beautiful. She was Miss Maryland. She was so beautiful that a total stranger came to the gate of her house on the Eastern Shore and shot himself dead beside the mailbox. He left her a note inside the mailbox. "I think you are very pretty," the note said.

Who Has Horses?

1. The Four Horsemen of the Apocalypse.
2. Helios, whose horses pull the sun. These include Amethea (no loiterer) and Erythreos (red producer).

3. The Pale Rider.
4. Pluto. One of his horses is named Abaster (away from the stars).
5. O'Donohue, whose horses are white waves that come on a windy day, topped with foam. Every seventh year on May Day, O'Donohue himself reappears and can be glimpsed gliding, to beautiful but wild music, over the lakes of Killarney on his own white horse. Fairies with flowers precede him.

The Steeplechase

A long time ago I was in love with a crazy boy, not John, who is dead now. Once we went to a Steeplechase. We had a box. There were three couples in this box. The girls wore corsages and light wool spring suits. I had a pink suit. Ann had a green suit. Mary Louise had a yellow suit. A friend of ours was riding in the race. He was very thin. He looked big from the front in his jodhpurs and very thin from the side when he went by on his horse, up out of the saddle, leaning forward.

I had been to the drugstore that day and the druggist had given me three free samples of a new banana perfume. I took the samples out of my purse and Mary Louise, Ann, and I put on the perfume. It was terrible. People in the neighboring boxes turned around. We were all laughing. Our friend won the big race, the Iroquois. His horse finished lengths and lengths ahead of the other horses. When he won, I wanted very much to kiss him. Instead I kissed the boy I was in love with, banana perfume and all.

On weekdays I get John off to his Body Shops, my children off to school, and go back to bed for an indeterminate length of time. Sometimes I go out to the branch library for a good look at back issues of *The Chronicle of the Horse*. I am most apt to cry in the afternoon. At dinner, I am competent and cheerful.

Mint Juleps

Our friend Carter had a mint julep party outdoors for her one hundred most intimate friends. One of the guests was the Arab psychiatrist Paul Fuad. I pulled him into a corner of the porch and made him listen.

"Do you want an appointment?" he said.

"No."

"Well, then."

"Social work?" he said.

"My motives could not be worse."

He kept inching away.

"Tell me what to do!"

"I think," Paul Fuad said sipping his drink, "that the thing to do is free your mind of horses."

I became indignant. "They are as good as anything else!" I snapped.

He stared at me inscrutably over the mint in his glass, beads of water on the glass beading up the picture of Citation winning the Derby on his Kentucky Derby glass.

I began to laugh.

"Why are you laughing now?" he asked.

I let him go. Arabs are not ironic.

Catherine the Great

We all know how Catherine the Great met her end. I think we know. Actually I am afraid to look her up at the branch library for fear it is not so. I think Catherine the Great was an insatiable nymphomaniac. I think no man could ever satisfy her. I think she took a fancy to a great white stallion in her stables and had him rigged up with an intricate system of pulleys to satisfy her insatiable lust. I think the experience was beyond her wildest dreams. Unfortunately, the system of pulleys failed. The great white stallion came crashing down and crushed her there on the stable floor.

The End

I Dream of Horses

In my dream I am walking through deep green grass that has no texture or weight; formless, it swirls in widening concentric circles about my disappearing feet. There are tall black tropical trees like thunderclouds that toss in the wind at the edge of the dream. I know they are over there. I am on a Stallion Hunt. I carry a stallion trap baited with olives and something horses love.

I set the trap. I place it in the center of the clearing where it disappears immediately into the swirling grass. I move back but keep clear of the tress. I know they are over there. I look at my watch. The stallions should be coming now. It is time for the stallions to show up. This place is supposed to be a favorite haunt of stallions. Where are they? I am growing dismayed and anxious.

Suddenly from the edge of the dream comes the tiny Eohippus or dawn horse, cantering gaily. He is eleven inches high. He canters along through the grass, going straight toward my trap. I stand; I am screaming at him; I am running to stop him. Running is hard in this kind of grass. He has reached the trap. I reach him with my hand outstretched. Luckily, the trap has disappeared.

The tiny Eohippus stands perfectly still but quivering all over. He stares up at me with his big dark eyes. I kneel beside him in the moving grass. I touch him. He steps forward, hesitates, backs off. The trees are over there. He steps forward again and nuzzles me with his warm nose. I look down. This unusual Eohippus has tiny perfect hooves already, each hoof corresponding to the nail of my big finger or third toe.

The French Revolution:
A Love Story

I can't believe I was in the bathroom messing around and missed the whole thing, the most exciting episode that absolutely ever happened at Martha G. Partlow Memorial Senior High. It just kills me. Lila Hawkins had to take her sinus pill and she asked Madame Jones if I could go with her. Madame Jones said *"Bien sûr,"* which is French for OK, and that is why we were in the bathroom and missed it. It is not the only thing I have missed, but since then I know what I missed before or what I am in the process of missing.

Anyway, by the time we got back in the room, Dr. Wheeler the principal was already there, and Miss Dujarnett the thousand-year-old fossil nurse from the school infirmary, and everybody in the class was crying and talking. "Sit down, sit down," Dr. Wheeler kept screaming. (He has a rage for order.) But nobody would. Most of the class was in a circle around Lucas Goodbar, passed out cold on the floor breathing real hard with the cord still around his neck, and blood coming from a couple of little cuts in his face. Glass from the broken window was all around him, and the window shade half covered his legs. Cold wind blew into the room.

The two biggest boys in the class, Cookie Leemaster and Cotton Quarles, each had one of King Edward Hartless' arms twisted behind his back, but King Edward wasn't trying to go anywhere.

He was staring out the window with that one rolling eye rolled over to the left, looking bored with all the racket, like he could see something a lot better somewhere else with that crazy rolling eye.

I have always bemoaned the lack of drama in my life, and then what do I do? Mess around with Lila Hawkins' sinus while life and death is going on in Room 302.

The first day of school, Madame Jones was late. We were all sitting in the seats looking around like you do on the first day. It was a big class, thirty-one of us. All the bad kids and the stupidest ones were in there, because that is what they do to new teachers.

I myself, Cassanora Clark, am quite intelligent although what my mother, who is PTA president, calls pleasingly plump.

I was secretly pleased to see King Edward Hartless sitting in the back row, as he was one of the more colorful characters in school and although he was not what I would call my type even if I had anything at all to do with boys, he made a fascinating study.

King Edward was the wildest boy in school. Everybody said so. He was always on the Absentee Hot List, which dopey Mr. Goodbar brought around every day. King Edward had some kind of unsavory family situation, I think. I don't know much about people like that. But Lila says his parents were divorced and had left him with an uncle, named Ralph, and they lived in the back of Ralph's Diner out on Route 41 away from town. They served beer there.

King Edward wore his shirts open at the neck so you could see he already had hair on his chest, brown curly stuff, and he wore boots before anybody else did, and blue jeans with a belt. King Edward was a hood.

He also had a combo. King Edward was the singer and lead guitar of King Edward and the Changing of the Guard, which was pretty good for a high school combo if you like that kind of music. I am partial to folk and classical music myself and have an excellent collection for somebody my age, but I must admit it moved me when I heard King Edward and the Changing of the Guard sing "Oh Yes, I'm The Great Pretender" on the Cerebral Palsy Telethon in August before school started. It was quite sensual.

Anyway, Madame Jones prissed in late on the first day, with the littlest skirt possibly ever seen at Martha G. Partlow, and yellow hair piled up on her head like a magazine. I guess she was very pretty in a tawdry sort of way. "*Bonjour, mes élèves,*" she said. I have had culture in the home and I daresay I was the only who knew what that meant.

Madame Jones sat on the desk, which hiked the skirt up some more in the front, and crossed her legs at the ankle. She pushed back her hair with one hand and we could all see that she had pierced ears. She leaned forward a little and started talking in French, very energetic, like she expected us to know what she was talking about. Everybody looked at each other and Norman Little yawned real loud. She went right on, waving her hands around like French people do in French movies, and then she switched to English and said, "In six weeks you will be able to understand every word I just said."

"Sure," said Hugo Weaver sarcastically. He said "sure" every chance he got.

Madame Jones held her hand straight out like Hitler. "*Fermez la bouche,*" she said, "which means shut up. First, I am Madame Jones, not Mrs. Jones, and anybody who calls me Mrs. gets two automatic zeros. This class is not going to be like any of your other classes. We will have no books and no homework."

Some of the more bourgeois kids clapped.

"*Fermez la bouche,*" said Madame Jones. "We will use a tape recorder, but primarily we will have conversations in class. The idea is to talk as much as possible."

I could see that Norman Little liked that.

"In French," continued Madame Jones.

"Sure," said Hugo Weaver.

"*Alors, nous allons commencer,*" announced Madame Jones. She walked back and forth across the room, displaying what Lucas Goodbar later wrote in the boys' locker room was a "high-class ass." "The French word for hello is *bonjour*," said Madame Jones. "*Bonjour,*" she repeated. "After me. *Bonjour.*"

"*Bonjour,*" we said.

"Louder!" cried Madame Jones. *"Plus haut! Bonjour!"*

"Bonjour!" we yelled.

"Bonjour," she said, waving her hands like Mr. Ledbetter in Boys' Choral.

"Bonjour!" we yelled.

The typing teacher across the hall walked over and closed our door. Madame Jones looked around the room and giggled, and that was that. With no effort at all, she was already the most popular teacher at Martha G. Partlow Senior High.

I have never courted popularity, myself. There were some girls in French I, like Kay Bankhead and Lucy Black, who were majorettes and couldn't even sit down without Norman Little and Cookie Leemaster falling all over themselves trying to get in the seat behind, or dropping pencils so they could get down and look up their skirts. And then there was Luella Green, not in our French class thank goodness, who was always Tardy in Home Ec. She would do it with anybody and had a million dates all the time. I heard that King Edward Hartless went out with her and I wouldn't be surprised. She was his type. I am more selective, as Mother says. But I must admit I had a hard time that first day of French class keeping my eyes off King Edward, mainly because of his one wall-eye. It gave his face such a unique although probably perverted appeal, like the way you have to stare at a cripple.

Everybody was talking about Madame Jones at lunch.

"We are not going to learn a thing," said Lucy, the majorette. "How does she think we can learn anything if we can't write?"

"I think she wears false eyelashes," said Lila.

"No, they're not. They're real," said another girl in our class.

"I'll tell you a secret," said Lucas Goodbar. He liked to gossip as much as a girl. "Madame Jones is divorced."

"How do you know?" I said.

"Because my father said, that's how," said Lucas. "So there." Lucas' father was the assistant principal, who never did much at all that I could see except hand out sharpened pencils when we took SCAT tests, on which I always did very well. Anyway,

Lucas had a thin, dark face, and a twitchy mouth, and eyes that watered a lot. He was rather mean although he was bright particularly in math. His mother had died the year before. Every day in the cafeteria old Lucas ate with the girls, even though nobody asked him.

I was clandestinely observing King Edward Hartless as I ate my vile plate lunch. He had an extraordinary profile. He was talking to the drummer of the Changing of the Guard, and while I watched he got a milk from the milk machine without paying for it.

King Edward is a juvenile delinquent, I realized. I was attracted and repelled.

We were speaking French in a week, exactly as Madame Jones had promised. We knew: *Bonjour*, *Au revoir*, *Il fait beau* (*froid*, *mauvais*, etc.), *Où vas-tu*? and many more.

Unfortunately, King Edward never progressed beyond "*Je m'appelle* King Edward Hartless," which means "My name is King Edward Hartless."

"*Combien font deux et deux*?" Madame Jones demanded, asking how much is two and two.

"*Je m'appelle* King Edward Hartless," he said. He was hopeless. King Edward's weirdo eyes would go dark every time he messed up, and he stared at Madame Jones all the time. It was the only class in school that King Edward never cut. Everybody said so, and old Rage-for-Order couldn't get over it. I wondered what he would think if he knew that Madame Jones used the familiar form of "you" all the time to us in class.

About this time I took to dreaming about King Edward every night. I would have died if anybody found out. He moved up to the second row, and I moved over so that right from where I sat I could look to the left, wearing my Op Art sunglasses so that nobody could tell where I was looking, and see little globs of sweat on those curly brown hairs at his neck, because he had just come from Phys Ed. It really turned me on, and it also made me sick to my stomach when I thought about it later.

In class I could not, absolutely could not, keep my eyes from looking at King Edward. They slid sideways in their sockets with a will of their own no matter how hard I tried, and fastened like clamps on that curly brown patch.

I even had pervert dreams about it, like one time I dreamed I invented a tie-on hair patch, for boys who didn't have any hair on their chests and were ashamed. It was a triangular piece of cloth with curly dog hair glued to it, and the boy could tie it around his neck like a housewife ties an apron. Even when I woke up I thought it was a good idea. But perverted. One thing about me is I am almost too intelligent for my own good.

Even while the mere sight of King Edward was enough to break out my face (I am not supposed to get emotionally wrought up because of acne), I despised him. Another night I dreamed he lived in a giant beer can.

All this was bad for my average in French. Madame Jones would ask me questions in class and sometimes I didn't even hear her.

"Est-ce que tu fais du français?" she asked one day, pointing her finger with pearly polish at me. "Cassanora! *Est-ce que tu fais du français?"* meaning do I take French, but by the time I got ready to answer, she had called on Lucas Goodbar.

"Oui, je fais du français," said Lucas. *"Quelquefois je fais du latin,"* meaning sometimes he takes Latin. It is just the kind of smart-aleck thing Lucas was always adding onto the ends of his sentences. I knew how to say *quelquefois* too, but I had my pride. There were some things that nobody but Lucas would do. He was Madame Jones' pet.

"Très bien," she said, *"très très bien,"* meaning very, very good. Teachers are terrible judges of character as a rule.

I sneaked a look at King Edward, and he was lounged back in his chair like a real king on a throne, staring at Lucas, looking real mean. It made me shiver all over.

One day after class King Edward walked right up to me out of the blue and said, "Can you help me some with my French?" I got so nervous I dropped my cable-knit sweater on the floor.

"Why me?" I said without meaning to. It was a stupid thing to say but as I am generally busy with my hobbies (reading, music, and water colors), I don't have many conversations with boys.

"Because you know more French than anybody in class except Lucas Goodbar," King Edward said. He picked up my sweater and handed it back, touching my left hand accidentally. I almost died. I looked into his face, into his dark brown eyes, and the wall-eye rolled off to one side. But even then I could not help thinking: King Edward said Franch instead of French. He has a hillbilly accent.

"Well, OK," I said. Then I panicked. I couldn't help him at my house, I remembered, because Mother would just die. Luckily I remembered about the Tri-Hi-Y Fellowship Hall. I was President of the Tri-Hi-Y Club at Martha G. Partlow.

"I've got a key to the Tri-Hi-Y Room," I said. "We could go there after school if you want to."

It was exactly like a real affair, with keys and everything.

"OK," said King Edward. He didn't even smile. I watched his hips walk off down the hall to the cafeteria: he is small but he is wiry, I thought. (It is a terrible thing to weigh more than the man that you love.)

I was nervous, later, in the Tri-Hi-Y Room. I almost didn't go, in fact, but once we got down to verbs it was all right. I went over and over *avoir* and *être*, meanwhile staring at the brown patch and hating myself.

"Thank you an awful lot, Cassanora," King Edward said when we got through. He didn't talk much at all but he looked at everything hard, I noticed.

"I'll help you any time," I said.

"Aw hell," King Edward said. "I don't know if it does any good or not. I guess the only thing I can really do is sing. You know that little song about Avignon?" His accent was atrocious.

Then to my total amazement, although as I have said King Edward had a reputation for being wild and liable to do anything, he sang it:

> *"Sur le point d'Avignon*
> *On y danse, on y danse.*
> *Sur le point d'Avignon*
> *On y danse tout en rond."*

It was such a finky thing to do, but it wasn't really finky when he did it. King Edward smiled, a long smile that never quite made it up to his eyes.

"I like that little song," he said. "Everybody dancing around and around."

I didn't know what to say. "Well, you'll probably do OK in French," I said.

"No," said King Edward. "Ralph told me one time I was born under a veil, and when you are born under a veil you can look ahead and see everything that's going to happen. I'm going to flunk."

"That is the wildest thing I ever heard in my life," I said. "You're crazy if you believe that."

"OK," he said, opening the door of the Tri-Hi-Y for me to go out. I looked sideways to thank him and when I did it he was staring at me, very hard, with even the wall-eye in focus. *What is going to happen to me?* I thought. For some reason I began to cry, but by then King Edward had lighted a cigarette (against the rules) and was walking off, cocky, down the hall. Maybe I am having a nervous breakdown, I thought, like Zelda Fitzgerald or Madame Bovary.

We studied all about French food in class, and practiced until we could order anything we wanted in French. Then Madame Jones took up money and brought some French food to class for us to eat. She brought mashed-up liver (*pâté*), egg pie (*quiche Lorraine*), and these little cakes named *petits fours*. It was all good but I am allergic to liver.

When she tried to give King Edward some more to eat, he turned red and said "No-thank-you-ma'am-it-was-real-good" very fast. I couldn't believe it since I had seen him steal a milk with my own eyes.

"*En français*, King Edward," said Madame Jones, but she smiled.

"Tell us about when you were in school in France," said Lucas. "What were the French men like? Were they fresh? What did they do?" He kept going on and on in a high thin voice.

Madame Jones turned a little pink and several kids giggled.

King Edward was staring at Lucas.

"Did they French kiss?" said Lucas, and everybody gasped like you do at a touchdown.

"Well honestly," began Madame Jones, throwing her head

back, but the bell rang then and we all left.

Something was wrong with King Edward that afternoon in the Tri-Hi-Y Room. Finally I said, "Look, if you are not going to try to understand this we might as well quit. It's really easy. You put *S* on adjectives that modify plural nouns, and *E* on adjectives that modify feminine nouns, so if you've got a plural feminine noun you put E and S both, like *les robes bleues*. See?"

"Jesus," said King Edward, and lit a cigarette right there in the Tri-Hi-Y Room. After all I am the President, and it made me furious.

"What's the matter with you?" I said. I hated him.

"Goddamn Madame Jones," he said. "Goddamn, god-damn." My mother and I live alone—Mother is widowed—and that was virtually the first time such language had been used in my presence, although of course I had read a lot of paperback books.

"Look," I started.

"She is going to marry Mr. Goodbar," King Edward said. "She really is going to marry him when school is out."

"Madame *Jones*?" I said. "How do you know that?"

"I know she is," King Edward said. He leaned back, sideways, and put his boots up on the chair across the aisle.

"How do you know?" I said. He wasn't even looking at me. I sat right across the aisle in the Tri-Hi-Y Room, in the chair next to his boots.

"I go over there a lot," he said.

"To her house?" I couldn't believe it.

"Yeah," he said, staring out the window. "I just park outside someplace and sit around."

"You mean you sit outside and watch her house?" I was disgusted and King Edward's hair looked greasier than ever where the sun hit it coming in through the window.

"Well I listen to the radio too," he said, like that made it all right. "I mean she lives by herself and after all a lady can't be too careful these days."

I stood up. "Get out!" I yelled. "Get out of the Tri-Hi-Y Fellowship Hall!" I was shaking all over. "Go on!"

King Edward looked at me, puzzled, the way he looked at

French irregular verbs. He pushed a long piece of hair back from his forehead with one of those slow movements that no other kids in school made.

"What's it to you?" he said.

I looked at him for a long time, into his dark sad eyes, one of which was fastened on me alone although the other wandered. In the Tri-Hi-Y Room you could have heard a pin drop, it was so quiet; there was no sound at all, nobody anywhere, not a noise except the faraway marches of band practice out on the football field. I don't know how long we stared at each other. It was the most meaningful moment of my life.

Then I got this crazy idea that I wanted to have him touch me. Just touch me, is all. I must have been temporarily insane. I got up and walked over to him where he sat with his feet braced, and all I noticed was what good care he took of his boots. They were so polished you could see your face in the toes. His nose was level with my breast, and I put my breast about an inch away from it. Then I felt like a fool with my own breast not even one inch away from somebody so common, so I backed off and went almost running out of the room. I looked back at him from the doorway. From the way his eyes looked, I didn't want to know whatever it is that you know when you are born under a veil. I left. That was the second and last time I ever saw King Edward Hartless alone.

At Christmas we had a French Class Christmas Party. Old Pencil-Sharpener Goodbar showed up, and grinned like a fool the whole time. He couldn't understand one word of the Christmas carols, naturally, since they were all in French. He must have made Madame Jones nervous, because everything she did was a little jerky.

Lucas Goodbar was awful, the way he had been lately. Norman Little had to stand up in front of the class to say a poem in French, "*La Fête de Noël et Moi*," and when he walked back to his seat Lucas tripped him and Norman fell flat on the floor and broke the rubber band on his braces. It wasn't funny at all and it messed up the party.

"Norman, *asseyez-vous*," said Madame Jones, who was mad at him. That mean sit down. She never got mad at Lucas, no matter what he did, and he did some real bad things. Lucas was starting to act real peculiar: his voice got higher and his face got whiter, all the time.

March was when it happened. Madame Jones was late for class as usual and we were all talking, and somebody asked Lucas when Madame Jones and his father were going to get married. "I don't know," Lucas said real loud, "but they make out all the time." He said it right in the middle of one of those big silences you get sometimes in large groups, and all the girls turned red.

King Edward Hartless got up from his seat and walked over to Lucas' desk. The rest of us just watched him. It was like a Western movie and I couldn't believe it was happening right in second period right in Martha G. Partlow.

"You're badmouthing her," King Edward said real low, but of course everyone heard him. "Now you take that back."

"No," squeaked Lucas. King Edward had grabbed both sides of Lucas' collar and rolled his face back and forth like a little ugly toy. "Take it back or I'll break every bone in your body," King Edward said. He had pulled Lucas about halfway out of his seat when in came Madame Jones. Everybody in class turned to stare at her: all the time, we thought.

"What is going on here?" she asked sharply. "King Edward, sit down."

He kept on holding Lucas about halfway up out of his desk and turned to look at her, the most pitiful thing.

"Sit down!" she repeated. "*Asseyez-vous*! Do you want me to call—"

King Edward let go of Lucas and slouched back across the room, slow, with everybody watching him.

"*Alors*," began Madame Jones. I looked at her good, at her hair piled up on top of her head, and I couldn't imagine what she would look like all spread out with old Pencil-Sharpener Goodbar, making out.

Madame Jones put us in groups of three or four, and then gave us five minutes to make up skits, something we did a lot. Some of the kids hated it but I myself had always had a lot of stage presence as well as elocution, and I didn't mind at all.

Lila, Johnny Hardy, and I were a group. We went second. I was a waitress and they ordered meals. Johnny Hardy ordered *neuf bières*, meaning nine beers, and everybody laughed.

"Sure," said Hugh Weaver.

Lucas was in a group with Brenda Stone Porter and Cookie Leemaster. The skits Lucas was in were always the best ones, a lot longer than anybody else's. Lucas had a lot of imagination but he didn't have any sense of humor. This time, Lucas and Brenda Stone and Cookie were in the back of the room whispering and getting ready all during everybody else's skits. You could tell it would be a real Academy Award show. Lucas always made "*très bien*" in skits.

King Edward was a student and Norman Little was the teacher in their group. King Edward blew his only line as usual, which was "*Où est le crayon?*," meaning where is the pencil. I was sure he had made another *mal*.

Finally it was time for Lucas. I remember as clear as anything: Lucas wore this queer light blue-and-white striped sweater, and his mouth twitched. "The French Revolution," he announced. Nothing happened. He had Brenda Stone at one corner of the room, and Cookie Leemaster was doing something with the window cord. Madame Jones sat in the chair at her desk. "*Es-tu prêt*, Lucas?" she asked, and Lucas said *oui* he was ready. "The French Revolution," he announced again.

That is when Lila and I went to the bathroom. I could just die every time I think about it. But from what the other kids in the class said, this is what happened.

Brenda Stone, who is a big loud cheerleader to begin with, came running from her side of the room yelling and screaming, I mean really screaming loud, and fell down in the middle of the floor saying "*Non, non, non*" at the top of her real healthy lungs.

Norman says Madame Jones tried to make her be quieter, but by then the skit was in full swing. Old Lucas came staggering over to the window, with his hands fixed like he was praying. "*Mon dieu!*" he yelled. "*Je suis innocent! Mon dieu!*"

Meanwhile Cookie Leemaster had pulled his pullover sweater up over his head, because he was the hangman. "*Vous allez mourir, monsieur*," Cookie yelled in a deep voice such as a hangman would have, meaning mister you will die. He grabbed Lucas by his skinny little arm and put the cord around his neck, while Brenda Stone continued to bat around on the floor.

Nobody has got straight what happened after that. King Edward Hartless got over to the window, though, real fast, and started choking Lucas with his bare hands. Everybody just sat there for a minute, thinking it was part of the French Revolution, and then they all realized at once that King Edward had already done his skit and that he was really trying to choke Lucas to death up there in the front of the room.

They said Lucas' face turned dark red and his eyes rolled way back in his head: it was awful. I would give anything to have been there. He started caving in at the knees, falling, and then the cord started choking him too like a real noose, until the rod broke and the whole mess came down on top of King Edward and Lucas, who by then were on the floor.

Nobody is sure who broke the window, whether it was King Edward himself or Cookie Leemaster trying to get him off Lucas. Madame Jones stood right in the center of the room and screamed.

"That King Edward is a strong little bastard," Cookie said after. "You sure wouldn't think it to look at him." Cookie was a hero for the next two days.

Madame Jones quit teaching right then, right in the middle of March, and married old Pencil-Sharpener Goodbar. I'm not sure exactly why she stopped teaching; it may have had something to do with some things I had told my mother, who is president of the PTA, about her methods. Now we have Mrs. G. O. Browning for French, and she is teaching us to write. We never do skits anymore.

King Edward got kicked out of school, of course, and nobody has heard from him since. He is not staying at Ralph's anymore, Norman says, and not even the Changing of the Guard knows where he has gone.

Somehow I think he is in California. I bet you anything that's where he is. I think about King Edward almost all the time now that he is gone. Sometimes I think I am going insane, I think about him so much. I bet King Edward was the only martyr that ever went to Martha G. Partlow Senior High, though, and lots of nights I have these dreams about him in California, singing and playing the electric guitar right in the middle of the Golden Gate Bridge.

> "Sur le pont d'Avignon
> On y danse, on y danse.
> Sur le pont d'Avignon
> On y danse tout en rond."

There has got to be a place where everybody dances round and round, and I dream I am there, dancing with King Edward, and then I wake up sitting right in the middle of the bed, hugging myself. My mother and I have been drinking Metrecal for supper lately, but I am still too fat.

Cakewalk

They call Florrie the "cake lady" now and don't think Stella doesn't know it, even though of course no one has dared to say it to her face. Stella's face is smooth, strong, and handsome still—you'd have to say she's a handsome woman, instead of a pretty one—but her face is proud and stand-offish, too, sealed up tight with Estèe Lauder makeup, ear to ear. Stella has run the cosmetics department at Belk's for twenty years and looks like it. Florrie, on the other hand, doesn't care what she looks like or what anybody thinks about it, either, and never has. Florrie wears running shoes, at her age, and wooly white athletic socks that fall in crinkles down around her ankles, and whatever else her eye lights on when she wakes up. At least that's what she looks like. Sometimes she'll have on one of those old flowered dresses that button all the way up the front, or sometimes she'll have on turquoise toreador pants or a felt skirt with a poodle on it—stuff she must have kept around for years and years, since she never throws anything at all away, stuff Stella wouldn't be caught dead in, as Stella frequently remarks to her husband, Claude, but whatever Florrie puts on, you can be sure she'll have white smudges all over it, at the skirt or on the sleeve, like she's been out in her own private snowfall. That's flour. She's always making those cakes. And then you can see her going through town carrying them so careful, her tired plump little face all crackled up and smiling, those Adidas just skimming the ground. She never wears a coat.

Oh Stella knows what they say! Just like Florrie is some poor soul on the order of Red Marcus' son who used to ride his blue bike around and around the Baptist Church until he either had a fit or somebody stopped him, or Martin Quesenberry's wife, Eloise, who is hooked on arthritis dope and has not come out of her nice Colonial frame house for eleven years, Stella knows the type and you do, too: a town character. It breaks Stella's heart. Because they were not raised to be town characters, the Ludington girls, they were brought up in considerable refinement thanks entirely to their sweet mother, Miss Bett, and not a day went by that she did not impress upon them in some subtle or some not-so-subtle way their obligations in this town as the crème de la crème, which is what she called them, which is what they were. Miss Bett learned this expression, and others, when she resided for one solid year in a tree-lined street in Europe in her youth. "Resided"—that's what she said.

Florrie and Stella resided in the big gray house on the corner of Lambert and Pine, the house with the gazebo, the hand-carved banisters and heart pine floors, the same house that Florrie has made a shambles of and lives in, to this day, in the most perverse manner Stella can think of. But in those days it was the loveliest house in town and the Ludington family had always lived there, "aloft," as Stella told Claude, "on the top rung of the social crust."

So Stella was born with a natural gift for elegance, and this is why she loves Belk's. She goes in to work twenty minutes early every day with her own key on a special key ring by itself, a shiny brass key ring that spells out STELLA. After she lets herself in, she goes straight to the cosmetics department where everything is elegant, gleaming glass counters cleaned the night before by the hired help, all the shiny little bottles and tubes and perfume displays arranged just so, and she pours the tea from her thermos into a china cup and puts the thermos out of sight under the counter and settles herself on her high pink tufted stool and slowly sips her tea; she uses a saucer, too. The cosmetics department rises like an island on a rose pink carpet in the center of the store, close to the accessories but not too close, a long way from the bedspreads. After Stella has been there for about ten minutes or so, everybody else comes trickling in, too, and she speaks to them pleasantly one by one and pities their makeup and the way they look so thrown together, some of them, with their slips showing and sleep at the edges of their eyes. Then, five minutes before Mr. Thomas slides open the huge glass door to the rest of the mall, just when she has reached the hand-painted violet at the bottom of the china cup, then comes the moment she has been waiting for, the reason she gets up one whole hour before she has to and does her makeup by artificial light, which is not the way to do it, anybody can tell you that, and leaves the house in the pitch black frosty morning with Claude still sleeping humped up in the bed: this is it, the moment when Mr. Thomas flicks that master switch and her chandelier comes on. Of course, the cosmetics department is the only section in the store that has a chandelier, and it's a real beauty, hundreds and hundreds and maybe thousands of glass teardrops glowing like a million little stars, and all those shiny tubes and bottles winking back the light. The chandelier is as big as a Volkswagen, hanging right down over Stella, dead center at the soul of Belk's. It's just beautiful; Stella sighs when it comes on.

She checks her merchandise, then, and maybe she'll add something new or drape a bright silk scarf around a mirror. Stella carries Erno Laszlo, Estée Lauder, Revlon, Clinique— all the most exclusive lines, and she sells to the very best people in town. Nobody else can afford these cosmetics, and Stella keeps it that way. The ladies she helps are the crème de la crème, so she never rushes them, and they will linger for hours sometimes in the sweet-smelling pink air of the cosmetics department, trying teal eyeliner or fuchsia blush, in the soft glow of the chandelier. Stella is calm, aloof, and refined, and it's a pleasure, in this day and age, to deal with someone like that. She doesn't seem to care if anybody buys anything or not, so the ladies buy and buy, just to *show* her. Stella makes a mint, her salary plus commissions, and whatever you read about in *Vogue*, she's already got it, she ordered it last month. If Pearls-in-Your-Bath are in, for instance, Stella has some pearls thrown out on black velvet in a tasteful little way to catch your eye, and the product set up in a pyramid at the side. Stella says she keeps one foot on the pulse of the future, and it's true. Stella has always stayed up with the times.

Florrie doesn't, though. If she made any real money from all those cakes, that would be different. But the way Stella figures it, Florrie just barely covers expenses. She won't use a mix, for one thing. And the way she gets herself up looking so awful, and the people she deals with—why, Florrie will make a cake for anybody, any class of person, and that's the plain truth, awful as it is. Stella shudders, thinking of it on this mid-October day, this cool nippy day with a jerky wind that whistles and whistles around the corner of Belk's although not one teardrop of the chandelier above Stella's cosmetics counter ever moves. Stella shudders, because today is the day she has circled in her mind to go over there (since she gets off early on Thursdays anyway) and try to talk some sense into Florrie for the umpteenth time.

She's got it all worked out in her head: if Florrie will quit making those embarrassing cakes and running around town like a mental person, Stella is prepared to be generous and let bygones be bygones, to let Florrie move in with her and Claude where she can do the cooking, since she likes to cook so much, and then they can sell Mama's house for a pretty penny. And all of this might be good for Claude, too, who has acted so funny since he retired from the electric company two years ago. Claude just bats around the house these days with his pajama top on over his slacks, leaving coffee cups any old place, which makes rings on all the furniture, smoking his pipe and smelling up the house, or taking that boat of his up to Kerr Lake and driving it around in the water all day by himself. It would be one thing if he were fishing, but he's not. He's just driving around in the water and looking back at the wake. Stella has colitis—that's why she's switched to tea instead of coffee—and the very thought of Claude out in that boat goes straight to her bowels. Well. At least she can go over and talk some sense into Florrie, something she's been trying to do ever since she can remember.

She can't remember a time when Florrie didn't need it,

either, but she *can* remember, or thinks she can, when Florrie started making those cakes. In fact Stella can recall precisely, because she's got such a good head for business, several cakes in particular, and she narrows her frosty green eyelids and totally ignores the tacky woman on the other side of the counter asking if they carry Cover Girl, which of course they do *not*, and recalls these cakes one by one.

To understand the circumstances of Florrie's first cake, which she made practically over her mama's dead body when she was in the eighth grade—it was the dessert for a Methodist Youth Fellowship Progressive Dinner—you have to understand the way they used to live then, in that fine old house on the corner of Lambert and Pine. The house was number one on the House Tour every year, and you couldn't find a speck of dust in it, either, or one thing out of place. That Miss Bett kept her house this way was a triumph of mind over matter, because she was not a well woman, ever, and it wore her out to keep things so straight. But she did it anyway, and held her head up high in the face of her husband's failings, and even the towels were ironed. So you can see why the idea of fifteen teenagers tromping in for dessert would have run her right up the wall.

"But Mama," Florrie said, "they're *coming*. It's all settled. We're going to have the first course at Rhonda's house, and the main course at Sue and Joey's, and then I invited them here for dessert. After that we'll go back to the church for the meeting."

"I never heard of such a thing," Miss Bett said. Miss Bett was a tall frail woman with jet black hair in a bun on the top of her head, and big dark eyes that could flash fire, as they did right then at Florrie. Miss Bett held famous dinner parties every year or so, which involved several weeks of preparations, all the silver polished and the china out, dinner parties that were so lovely that she had to go to bed for a day or two afterward to recover. "A Progressive Dinner!" she snorted. "The very idea!"

"Well, they're coming," Florrie said sweetly. That was her way—she never argued with her mother, or cried, just acted so sweet and did whatever she wanted to do. Stella wasn't fooled by this and neither was Miss Bett, but Florrie had every-body else in town eating out of the palm of her hand, including, of course, her daddy.

"Come on, Bett," Oliver Ludington said, standing in the kitchen doorway. "Don't embarrass her."

"I would talk about embarrassment if I were you," Miss Bett said. She stared at him until he said something under his breath and started to turn away, and then she looked back at her two daughters just in time to see Florrie give him a wink. That wink was the last straw.

"All right." She bit off the words. "Since Florrie has invited fifteen perfect strangers into our home, we will entertain them properly. Stella," she directed, "go out and cut some glads and some of those snapdragons next to the lily pond."

Florrie giggled. "We don't have to have *flowers*," she said.

"*Stella!*" said Miss Bett, and Stella went out, furious because she was three years older and had never joined the MYF in the first place, even though she was more religious than Florrie, and now she had to cut the flowers.

Miss Bett began removing vases from the sideboard, con-sidering them one by one.

"I'll just make a cake," Florrie suggested. She knew it would take her mother hours to arrange the flowers.

"You've never made a cake in your life," said Miss Bett. "You don't know the first thing about it."

"I won't make a mess," Florrie said.

"Florrie—" their mother began.

But Oliver Ludington, from the parlor, said, "That's all right, honey, Bessie can clean it up."

"Bessie doesn't come until *Monday*," Miss Bett reminded everybody, and of course it was only Sunday afternoon.

"I think I'll make a yellow cake with white icing," Florrie said. She had taken all the cookbooks out of their drawer and piled them on the table in a heap, and now she was flipping through them in her disorganized way. "Where's that big flat cake pan?"

A sound that could have been a laugh, or maybe a cough, came from the parlor as Miss Bett found the pan and slammed it out on the table for Florrie.

"Stella, don't put the flowers right down on the counter like that, honey, put them on *newspaper*, they could have anything on them, and then please take sixteen salad forks out of the silver chest and polish them."

"*Mama*," Stella said, but after one look at Miss Bett, she did it.

By the time the members of the MYF arrived three hours later, the dining room looked just like a picture, silver forks and pink linen on the table and flowers in a cut-glass vase from Europe in the center. Stella was fit to be tied and refused to have dessert with the group, even though Florrie begged her, and Miss Bett had taken to her bed with a sick headache after one look at Florrie's cake. The cake would have been fine if Florrie had not gotten into the food coloring, which was never used in that house except at Christmas when Miss Bett made cookies for the help. But Florrie had found it, and she had tinted some of the white icing yellow and had made a great big wobbly cross in the center of the cake. Then she tinted the rest of the icing dark blue and wrote MYF on the cross, and put a little blue border all around its sides.

"Oh!" Miss Bett shrieked, and her hand fluttered up to her high pale forehead, and she turned without a word and climbed the steps, clutching the handsome banister all the way.

Florrie had cleaned up the kitchen the best she could, not really knowing how to do it, but she couldn't get the blue food coloring off her fingers so they stayed that way for the Progressive Dinner, even though she looked very nice otherwise, with her curly blond hair pinned back out of her eyes by silver barrettes, and wearing her pleated skirt. Oliver Ludington went upstairs and took a bath, singing "Bicycle Built for Two" as loud as he could, and then he appeared at the door in a sparkling white shirt, a red bow tie, and his best seersucker suit, just in time to welcome the whole Progressive Dinner to his house. "Come right in!" He bowed. "Glad to have you," he said, and Florrie smiled her full happy smile at him, showing her dimples, and giggled "Oh Daddy!" as she came through the hall trailed by the whole MYF in which all the boys had a crush on her, even then, and even then she knew how to flirt back, and laugh, and shake her blond curls, but that's *all* she did in those days—it was later, in high school, that boys became a problem.

* * *

Oliver Ludington died when Florrie was sixteen and Stella was off at college. He died of cirrhosis of the liver, as everyone knew he would, and it was a funny thing how many people showed up for his funeral, filling up the whole Methodist Church and then spilling out to fill up all that space between the church and the street. It was awful how Florrie took on. Miss Bett and Stella cried too, into their handkerchiefs, but to tell the truth everybody expected Miss Bett to be *relieved*, after it was all over, since Oliver Ludington drank so and since she had never been happy with the way he had refused to practice law and taught at the high school instead. But Miss Bett was not relieved, or at least she didn't seem to be. After Oliver died, all that fine dark fire went right out of her, and she crept around like a pastel ghost of herself for the rest of her life. It was like she had used herself completely up in her long constant struggle with Oliver, and lacking anybody to fight with or try to raise up by their bootstraps, she paled and died back like one of the flowers in her own garden, going to seed. She let the house go, too, even though Bessie still came in. The house seemed to sag at all its corners, the gazebo started to peel, worn places in the upholstery were left unrepaired, and a loose shutter flapped in the wind. She didn't even try to control Florrie, who went out with any boy who asked her, and when Stella tried to talk some sense into her, she didn't seem to hear.

"Mama," said Stella, just home from business school where she had a straight A average, "you have got to do something about Florrie. She's getting a *reputation*." Stella paused significantly, but her mother's dark eyes were looking beyond her face. "I might as well come right out and say it, Mother, I think she's fast. And Daddy used to think she was so smart, but look at her grades now! They're terrible, and she'll never make it to college at the rate she's going. Besides, I don't like the crowd she hangs around with, for instance that Barbara Whitley. Those people are common."

Miss Bett's fingers trembled on her lap, like she was brushing some insect, or some speck, off the flowered voile. "You haven't asked me how my stomach is," she said to Stella.

Stella sat straight up in her chair. "Well, how *is* it?" she said.

"I have my good days and I have my bad days," Miss Bett

told her. "I just eat like a bird. Sometimes I have a little rice or a breast of chicken"—but just then Florrie came in from the kitchen with her lipstick on crooked, bringing her mama some tea, and Miss Bett sighed like she was dying and then drank it up in one gulp.

"Come on and go to the sidewalk carnival," Florrie said to Stella. "It's for the Fire Department, and they've got a band."

"I think somebody should stay here with Mama," Stella said.

"I think I could stand another cup of tea with a little more lemon in it," Miss Bett said, and then Stella decided to go after all, and she changed her dress while Florrie fixed Miss Bett's tea.

Florrie had made a cake for the carnival, a white sheet cake with yellow icing and a fire engine outlined on it in red, the engine's wheels made out of chocolate nonpareils. The sisters walked downtown along the new sidewalk and Stella thought how the town was growing since the aluminum company had come, and how many new faces she saw. Everybody spoke to Florrie, though, and stopped to admire her cake, and Florrie introduced them all, complete strangers, to Stella. "She's away at school," Florrie would say.

"I wish you wouldn't do that," Stella told her finally, because she could tell after twenty minutes or so that there was no one she wanted to meet.

The square had been roped off for the carnival, and Florrie took her cake carefully up to the table in the center of it, a long table draped with red, white, and blue, and put it right down in the middle. Everybody went "ooh, ah," and Stella turned away and went to sit on the steps of the North Carolina National Bank where to her surprise she fell into a conversation with Claude Lambeth, a boy she hadn't seen since high school, a tall serious-looking boy who was studying electrical engineering at State. Now Stella was a beauty at that time. She had Miss Bett's looks and her own way of walking so straight and inclining her head. Stella and Claude Lambeth sat on the high steps of the bank, back from the action, and watched the crowd mill around and watched the kids dancing in front of the fountain to the band. They had a lot in common, Stella learned, as they talked and talked and watched the dancing.

Florrie was like a little whirlwind out there. First she went with one and then another, and even Stella had to admit she was pretty, or would have been if her hair didn't fly out so much on the turns and she didn't look quite so messy in general.

"That's your sister, isn't it?" Claude Lambeth said to Stella, and Stella said yes it was. Claude Lambeth just shook his head, and then later, at the cakewalk, he shook it again when the music stopped and five or six boys jumped on the painted red dot for Florrie's cake and the right to walk her home. The boy who ended up on the bottom was Harliss Reeves, who was generally up to no good, and when the whole cakewalk was over, Claude Lambeth told Harliss Reeves thanks anyway, he had promised their mother that he would drive Florrie and Stella home in his car. And he did, leaving Harliss on the sidewalk with his cake in both hands and his mouth wide open, Florrie mouthing apologies at him through the closed glass window of Claude Lambeth's car. "What'd you do *that* for?" she screamed at Claude, jerking her arm away from Stella, but Stella was taken with Claude and approved his action with all her heart.

Which was broken when Claude Lambeth failed to write to her and dated her little sister instead, all that spring and summer while Stella graduated and then worked so hard in her first job as a teller trainee in Charlotte. Stella was so mad she wouldn't come home at all, not even to try to talk some sense into Florrie when her mama wrote that Florrie refused to go to college and was selling toys in the five-and-dime, but then her mama wrote that Florrie and that nice Claude Lambeth were unfortunately no longer seeing each other, and Stella knew he had seen the light. She came home for a visit and married him on the spot, and Florrie made them a three-tiered Lady Baltimore wedding cake.

"You ought to charge," Stella told her, eyeing the cake at her wedding reception. "You'll never get anywhere at the five-and-dime," she said, and Florrie stopped playing with all their squealing little girl cousins long enough to say maybe she would.

Florrie never had a wedding cake of her own, poor thing, or a wedding reception either—she ran off in a snowstorm two years later with Earl Mingo, a drifter from northern Florida, and married him in a J.P.'s office in the middle of the night in Spartanburg, South Carolina, under a bare hanging light bulb. Now Earl Mingo was good looking, you would have to say that—but who knows what else she saw in him? Because Florrie could have had her pick in this town, and she didn't, she ran off with Earl Mingo instead, a man with Indian blood in him who had never made a decent living for himself or anybody else. He painted houses, or so he said, but if it was too cold, or too hot, or he didn't like the color of paint you had picked out, forget it. Earl Mingo kept guns and he went hunting a lot, out in the river woods or up on the mountain, and sometimes when you were trying to hire him he'd stare right past you, to where the road went off in the trees. Everybody knew who he was. He had men friends, hunting buddies, but they never asked him over for dinner, and neither did anyone else.

Stella didn't speak to Florrie for months after she did it, and Miss Bett had to be hospitalized it was such a shock. After her mother got out of the hospital, Stella used to drive over there to pick up Miss Bett and take her to church—of course Florrie and Earl didn't attend—and then she would drop her off again, but finally when Miss Bett told Stella that Florrie was pregnant, she decided to walk back in that house, meet Earl Mingo face to face, and make peace. Because Stella had had a baby herself by then, little Dawn Elizabeth, and this had softened her heart.

So finally, on this particular Sunday after church, Stella parked the car and walked her mother right up to the door in the pale March sunlight, her hand under Miss Bett's arm, and she couldn't help but notice now nobody had ever fixed that shutter, and how dirty the carpet was in the front hall. While her mother went upstairs to lie down, Stella stood at the last step, holding on to the banister, and hollered for Florrie.

Nobody answered.

But Stella smelled coffee and so she pressed her black patent leather purse up tight against her bosom and put her lips in one thin line and headed back toward the kitchen without another word. Forgive and forget, she thought. The swinging kitchen door was closed. When Stella pushed it open, the first thing she noticed was the *color*, of course, which her mother had never said the first word about and which was a big surprise as you can imagine, her mama's nice white kitchen painted bright blue like the sky. Now if it had been a kitchen color that would be one thing, such as pale blue or beige or yellow, but whoever heard of a sky blue kitchen? Even the cabinets were blue. Stella was too surprised to say a word, so she kept her mouth shut and blinked, and then she saw what she would have seen right away if that color hadn't been such a shock: Earl Mingo seated big as life at the kitchen table with Florrie on his lap, both their faces hidden by Florrie's tumbling yellow hair. Florrie was laughing and Earl Mingo was saying something too low for Stella to hear. Earl Mingo didn't even have a shirt on, and the kitchen table was cluttered with dishes that no one had bothered to wash.

When Stella said "Good morning!" though, Florrie jumped up giggling and pulled the tie of her pink chenille robe around her and tied it as fast as she could, but not before Stella could see she was naked as a jaybird underneath. This was in the *afternoon*, close to one o'clock.

"Stella, this is Earl," Florrie said exactly as if people ran around in nothing but pink chenille robes all day long.

"I'm pleased to meet you." Earl stood up in his bare chest and stuck out his hand to Stella, who seized it in her confusion and pumped it up and down too long. Later, she hoped Earl Mingo didn't think she meant anything by that because she could see in one glance that he was the kind of man who thinks a woman is only good for one thing, and Stella was not that kind of woman by a long shot.

Earl Mingo stood over six feet tall, with black hair, too long, brushed straight back from his high dark forehead and black eyes that looked right through you. He had a big nose, straight thick eyebrows, a hard chin and a thin crooked mouth that turned up at the corners, sometimes, in the wildest grin. When Earl Mingo grinned, he showed the prettiest, whitest teeth you can imagine on a man. He grinned at Stella like he was just delighted to meet her after all. "Have a cup of coffee," he said.

"Why don't you take off your hat and sit down," Florrie said, which is what she and Earl proceeded to do themselves, only this time Florrie sat in a separate chair. "That's a pretty hat," Florrie said. "I like that little veil."

"I'd just love to stay but I can't." Stella was lying through her teeth. "Claude is watching Dawn Elizabeth and I have to get right back. I just wanted to run in and say I'm real happy about the baby, Florrie, and I never have said congratulations either, so congratulations." Stella's eyes filled up with tears then—she had been having those crying spells ever since Dawn Elizabeth was born—and Florrie jumped right up and hugged her on the spot. Stella remembered holding her little sister by the hand when she started first grade, walking Florrie to school.

"Well, I've got to go," Stella said finally, and then for no reason at all she said, backing out that bright blue kitchen door, "You all be careful, now," and Earl Mingo threw back his head and laughed.

There comes a time in a woman's life when the children take over, and what you do is what you have to, and it seems like the days go by so slow then while you're home with them, and nothing ever really gets done around the house before you have to go off and do something else that doesn't ever get done either, and it can take you all day long to hem a skirt. Every day lasts a long, long time. But then before you know it, it's all over, those days gone like a fog on the mountain, and the kids are all in school and there you are with this awful light empty feeling in your stomach like the beginning of cramps, when you sit in the chair where you used to nurse the baby and listen to the radio news.

Not that Stella ever nursed Dawn Elizabeth or Robert either one, but Florrie had two babies in a row and nursed them all over town. Anyway, with Robert in school at last, Stella had her hair frosted, bought some new shoes, took a part-time job in the accounting department at Belk's, and started working her way up into her present job in the cosmetics department. It was like she just woke up from a long, long sleep. She had done her duty and stayed home with those babies, and then she went back to the real world where she belonged. Not that Stella ever neglected those kids while she worked: she had them organized like the army, the whole family. Everybody had a chore, and she and Claude gave them every advantage in the world—piano lessons, dancing lessons, braces, you name it. Claude advanced steadily in his job at the electric company, a promotion every six years, and they built a nice brick ranch-style house with wall-to-wall carpeting and a flagstone patio. Claude was elected president of the Kiwanis Club, and Stella went on buying trips to New York City, where she stayed in hotels by herself.

And Florrie? Florrie never could seem to understand that those baby days were over. She had Earlene—six months after she got married—and then she had Earl Junior and then she had Paul who was born too soon and died, and anybody else would have left it at that. But nine years later, along came Bobby Joe, and then Floyd, and Florrie seemed tickled pink. She raised her children in the scatterbrained way she did everything else, and they ran loose like wild Indians and stayed up as late as they pleased on a school night, and spent all their money on gum. Then when they got to be older, they used to have all the other kids in town over there in that big house, too, dancing to the radio in the parlor and who knows what all, smoking cigarettes out in the yard. Florrie was always right there in the middle of it, making a cake as often as not.

Because her business had grown and grown—she never gave it up even when she had two of them in diapers at one time. And she never switched to cake mixes either, although she would have saved herself hours if she had. Florrie still made plenty of birthday cakes with roses on them, and happy anniversary cakes with bells, and seasonal cakes such as a green tree cake for Christmas with candy ornaments on it, or a chocolate Yule log, or an orange pumpkin cake for Halloween, and she had four different sizes of heart molds she used for Valentine's Day. But the town was growing and changing all the time, and you could tell it by Florrie's cakes. After the new country club opened up, she made a cake for Dolph Tillotson's birthday that was just like a nine-hole golf course, a huge green sheet cake with hills and valleys and little dime store mirrors for the water hazards, flags on all the greens, and a tiny sugar golf ball near the cup on the seventh hole. When the country club team won the state swim meet, they ordered an Olympic pool cake with a chocolate board and twelve different lap lanes. Once she worked for two solid days on a retirement cake for the head of the secretarial pool out at the aluminum plant. This cake involved a lot of oblong layers assembled just so to form a giant typewriter with Necco wafers as keys. The sheet of paper in the blue typewriter was smooth white icing, and on it Florrie had put "We'll Miss You, Miss Hugh" in black letters that looked like typing. When the new Chevrolet agency opened, she filled an order for a chocolate convertible; and after the community college started up, she made cakes and cakes for the students, featuring anything they told her to write, such as "Give 'Em Hell, Michelle" on a spice cake for a roommate's birthday.

The cake business and the children kept Florrie happy then, or seemed to, a good thing since Earl Mingo did not amount to a hill of beans, which surprised nobody. He painted houses for a while, and then he put in insulation, and then he went away working on a pipeline. In between jobs he would go off hunting by himself, or so he said, and stay gone for as long as a month. Then he'd show up again, broke and grinning, and Florrie would be so happy to see him and all the children would be too, and things would go on like that for a while before Earl Mingo went off again.

It was a marriage that caused a lot of talk in the beginning, talk that started up again every time Earl Mingo went away and then died back every time he came home, but since he kept doing it, the talk slacked off and finally stopped altogether and everybody just accepted the way it was with them, the way he came and went. Since it didn't seem to bother Florrie, it stopped bothering everybody else too—except Stella, who felt that Florrie had stepped off the upper crust straight into scum. Into *lowlife*, which is where in her opinion Florrie had been heading all along.

For years Miss Bett had her own rooms upstairs, with her pressed flowers and her pictures from Europe in silver frames, her little brocade settee and her Oriental rug and her gold-tasseled bed. So many of the other fine things in the rest of the house had been broken by Florrie's children. Which wasn't their *fault*, exactly, since nobody ever taught them any better or ever told them "no" in all their lives.

"It's just a madhouse over here!" Stella said, not for the

first time, one day after work when she was sitting with her mama in what used to be called the east parlor, looking out on the front yard where Earl Junior and a whole gang of boys were playing football in spite of the boxwood hedges on either side of the walk. Stella and Miss Bett watched through the wavy French doors as Earl Junior and his friends caught the ball, and ran, and fell down in a pile and then got up. They watched as Earl Junior and his friends waved their arms frantically and shouted at one another, the breath of their words hanging white in the cold fall air. Sometimes they had a fight, but nobody stepped in to stop it, and after a while they would get tired of fighting it seemed, and roll over on their backs and start laughing. Stella was glad that her own son, Robert, was not out in that pile of boys. In the west parlor, Earlene was playing the piano—practically the only stick of furniture in that room that was left in one piece—practicing for a talent show at school. Her fingers ran over the same thing again and again, a tinkly little melody that got on Stella's nerves. Floyd and Bobby Joe were wrestling in the hall. Every now and then they rolled past the east parlor door, for all the world like two little monkeys. Back in the kitchen the TV set was on, Florrie watching her stories and smoking cigarettes, no doubt, while she cooked. Earl Mingo was gone.

Cold sunlight came in through those high French doors and fell across the worn blue carpet, pale fine golden sunlight that reminded Stella suddenly of their childhood in such a way that it caused her to suck in her breath so hard it hurt her chest, and blurt out something she didn't even know she'd been thinking about until she said it out loud.

"Mama," she said, "you don't have to stay here, you know. You could come to live with Claude and me, we'd be glad to have you."

Miss Bett looked so pitiful and small, her eyes like puddles in her little white face. She's *shrunk*! Stella noticed. She's shrinking up like a little old blow-up doll, and no one has noticed but me. "*Mama*," Stella said. "We could build you a little apartment over the garage."

"I had a bad day yesterday," Miss Bett said, looking past Stella out the French doors where Earl Junior was catching a pass. "Everything went through me like a sieve."

"Wouldn't you like to have your own apartment, Mama?" Stella went on. "Wouldn't you like to have some peace?"

"I'd like a little peace." Miss Bett said this like she was in a dream.

"Well then!" Stella stood up. "I'll just talk to Florrie about it, and we'll—"

"No!" Miss Bett got all excited suddenly and twisted her hands around and around in her lap. She said it with such force that Stella stopped, halfway out the door.

"We'd love to have you," Stella said.

"I—" Miss Bett said. "I—" She moved her little blue hand in a circle through the sunlight, then let it drop back in her lap. She looked straight at Stella. "I'll try to stand it a little longer," she said.

"We'll buy you a new TV."

Miss Bett lifted her head the way she used to, and touched a white wisp of her hair.

"I'll just have to bear it," she said.

But Stella sailed right past her into the kitchen where, sure enough, Florrie was sitting at the kitchen table reading a magazine and smoking a cigarette. The table was half covered up with newspapers and Popsicle sticks and glue.

"What's all that?" Stella pointed at the mess.

"Earl Junior is making this little old theater, like Shakespeare had, for school. It's the cutest thing," Florrie said.

"Listen." Stella sat down and started right in. "Listen here, I'm worried about Mother."

"*Mother*?" Florrie said it like she was surprised.

"I think she needs a change." Stella was going to be tactful, but then she just burst into tears. "Poor little thing. She's *shrinking*, Florrie. I swear she's just shrinking away."

Florrie put her cigarette out and giggled. "She's not shrinking, Stella," she said.

"But what do you think about her *health*, Florrie? Now really—I wouldn't be surprised if it turned out to be all mental myself, if you want to know. I hope you won't take this wrong, but I just don't think it's good for her to live under such a strain. I don't think there's a thing wrong with her stomach, if you want to know what I think. I think if she could get a little peace and quiet, and if she had some *hobbies* or something—"

Florrie threw back her head and laughed. "I can just see Mama with a hobby!" she said. "Lord! Mama's already got a hobby, if you ask me."

"No, *really*, Florrie," Stella said. "Wouldn't it be a whole lot easier for you and Earl if she came and lived over our garage?" Floyd came in the kitchen crying then, and Florrie got him a Coke, and Stella went on. "Just think about it. Think about how much easier your life would be. What do you think about her health, anyway? I've been meaning to ask you."

Florrie looked at Stella. "Well, she has her good days and she has her bad days," Florrie said. "Sometimes everything goes through her like a sieve."

"*Oh!*" Stella was furious. "I can't talk to you. You're as bad as she is!" Stella picked up her pocketbook and flounced out of there, right past Earlene playing the piano and Floyd and Bobby wrestling in the hall and her mother all shrunk up to nothing in the sunlight on the sofa in the east parlor; Stella sailed straight out the front door just as Earl Junior hollered "Hike!"

So Miss Bett lived with Florrie and Earl until she died of heart failure, and when she did, it was all Stella could do to persuade Florrie to let them bury her mama decently. Florrie wanted Miss Bett put in a pine box, of all things, where the worms could get in. Then Florrie revealed that in fact this was the way she and Earl Mingo had buried Paul, the baby who had died so long ago. Stella and Florrie had a big argument about all of this in front of everybody, right there in the funeral home, but since Earl Mingo was out of town and Earlene had gone off to college, Florrie had no one to take her side and finally Claude just gave Mr. Morrow a check and that settled it, or seemed to, since Florrie did not mention the pine box or the worms again though she cried for three solid weeks, despite the fact that Miss Bett had left her the whole house out of pity.

Lord knows where Florrie got such ideas in the first place, although you can be sure she passed them along to Earlene, who turned into a hippie beatnik and won a full scholarship to the North Carolina School of Arts while she was still in high school and went there, too, came home for vacations wearing purple tights and turtleneck sweaters and necklaces made out of string. Turned into a vegetarian and went away to college up North, where she majored in drama. Now that was Earlene.

Earl Junior was a horse of a different color. No brains to speak of, a big grin like his daddy, always wrecking a car or getting a girl in trouble. Earl Junior got a football scholarship to N.C. State where he played second string until his knee gave out, and then he quit school and got a job as some kind of salesman, nothing you would be proud of. But Earl Junior liked to travel, just like Earl. You would have thought Earl Junior owned all of North Carolina, South Carolina, Virginia, and Tennessee, the way he called it his "territory."

Bobby Joe and Floyd were boys that anybody would be proud of, though, in the Boy Scouts and on the Junior High basketball team for instance, boys with brushed-back sandy hair and steady gray eyes, who mowed everybody's grass on Saturdays. Stella was glad to see that those two were turning out so well in spite of the way they were raised with no advantages to speak of, and as years drew into years and it became perfectly clear who had succeeded and who had not, she pitied Florrie, and tried to be extra nice to her sometimes—bringing them a country ham just before Christmas, for instance, or having oranges sent—things that Florrie often failed to notice, scatterbrained as she was. Because there is a kind of flyaway manner that might be fetching in a young girl, but goes sour when the years mount up, and Florrie was pushing forty. She should have known how to say "thank you" by then. Bobby Joe and Floyd were almost through with high school the year that the worst thing that *could* happen, *did*.

Earlene had always been Florrie's favorite, in a way, her being the only girl, and this made it that much worse all the way around: Earlene was the *last* one, the very last person you would pick to be the agent of her mother's doom. But you know how Earlene changed when she went off to school, so you can imagine what her friends would be like: tall skinny girls with wild curly hair or long drooping hair and big eyes, like those pictures of foreign children you see in the drugstore, and of course Earlene was exactly like the rest of Florrie's children—sooner or later, she brought every one of them home.

Elizabeth Blackwell was the daughter of two Duke professors, Dr. Blackwell and Dr. Blackwell, of the History Department. You would never have guessed what was going to happen if you had ever seen her or heard her name, which sounded so well-bred and nice. But Elizabeth Blackwell wore blue jeans day in and day out when she was visiting Earlene, and she had light red hair so long she could sit on it if it hadn't been braided in one long thick plait down the back of her lumberjack shirt. Whenever Elizabeth came to visit Earlene, all she wanted to do was go hiking up on the mountain with Earlene and Floyd and Bobby Joe, and sometimes Earl went too, if he was home. Elizabeth Blackwell wore big square boots from the army-navy store, boots exactly like a man's, and no makeup at all on her pale freckled face, which would have been pretty if she had known what to do with it, especially those big eyes that were such an unusual color, no color really, something in between green and gray. She was not feminine at all, so when she and Earl Mingo ran away together it was the biggest shock in the world to everybody.

Except Earlene, who urged everybody not to feel harsh toward her friend because, she said, Elizabeth Blackwell was pregnant, and furthermore it was Earl Mingo's child. Earl Mingo must have been almost fifty by then, and Elizabeth Blackwell was nineteen years old. Now who can understand a thing like that? Not Bobby Joe, who shot out the new streetlight on the corner of Lambert and Pine with his daddy's Remington pump shotgun and then threw the shotgun itself in the river; not Floyd, who got a twitch in one eye, clammed up in all his classes at the high school, and started studying so hard he beat out Louise Watson for valedictorian of the class; not even Earlene, who took a week off from college to come home and cry and tell everybody it was all her fault. Nobody could understand it except possibly Florrie herself, who of course had known Earl Mingo better than anyone else and did not seem all that surprised. It made you wonder what else had gone on through all those years, and exactly what other crosses Florrie had had to bear.

"I would just die if it was Claude," Stella said several days after it happened, one night when she had come over to commiserate with her sister and find out more details if she could. "But of course Claude would never do anything like that," Stella added. "It would never enter Claude's mind."

Florrie stood back from the wedding cake she was working on and looked at Stella. "You never know what's going to happen in this world," she said. Florrie sounded like she knew a secret, which made her sister mad.

"Well, I know! Claude and I have been married for twenty-six years, and I guess I ought to know by now."

Florrie smiled. Her smile was still as pretty as ever, like there might be a giggle coming right along behind it, but she had aged a lot around the eyes, and that night her eyes were all red. Her hair had a lot of gray mixed in with the blond by that time, and she wore it chopped off just any old way. Florrie had six different-sized layers of white cake already baked, and she was building them up, pink icing between each layer. Floyd sat in the corner in his daddy's chair, reading a library book.

"Who's that cake for?" Stella asked.

"Jennifer Alley and Mark Priest," Florrie said. "Look here what they got in Raleigh for me to put on the top." She showed Stella the bride and groom in cellophane wrapping, a little couple so lifelike they might have been real, the bride in a satin dress.

"Lord, I wish you'd look at that," Stella said. "Look at that little old veil."

Florrie smiled. "Real seed pearls," she said.

"But Florrie—" Stella looked at her watch. "Isn't the wedding tomorrow?" Stella *knew* it was, actually, because she and Claude had been invited, but of course Florrie had not.

"Noon," Florrie said. She rubbed her hand across her forehead, leaving a white streak of flour.

"Are you going to get it done in time?" Stella asked as Florrie spread the smooth white icing over the whole thing and then mixed up more pink and put it in her pastry tube.

"Sure," Florrie said.

"If I were you, I'd just go to bed and get up in the morning and finish it," Stella said.

"I like to make my wedding cakes at night," Florrie said. "You know I always do it this way."

"That's going to take you all night, though."

"Well." Florrie started on the tiny top layer, making pink bows all around the edge. "Light me a cigarette, honey, will you?" she said to Floyd, who did.

Stella sat up straight in the kitchen chair and put her mouth together in a line, but she kept it shut until Bobby Joe came in the kitchen for a Coke and told her hello, and then she said, "Listen, that's another reason I came over here tonight. Claude said for me to tell you that if you want to go off to school next year, Bobby Joe, you just let us know and we'll take care of it." Stella had been against this when Claude first brought it up, but now she was glad she had it to say, since everything was so pathetic over here at Florrie's. Floyd had a scholarship, of course, already. Floyd was a brain. "If you want to go to college, that is," Stella said for emphasis, since Bobby Joe was just standing there in the middle of the kitchen like he hadn't heard her right.

Bobby Joe stared at his aunt and then he popped off his pop top real loud. "Thanks but no thanks," he said.

Well! Bobby Joe took a long drink out of the can and Stella stood up. "If that's how you feel about it," she said, "*all right*."

Florrie was crying again without seeming to notice it, the tears leaking out as slow as Christmas, her blue eyes filling while she shaped three little red roses about each pink bow on the cake, crying right in front of her sons without a bit of shame.

Stella, who knew when she wasn't wanted, left. But the next day at Jennifer and Mark Priest's wedding reception, Stella couldn't eat *one bite* of that cake; it stuck fast in her throat, and thinking about Florrie gave her indigestion anyway, Florrie bent hunchbacked over that great huge cake the night before, making those tiny red roses.

And Lord knows whatever happened to Earl Mingo, or to Elizabeth Blackwell, or to that baby she either did or did not have. Nobody ever saw or heard from them again except for four postcards that Earl sent back over the next couple of years, from Disney World, from Mammoth Cave, from Death Valley, from Las Vegas—like that. He didn't write a thing on any of them except "Love, Earl Mingo." Florrie kept each one around for a while and then she threw it away, and kept on with her business, living hand-to-mouth some way, nobody knew quite how except that she had made some money when she sold off most of the backyard to Allstate Insurance, which tore up the gazebo and the fish pond and built a three-story brick office building on it right jam-up against that fine old house, and then Claude dropped by and did little odd jobs around the house that needed doing, and that was a savings, too. Other people came by all the time to see her. It seemed like there was always somebody in that kitchen having coffee with Florrie if it was winter, or Coke if it was summer, but then of course she had Earlene's children, Dolly and Bill, to take care of too, while Earlene was having a nervous breakdown after her divorce. Florrie took them in without a word and they lived with her for three years, which is how long it took Earlene to get her feet back on the ground, give up art, and get her license in real estate. Floyd is gone for good: he teaches at the college in Greensboro. Bobby Joe has never amounted to much, like Earl Junior who runs a Midget Golf in Myrtle Beach now. Bobby Joe is still in town. He lives in an apartment near the country club and works in a men's store at the mall, all dressed up like a swinging single in open-neck shirts and gold neck chains, still coming over to see his mama every day or so, breezing in through the screen porch door. Earl Junior's ex-wife, Johnnie Sue, came to visit about two years ago and brought their little boy, Chip, and she has stayed with Florrie ever since, leaving Chip with his grandmother while she teaches tap dancing at Arthur Murray's studio in Raleigh.

Johnnie Sue is not even related to Florrie, so who ever heard of such an arrangement? Stella shakes her head, thinking about it, and smokes a Silva Thin in the car as she drives across town from Belk's to Florrie's house through the fine October day, the leaves all red and golden, swirling down with the wind against the windshield of Stella's new car. Florrie's house is almost the only one left standing on Lambert Street since it has been zoned commercial, and it looks so funny now with the Allstate Building rising up behind it and the Rexall Drugstore next door.

"It's real convenient," Florrie says when Stella mentions the Rexall, again, as tactfully as possible. "I just send Chip right over whenever there's something we need."

Stella sighs. This will be harder than she thought. She had hoped to find Florrie by herself, for one thing, but Chip is home with a cold and she can hear him upstairs right now, banging things around and singing in his high, thin voice. Chip is a hyperactive child who has to take pills every day of his life. Not a thing like Stella's own well-behaved grandchildren, who unfortunately live so far away. Well. At least nobody else is here, even though the table is littered with coffee cups and there's a strong smell of smoke, like pipe smoke, in the air. Florrie, who doesn't keep up with a thing, probably doesn't even know about room deodorizer sprays. Or no-wax wax, obviously, since the floor has clearly not been touched in ages. Stella sighs, taking a kitchen chair, at the memory of how this floor used to shine and how the sun coming in that kitchen window through the starched white curtains just gleamed on the white windowsill. Now the windowsill is blue and you can't even see it for the mess of African violets up there, and the windows have no curtains at all. It gives Stella a start. It's funny how you can be in a place for years and stop really noticing anything, and then one day suddenly you see it all, plain as day, before your face: things you haven't thought to see for years. She looks around Florrie's kitchen and notices Chip's Lego blocks all piled up in the corner, a pile of laundry in Earl's chair, the sink full of dirty dishes, a crack in the pane of the door—and then Stella's eyes travel back to the kitchen table and she sees what she must have seen when she first came in, or what she saw and didn't notice: smack in the middle of the table, on an ironstone platter, sits Florrie's weirdest cake yet.

This cake is shaped like a giant autumn leaf and it looks like a real leaf exactly, with icing that starts off red in the center and changes from flame to orange, to yellow, to gold. It's hard to tell where one color leaves off and turns into another, the way they flow together in the icing, and the icing itself seems to crinkle up, like a real leaf does, at all the edges of the cake.

"Mercy!" Stella says.

"I just made that this morning," Florrie remarks. She pushes the ironstone platter across the table so Stella can get a better look, but Stella scoots farther back in her chair. She can hear

Chip coming down the stairs now, making a terrible racket, dragging something along behind him on his way.

"You want to know how I did it?" Florrie says. "I just thought it up today. What I did was, I made one big square cake, that's the middle of the leaf only you can't tell under all the icing, and a couple of little square cakes, and then I cut those all up to get the angles, see, for all the points of the leaves. Come here, honey," she says to Chip. "Let me blow your nose in this napkin. Now blow."

Stella looks away from them but there is no place for her to look in this kitchen, nothing her eye can light on without pain.

"Pretty!" Chip points at the cake. Chip is skinny, too small for his age, with thin light brown hair that sticks up on his head like straw.

"You should have seen what I made for his class," Florrie says to Stella. "It was back when they were doing their science projects about volcanos, and I made them a cake like Mount St. Helen's and took it over there and you should have seen them, they got the biggest kick out of it! Didn't you, Chip?"

"Va-ROOM!" Chip acts like a volcano. Then he falls down on the floor.

Florrie smiles down at him, then up at Stella. "Aren't you off early?" she asks.

"Well, yes, I am," Stella begins. "I certainly am. But as a matter of fact I came over here for a special reason, Florrie, there's something I wanted to talk to you about. If you could maybe—" Stella raises her eyebrows and looks hard at Chip.

"Why don't you go over there and play some Legos?" Florrie asks him, pointing.

"No," Chip says. He starts singing again in his high little voice.

"I bet you could make a submarine," Florrie says, "like you were telling me about."

"No," Chip says, kicking the floor, but then he looks up and says he might like to go outside.

"I thought he had a cold," Stella says.

"He does. But I guess one little bike ride wouldn't make it any worse than it is already. OK," Florrie tells Chip. "Go on. But I want you back here in fifteen minutes."

225

Chip gives a whoop and runs out the door without a jacket; it will be a wonder if he lives to grow up at all.

"Now then." Florrie folds her hands in her lap and yawns and looks at Stella. "What is it?"

"Well, I've been thinking," Stella says, "about you living over here in this big old house with not even any real relatives to speak of, living with strangers, and how this property is zoned commercial now and we could make a pretty penny if we went ahead and sold it while the real estate market is so high—"

"This is my house," Florrie interrupts.

"Well, I know it is," Stella says, "but it's just so much for you to try to keep up, and if you sold it and moved in with Claude and me, why we could pool all our resources so to speak and none of us would ever have to worry about a thing."

"Moved in with Claude and you?" For some reason Florrie is grinning and then she's laughing out loud. It gives Stella a chill to see her; she knows that her suspicions are all true and Florrie's gone mental at last.

"Moved in with Claude and you?" Florrie keeps saying this over and over, and laughing.

"Now this is serious," Stella tells her. "I don't see anything funny here at all. When I think of you over here with strangers—"

"They're not strangers," Florrie says. "Chip is my very own grandson as you very well know, and Johnnie Sue is Earl Junior's ex-wife."

"You might as well be running a boardinghouse!"

"Now there's an idea," Florrie says, and it's hard to tell from her face whether she's serious or not, the way her eyes are shining so blue and crinkling up like that at the corners. "I hadn't thought of a boardinghouse." She smiles.

"Oh Florrie!" Stella bursts out. "Don't you see? If you came to live with us you wouldn't have to make these ridiculous cakes and drag them all over town."

"I like making cakes," Florrie says.

"Well, I know you do, but that's neither here nor there. The fact is, Florrie, and I might as well just tell you, the fact is you are going around here acting like a crazy old woman, whether you know it or not, and it's just real embarrassing for everybody in this family, and I'm telling you how you can stop. We can sell this house, you can come live with us. You're just a spectacle of yourself, Florrie, whether you know it or not."

"Does Claude know you came over here to tell me this?"

"Claude!" Stella bristles. "What does Claude have to do with anything?" Then Stella squints through her frosted eyelids, and drums her long red nails on the kitchen table. "Oh! I get it!" she said. "You're still jealous, aren't you? And I came over here prepared to let bygones be bygones."

"What bygones?" Florrie's eyes are bright, bright blue, and she has a deep spot of color, like rouge, on each cheek. "What bygones?" she repeats.

"Well," Stella says, "I guess the dog is out of the bag now! I mean I know exactly how you feel. Don't you think for one minute I don't know. I know you are jealous of me and always have been. You are jealous of my position at Belk's and my house and you resent our place in the community, mine and Claude's, and don't try to deny it. You always have. Don't try to tell me. I know you resent how Robert and Dawn Elizabeth have turned out so well, and all of that, but mainly I know that you're still mad that you never got Claude in the first place, that Claude picked me over you."

"What?" Florrie says. "That Claude what?"

"You know what," Stella says.

Florrie sits looking at Stella for one long minute as the wind picks up again outside and rattles the kitchen window. Florrie looks at Stella with her mouth open, and then her mouth curves up and she's laughing, laughing to beat the band. "Lord, Stella!" Florrie is wiping her eyes.

Stella stands up and puts on her coat. "If that's how you feel about it," she says.

"I can't move over there," Florrie finally manages to say. "It would never work out, Stella, believe me." Then she's laughing again—it's clear just how mental she is.

Some people are beyond help. So Stella says, "Well," almost to herself. "Nobody can say I didn't try." This ought to give her some satisfaction, but it does not. She stands on one side of the table and Florrie stands on the other, with that crazy cake between them.

"Who'd you make *that* for, anyway?" Stella asks, jerking her head toward it.

"Why, nobody," Florrie tells her. "Just nobody at all."

Stella shakes her head.

"But you can have it if you want it," Florrie says. "Go on, take it, you and Claude can have it for dinner."

"What kind is it?"

"Carrot cake." Florrie picks up the ironstone platter like she's fixing to wrap it up.

"You know I can't touch roughage." Stella sighs, leaving, but Florrie follows her out to the car still holding that cake while Chip rides by on a bike that used to be Floyd's, trailing his high wordless song out behind him in the wind, and real leaves fall all around them. Stella doesn't doubt for one minute that if Johnny Sue and Chip don't cut a piece of that cake within the next few hours, Florrie will go right out in the street and give it to the very next person who happens along. Chip puts his feet up on the handlebars, and waves both hands in the air. Stella turns her collar up against the wind: the first signs of a woman's age may be found around her eyes, on her hands, and at her throat.

Stella gets in her car and decides to drive back over to Belk's for a little while, to put her new Venetian Court Colors display beneath the twinkling lights of her beautiful chandelier; while Claude, out driving his boat around and around in big slow circles at Kerr Lake, doesn't even pretend to fish but stares back at the long smooth trail of the wake on the cold blue water, with a little smile on his face as he thinks of Florrie; and Florrie stands out in the patchy grass of her front yard with the leaf cake still cradled in her bare arms, admiring the way the sunlight shines off the icing, thinking about Earl Mingo and thinking too about Earl's child off someplace in this world, that child related to her by more than blood it seems to Florrie, that child maybe squinting out at the sky right now like Earl did, through God knows what color of eyes.